"*Black Dragonfly* is a lavish, beautiful testimony to the life and achievements of Lafcadio Hearn, the Irish man who in the nineteenth century opened our eyes to Japan's extraordinary art and literature, and to its rituals, sometimes exquisite, sometimes scarifying, always uniquely the country's own. Jean Pasley acutely imagines the dramatic twists and turns of Hearn's tumultuous life, deeply sympathetic to the vicissitudes of his appalling childhood, in profound contact with his development as a man desperately seeking refuge, finding it in the secrets and stories of his beloved Japan. He marries Koizumi Setsuko, their love lies at the core of this remarkable book, the prose delicate at times as a gesture from the tea ceremony, and cutting as a samurai sword when the narrative shows its edge. Pasley is a true writer, and *Black Dragonfly* a book to read and remember."

Frank McGuinness, Playwright

BLACK DRAGONFLY

A

novel

by

JEAN PASLEY

Inspired by and incorporating the work of

Lafcadio Hearn (1850–1904)

BALESTIER PRESS
LONDON · SINGAPORE

Balestier Press
Centurion House, London TW18 4AX
www.balestier.com

Black Dragonfly
Copyright © Jean Pasley, 2021

A CIP catalogue record for this book
is available from the British Library.

ISBN 978 1 913891 05 3

Cover design by Sarah and Schooling
Map design by Niall MacBride

This book is a work of fiction, although based on the life and
work of Lafcadio Hearn. The Afterword contains an explanation of
the treatment of his work and the portrayal of events.

Jean Pasley asserts her right to be identified as the author of this
work in accordance with The Copyright, Designs and Patent's Act 1988.

'The dead are not dead.

They live in all of us and move us

and stir faintly with every heartbeat.'

Lafcadio Hearn

For my Mother

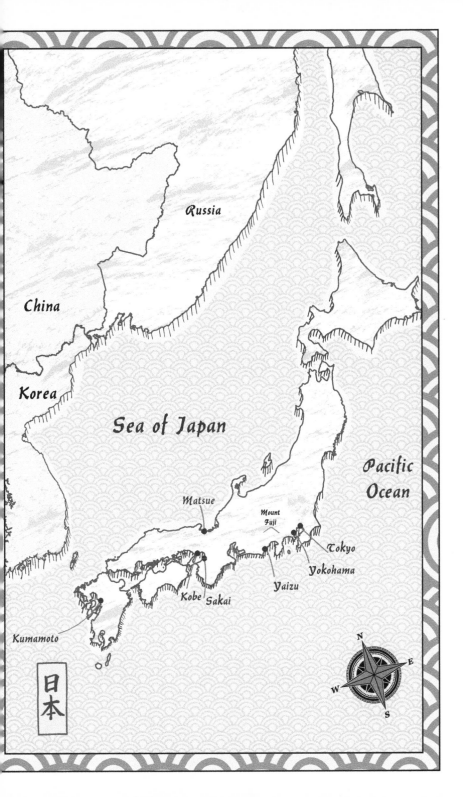

PROLOGUE

Dublin, Ireland, 1854

There is something wrong. She is holding him too tightly and she squeezes even harder when the clip-clop of horse hooves is heard on the road outside. Servants carry her travelling trunk out of the house. She releases him, cups his chin in her hand and tilts his face up to hers.

"You will be a good boy, Patricio."

"Where are you going?"

"Away. Just for a little while."

He feels soft kisses on both cheeks and then she is gone. Aunt Sarah grabs his hand and restrains him when he tries to follow her.

"Mama, Mama," he calls.

The front door closes. He yanks his hand free and runs into the library where, through the great sash window, he sees his mother getting into a carriage.

"Mama," he screams.

He can see her inside, bowed and shaking, and he bangs on the windowpane with his little fists but she does not seem to hear him. A servant closes the carriage door. Sobs blur his vision. Panic silences the world. The horses move off; their hooves make no sound as they strike the ground. The carriage glides away. He watches it grow fainter and fainter until it disappears into the misty morning.

"Take the child to his room, Catherine," says Aunt Sarah.

The maid, a robust country girl, pulls the hysterical four-year-old away from the window. She picks him up and tries to console him but he continues to sob and struggle in her arms.

"Get him some proper clothes and give him a haircut. He looks foreign enough without those ghastly earrings. Get rid of them."

"Yes, Ma'am."

As the maid carries him up the stairs, he turns away from the picture on the wall. The people in it are sad; one of them is up in the air with his arms stretched out and there is blood on his face. Through the bannisters he sees his aunt's pale, wrinkled face watching him from below. She sighs and walks away.

~

The brass bedposts glimmer in the light from the oil lamp on the bedside table. Another agonised face of Christ on the cross stares down at the boy as he kneels by his bed. Beside him, sitting erect in a straight-backed chair, Aunt Sarah prompts.

"Pray for..." she says.

"Pray for... for..."

"Us sinners now and..."

"And..."

"And at the hour of our death. Amen."

"Amen."

They bless themselves. Her rosary beads disappear into the folds of her voluminous black skirt. She stands up and reaches for the oil lamp.

"Please don't take it away. Please don't. The ghosts—"

"There are no ghosts, child. Get into bed."

"There are. I've seen them."

"You must never speak of such things. Now get into bed."

He obeys.

"But, Auntie, I'm afraid—"

"Nothing will hurt you. Go to sleep."

Despite his pleas, she leaves, taking the lamp with her and he is left alone in the dark. It is useless to try to escape because she locks the door every night. As her footsteps recede, he clutches the bed clothes tight to his chin and imagines monsters on the landing stomping towards his room. He does not know that the heavy rhythmic thumping in his ears is his own heartbeat. The house creaks and groans and wind roars in the chimney. When his eyes adjust to the black night, he sees over the top of the sheet ugly creatures lurking in the shadows; more are coming down the chimney. He inches back on the bed until he is pressed against the wall and waits for them to come and get him. They yank at the bedclothes. He screams and screams but no one comes to save him.

He remains petrified until the first rays of dawn light filter through the narrow gap in the shutters – only then does he fall asleep. And he dreams of a vast blue sky and a sun larger and brighter than the one rising outside his window. His mother's long blue-black hair tickles his face as she dangles him over the water. Gentle waves cool his feet and he giggles with delight. Somewhere in the distance a bell rings. He covers his ears and clings to the image of his mother, happy, laughing under a glorious sun. In dreams she is always well. In dreams he is loved. The image fades. He hides under the bedclothes, but try as he might, he cannot re-enter the dream. The bell rings six more times with a deep resonant peal that gradually grows louder and louder. He hears the click of the key turning in the lock and looks out hopefully from under the blankets.

Months pass. His mother does not come back. He cannot remember her face clearly; what lingers is a memory of beautiful dark eyes and brown skin like his, and a desperate longing for a warmer, sunnier place. The house he has been left in is cold and dark. He suffers from nightmares almost every night and even when he wakes up he can still see monsters lurking in the shadows, crawling up the walls, across the ceiling and down the other side. They soon fade but for several moments they appear real to him. Sometimes at twilight ghosts follow him, reaching long dim hands after him up through the shadowy spaces of the deep stairwells. Nobody believes him when he speaks about it. His aunt, the servants, even visitors tell him that ghosts do not exist. He wonders if ghosts are afraid of big people and show themselves only to him because he is weak and little. Or is everybody lying? He grows distrustful and becomes almost as frightened of the adults as he is of the ghosts.

~

One autumn day he is sitting by the stove in the kitchen trying to keep warm when a sudden gust of wind rattles the window. He jumps with fright. The maid, who is polishing silver on the long refectory table, casts an amused glance in his direction.

"It's just the fairies, Patrick. Don't mind them. Come over here and help me."

His ears have attuned to her strange accent, and he moves to the table where he lines up shiny forks and spoons in a straight line while she tells him about fairies who live in black mountain lakes.

"They have frogs for watchdogs and they come down the mountains at night to steal sleeping children from their beds."

He listens, growing more fearful by the second.

"One day I was here with a big pot of boiling water on the fire, and a fairy fell down the chimney and into the water. He let out a fierce yell and leapt out of the pot. The next minute the kitchen was full of fairies and they were raging with me. They thought I'd scalded their friend, and they were about to do me mischief when he told them what had happened."

His eyes widen and his knuckles turn white as he squeezes the spoon in his hand.

"You must keep a watchful eye, Patrick. There are fairies everywhere. They like to creep up on you."

He notices a distorted reflection in the silver spoon he is holding and he reels around in terror. The maid laughs. Aunt Sarah appears in the doorway looking cross.

"Your father is here, child. He's waiting for you upstairs."

As he leaves the kitchen she scolds the maid.

"Did I not forbid you to tell the child fairy tales of any kind? You know it will bring on attacks of sobbing and trembling. Really, Catherine, what were you thinking?"

"Sorry, Ma'am. I meant no harm. It won't happen ag…"

He trudges slowly up the stairs trying to remember the last time he saw his father. He is afraid of this solemn man who rarely smiles or laughs but that day he is cheerful and they visit a lady: the loveliest lady he has ever seen. She is tall and beautiful, and she kisses him and gives him a toy gun and a book about a little fellow called David who killed a giant. They ride in a barouche with her two pretty daughters through the city, across a wide river to a large park. It is far away, further than he has ever been. And they take a walk and see deer with enormous antlers. It has not rained for a while and a carpet of fallen leaves covers the ground. The children run on ahead through a blaze of colour, kicking up leaves as they go. When he looks back he sees his father and the lady laughing together.

On the way home, his father buys him plum cakes.

"Now, Patrick, you mustn't tell Aunt Sarah about today. Promise me you won't tell."

"I promise."

"It'll be our secret."

"Yes, Papa."

Somehow Aunt Sarah finds out about the lovely lady with the golden hair and she is angry. The toy gun and the book vanish.

After that, he has only fleeting images of his father. He goes away to fight a war in some place called Crimea. And then he comes back again. He remembers seeing him riding up to the house in his bright red soldier's uniform with the gold braid on the shoulders. He remembers being lifted up and seated in front of him on the saddle and riding around the neighbourhood. He remembers him coming to dine with other officers, men in shiny boots with big hearty laughs. These visits are rare but the memories are clear because there are seldom men in the house. He likes to hide under the table and listen to their manly talk of far-away places, battles and sieges.

~

When he is seven years old, he hears a knock on the front door of his aunt's seaside cottage in Tramore. He is upstairs playing with his armies of tin soldiers, bombarding the enemy forces with peas shot from a toy cannon, killing time, waiting for the tide to come in so that he can go swimming. He is happiest when he is in the water – the only place where his puny body excels – away from bullying children who call him names and taunt him because he is different. Voices are raised downstairs. He sneaks out onto the upstairs landing and listens to the heated exchange between his father and his aunt.

"No, you cannot come in. It is an unpardonable sin, Charles Hearn. How could you?"

"It's done."

"I cannot forgive you."

"If you won't accept my new wife, I shall have to live with that but—"

"God forgive you."

She moves to close the door but he jams it open with his foot.

"We sail for India in two days' time. At least allow me to say goodbye to my son."

She lets out a distraught sigh.

"Wait here."

He steps away. She closes the door and calls out.

"Patrick."

His father holds his hand as they walk along the sandy beach together. He is used to him suddenly appearing and then going away. Today he is even more dour than usual and he is mumbling something

6

about the family being annoyed with him.

"Aunt Sarah has made you her heir. Do you know what that means?"

"No."

"She's a very rich lady and she has no children. Everything she owns will be yours one day: the houses, the estates and all her money. It means you will never want for anything. It's more than your mother and I could have ever hoped for you."

Patrick is not listening; he has a battle to finish and the sun has come out and the tide is almost in.

"Her one condition was that you be brought up as a Roman Catholic. I would like to have spared you that, but you can make your own mind up when you're older."

"Can I go swimming?"

His father nods and lets go of his hand. The boy undresses as he charges towards the sea, leaving a trail of discarded clothes behind him. His father watches him go, a delicate little boy, so quick and light his feet leave almost no prints in the sand.

Patrick looks back just once and sees a lone figure, still and shimmering in the dazzle of the midday sun. He waves a thin little arm and then vanishes into the water. He swims until he exhausts himself and then floats on his back, rolling with the gently undulating tidal movement beneath him. Drifting under a cloudless sky, he feels safe and at home. Somewhere in the distance seagulls cry. Water gurgles in his ears. He tilts his head sideways and sees his father walking away, a shrinking splash of red on a long golden beach, growing smaller and smaller with every step. He does not know that he will never see his father again.

CHAPTER ONE

New York, 1889

Hearn passed yet another building site. The city was spreading, buildings shooting up everywhere. High above, men heaved steel beams into place; their shouts and roars faint above the clatter and clang of the street. He stepped off the kerb to cross. His movements lacked the confidence of a man at ease in the city and, as he weaved his way through traffic, he was honked at twice before he reached the safety of the other side. He stopped a passer-by to ask for directions. With all the noise, the woman could not hear him and she kept going but not without an apprehensive glance at his dishevelled appearance.

He looked around for a familiar landmark but there was none; the buildings all looked the same. He stopped in a doorway to take a breath and pulled his threadbare coat tightly around himself. A tantalising memory of Saint Pierre called to him. He should never have left. Closing his eyes, he tried to imagine that he was back there, on warm sand, beneath a giant palm. Some of them were over two hundred feet high, much more impressive in his mind than any of the towering skyscrapers that surrounded him. A blast of sleet whipped his face and turning his head sideways he scanned a street sign with his one functioning eye. He then realised where he was, and it was far from where he was supposed to be. He cursed out loud, turned and went back the way he had come.

One hour later, and drenched to the skin, he found the apartment building. The doorman showed him to the service elevator. He arrived at the party through the kitchen and almost turned on his heel and left when he saw that half of literary New York were there, seated around a table bedecked with crisp white linen, silver and crystal. Heads turned, eager eyes appraised him and quickly dimmed with disappointment. He was aware that he produced a disagreeable impression; his diminutive stature, dusky complexion and bulging eye did not endear him to people.

"I lost my way," he said.

Elizabeth Cochrane, his hostess, a handsome socialite in her late forties, made light of it, relieved him of his coat and the wide-brimmed hat that was dripping onto her expensive rug, escorted him to the seat of honour and introduced him to her guests as the next Victor Hugo, a veritable genius in their midst.

"I do not consider myself a genius, Mrs Cochrane, far from it," he said.

The guests waited for him to continue and to redeem himself with his brilliant intellect and witty turn of phrase, whereupon they would forgive him his bizarre appearance, but he was too miserable to either talk or eat.

"Lafcadio... It's an unusual name for an Irishman," said one of the guests in an attempt to engage him in conversation.

"It's Greek," he replied.

The guest waited for further explanation but none came. The hostess answered for him.

"Lafcadio's mother was Greek. He was born on Lefkada, a charming little island in the Ionian Sea."

She turned a smiling face to Hearn confident that she had given him an opening to speak about a subject he loved: his birth island, home of the ancient gods. The first time she met him, he had spoken at length, and with great affection, about the island with its cypress trees and olive groves and the famous white cliffs where, legend had it, Sappho jumped to her death following her lover's rejection. All eyes were on him: a pack of hungry dogs anticipating a feast of eloquence and erudition. He remained silent.

"I believe that on a clear day you can see Ithaca from there," said the hostess in an effort to encourage him to speak. "Isn't that right, Lafcadio?"

"Yes," he said.

Her fixed smile became strained when she realised that he was not going to elaborate.

"Lafcadio Hearn," said another of the guests. "It has an exotic ring to it. I mean, it's more intriguing, more inviting than Patrick, or Paddy Hearn?"

This remark elicited amused chuckles around the table but it annoyed Hearn. He wished he had stayed at home. Hunger and solitude would have been far preferable afternoon companions. An awkward silence, heavy with diminishing expectations, weighed on the room. Dubious looks were exchanged. Eyebrows raised, just a hint. A pompous little man, plump in his bespoke suit, attempted to draw him out.

"May I congratulate you on your latest publication, Mr Hearn. *Chita* is a profound and wonderful book, an ingenious blend of the ghostly realm and the earthly world. Tell me, is it autobiographical? It is, after all, about an orphaned child, and I know that your father died when you were very young and that your mother left when you were just a baby, so I'm assuming…"

It was not a question; it was merely an opportunity for him to shamelessly display his own superficial knowledge. Head bowed, Hearn toyed with his food. Mrs Cochrane could see that he was not happy. She leaned in and whispered to him.

"You look poorly, Lafcadio. Are you ill?"

"I shouldn't have come. I think I might be coming down with something – influenza perhaps. Would you mind very much if I left?"

"Oh, dear… But of course. I'll have Benjamin drive you home."

"That would be most kind."

He really was exhausted when he arrived back at William Patten's apartment, where he had been staying for the past month. William was an art editor at Harper's, and they had become friends when planning the illustrations for one of Hearn's earlier books. On his return from Martinique, William had given him a key and told him that the couch was his for as long as he liked.

"I thought you hated parties," said William, who had seen the chauffeur-driven car pull up outside.

"I do. They are the most horrible condemnation to mental suffering that could ever be inflicted upon one."

"Then why did you go?"

William moved to the kitchen. Hearn followed and stood in the doorway.

"It was meant to be only me and Madam bloody Cochrane's two pretty nieces; that I might have enjoyed. There were fourteen other ghastly guests. You should have heard them torturing their feeble brains for something intelligent to say."

William laughed.

"This city is driving me crazy," said Hearn.

"You'll get used to it."

"I have no intention of getting used to this so-called civilisation."

"You'd prefer to be with your savages in the jungle, would you?"

"There's a lot to be said for savagery."

"Sit down. Chicken and beans? I made enough for both of us."

"Thanks but I'm not hungry."

Hearn sat beside the stove and warmed his hands. William felt sorry for him. He had arrived during one of New York's particularly cold spells. Most nights, he could hear Hearn coughing. Sometimes he thought he heard him weeping, but that was not the kind of thing he felt was appropriate to mention.

"I have to get out of here. I'm thinking of going to Japan—"

"Japan! Why on earth—?"

"Because until recently it was closed to the outside world for two hundred years. Can you imagine what an intriguing cultural study it would make? But it's so expensive. Do you think Harper's would—?"

"There are lots of books on Japan, Hearn. Too many. I doubt there's anything new there that hasn't already been written about."

"I wouldn't expect to discover anything totally new."

"Well, I doubt if Harper's would fund a vacation for you."

"It wouldn't be a vacation. I'd work from the minute I arrived. I'd try to create in the mind of the reader a vivid impression of living there, not simply as an observer, but as one taking part in the daily life of the ordinary Japanese people. On second thoughts, I'll have some of that chicken please."

William dished up the food and sat with him.

"Surely you wouldn't live there, would you?"

"Why not? For a year or two at least."

"Are you mad?"

"Possibly. But I could make some money and then retire and live with my preferred company."

"Monkeys and parrots."

A hint of longing flashed across Hearn's face.

"Oh, William, you cannot imagine how much I crave a warm climate. I can't work here. Cold numbs thought and shrivels up the little wings of dreams."

William loved listening to Hearn, who read widely and could wax lyrical on almost any subject; his was a huge intellect trapped in a tiny body. William could not imagine what it would be like to be so small, to be always looking up at people, to be so physically vulnerable. He suspected that perhaps Hearn's stature – at just over five foot tall – accounted for his defensive nature. If he sensed criticism of any sort, he would turn on you in a second. William forgave his frequent outbursts because there was usually an element of truth in what he was saying. He cut his victims down with such style that sometimes it took them a few moments to realise that they had been insulted.

When Hearn was on form he was hugely entertaining. It was partly why he was a much sought-after guest at luncheon and dinner parties. Hearn could be merciless with people; he saved his sympathy for the stray cats he shared his breakfast with.

"Have you talked to Alden about Japan?"

"We're not exactly on the best of terms, William."

"No, no, he likes you. Isn't he minding your library?"

"Yes, but—"

"Oh, come on, he's not minding two thousand books for somebody he doesn't like. He has great respect for you."

"So much respect that he edits my work until there is nothing left of me in it."

"You do exaggerate, Hearn. Don't be so pessimistic. Write a proposal and I'll pass it on to him. If he likes it, then you can decide whether you want to talk to him or not."

Later that night, after William had gone to bed, and motivated solely by the prospect of escaping New York, he began drafting his Japan proposal. Three weeks later he was sitting in Alden's office waiting to hear the verdict.

Alden was shocked by Hearn's appearance: he was in even more disarray than he had been the last time he saw him. The oversized coat he was wearing had probably been purloined from his unfortunate host and it made him look even more pathetic than usual. Alden picked up the proposal and leafed through it, wondering what to do. The idea was sound but could he trust Hearn to deliver?

Having been summoned, Hearn believed that Alden had already made up his mind and was going to commission the work. He watched him peruse the proposal and was irritated at the thought that Alden was waiting for him to plead his case and when he did, the magnanimous editor would take pleasure in informing the writer that he was to be saved from penury for another short while and he would expect him to be appropriately grateful. The situation was deeply distasteful to Hearn. He had no intention of begging but, to make Japan at all feasible, he needed an advance and so he hid his impatience and waited politely until Alden broke the silence.

"I hear the women are flat as pancakes."

Hearn assumed from this clumsy attempt at manly camaraderie that the advance was his and a chink of light appeared at the end of the dark, dismal tunnel.

"I have heard that remarked upon," said Hearn, forcing a smile.

"But I'm sure they have other compensating attributes."

"You'll be sure to let us know, won't you," said Alden, giving him a conspiratorial wink. "Spice it up a bit, but tastefully. It must be tasteful. Do it the way you wrote about those West Indian women. You certainly enjoyed yourself there, didn't you?"

"I'm a single man. Why shouldn't I do what nature intended me to do?"

"Do you not worry about your immortal soul?"

"Time enough for that," said Hearn, not wanting to offend his Christian sensibilities – at least not before he had the cheque in his hand – by telling him that he didn't believe in hell and damnation or any of that oppressive Christian mumbo jumbo. "Don't worry, I won't disappoint you."

Alden glanced over the proposal again. It was tempting but Hearn's track record was not great, especially when he was paid in advance. He had commissioned him to go to the West Indies and Hearn repaid him by invariably missing deadlines. Many of his articles were overwritten and required strenuous editing. Some were unsuitable for publication; his adoration of the female form evident to an almost unhealthy degree. Others were brilliant. Despite his poor eyesight, his observations and attention to detail were extraordinary. There was no doubt that Hearn was talented but he was unreliable and slow, a painstaking artist not a journalist. He could vanish into Japan with Harper's money and then deliver little or nothing of use.

While Alden still wavered back and forth as to whether or not to commission the project, Hearn thought how amazing it was the way so many educated, intelligent people clung to Christian mythology. As a precocious young man he had taken great pleasure in provoking his Jesuit mentors. He would challenge the basis of their religion and delight in watching them struggle to logically defend themselves. When they failed, the word 'faith' would be bandied about. There was no arguing with blind faith, but he believed that being sceptical enabled him to enjoy life better. He liked to think that he lived like the ancients, without fear of eternal torment in Lucifer's fiery furnace. Alden's words interrupted his thoughts.

"…a private enterprise."

"Sorry, what did you say?"

"I said that I approve of the idea but only as a private enterprise."

Hearn felt all the energy drain from his body.

"I can't give you a definite commitment but I'm sure we'll be able to use your articles. I mean, if anybody is going to write about the Japanese, it should be you. They're very strange people. I know your studies will be a revelation."

Hearn was stunned. Had he heard correctly? Had Alden just said he couldn't give him a definite commitment?

"Do you know Chamberlain?" asked Alden.

"Who?"

"Basil Hall Chamberlain, Professor of English at the Imperial University in Tokyo."

"Oh, of course, I know of him. I've read most of his work."

"He's been in Japan quite a while. He might be useful to you. I'll give you a letter of introduction."

"Thank you. That would be helpful and…" he said, though he already knew it was hopeless to ask, "I will need an advance."

"I'm sorry but there can be no advance. We will agree with the rates and terms for any work you send us that we publish. That's the best I can do."

Hearn was dumbstruck. He needed money now. How else was he going to get to Japan? The project was doomed before it had even begun. Alden walked him to the door.

"Now, about your library, what do you want me to do with it? It's taking up rather a lot of space in my cellar."

"Just mind it for a while longer, please."

"Send me a forwarding address when you're settled in and I'll arrange the shipping. There are some valuable first editions there, you know."

"Yes, I know that."

"Well, good luck. I look forward to receiving some literary gems from the Orient."

Alden shook Hearn's limp, deflated hand and sent him on his way. He left Harper's Publishing House in a daze and was almost run over as he crossed Franklin Square. Snow fell. It was a light fall and left a mess of slippery slush on the pavement. Trudging home, he cursed himself yet again for having left Saint Pierre. He felt like an outcast from heaven and quickly sank into a familiar despondency. Better a pauper there than this. Being in a big city without money was hell on earth.

Back in William's apartment, he stood at the window of the cosy parlour and peered out at the cold, grey world. The crumbs he had placed on the windowsill earlier were still there; even the little birds on the telegraph wires outside turned their feathered backs to him. Perhaps it was for the best. He could stay put, or maybe head south to one of the warmer states. Memories of earlier disastrous travels surfaced. How many times had he rashly set out only to become penniless, sick and almost starve to death before eventually finding his feet. At forty, he was too old to go through it again. And it could be worse in Japan, such an alien place and so far away from friends who were well-disposed towards him, friends who had helped him out, even saved his life, in the past. No, without an advance from Harper's, he would not go. He could not go. The future looked bleak. He had no money to rent a place of his own and he could not stay in William's apartment for much longer; he had more than overstayed his welcome. He was running out of friends to borrow money from and he had no idea of what to do next.

Wallowing in despair, his thoughts turned to Henry Molyneux Hearn, the man responsible for his impoverished state. He still remembered the first time he met the bastard. It had been during one of those idyllic summers in Aunt Sarah's seaside cottage in Tramore, a small coastal town in Ireland's sunny south east. He was eight or nine at the time and they had gone to visit Molyneux, a distant and much older cousin, who lived nearby. Hearn had hated him on sight. Aunt Sarah had been charmed by Molyneux's devout Catholicism and rewarded him over the next few years by investing in his various businesses. It was Molyneux who convinced her to send him away to school in England. He took control of her finances and ruined her, whether through stupidity or unscrupulousness Hearn never could decide, but by the time he finished school there was nothing left. Patrick L. Hearn was heir to nothing.

Having bankrupted his aunt, Molyneux then bought the teenage Hearn a one-way ticket to America and promised him that relatives in Cincinnati would look after him. They shut the door in his face. Until then he had led a pampered life, and he was totally unprepared for the harsh realities of the world. His first few months there were a nightmare: trawling the streets for work, homeless, filthy, starving and utterly alone. One night, some stable boys took pity on him and let him sleep in a barn. He remembered rolling his clothes into a bundle to use as a pillow and nestling down in a glorious bed of hay. Below the loft, horses stirred heavily and pawed the ground. He wondered how it was they could earn their keep, how these dumb beasts could stay glossy, warm and beautiful and be of value and of use in the world, whereas he, who knew so many things and even spoke several languages, was useless and of no value to anybody. Not much has changed, he thought. Twenty years on, he was still of little or no value to anybody and certainly not to the editor at Harper's.

One night, early in January, Hearn was in the parlour reading when William came home and plonked a large parcel down on the desk in front of him.

"Open it."

Hearn removed the wrapping to find a book of woodblock prints by Hokusai Katsushika, a famous Japanese painter, print maker and book illustrator.

"A fine book. It's handsome," said Hearn.

"Think of it as a belated Christmas present," said William.

"Oh... Well, thank you."

William poured two glasses of whisky, handed him one and sat on the couch with a grin on his face.

"What?" asked Hearn.

"I've found an investor for you: Sir William Van Horne, the president of the Canadian Pacific Railroad Company and Steamship Lines."

Hearn seemed dubious.

"He's a huge collector of Asian art; he read that book you wrote about Chinese ghosts and he's prepared to fund the trip."

This good news did not elicit the expected joyful response.

"He's offering you an advance of $250 and free passage to Japan on one of his steamships."

"What does he want from me?" asked Hearn.

"He wants you to use your considerable talents to write about the joys of travelling to the East on one of his steamships. You'll travel first class."

"Considerable talents! Really, William, I am mediocre at best. I only pursue this career because I can do nothing else."

Hearn could not stand working for other people. He hated the very idea of it. He could not even stay in one place for long. He could not stay anywhere without getting into trouble. And why he continued to write he had no idea. When he looked at others who had achieved success in this line he found they generally hanged themselves or starved to death, while their publishers made enormous fortunes and worldwide reputations after the unfortunate, idealistic writers were dead.

"And you'd have company. Weldon wants to go with you. He'd do the illustrations."

Hearn had met Weldon, a colleague of William's, once or twice before. The effort of sustained sociability with that cocky young man would be deeply unpleasant for him and, more than likely, distressing for Weldon – not that he was at all concerned for him.

"I travel alone. Anyway $250 is not enough," said Hearn. "It wouldn't last long and I've no idea of what I'd be letting myself in for over there."

"What do you mean it's not enough? You'll have royalties from *Chita* coming in—"

"If it sells."

"It'll sell. And there'll be more from the new edition of the West Indies book. And Harper's will pay you when you start to produce work."

"If bloody Alden deems it worthy. He deals in books precisely as one would deal in hay or pork."

"Jesus Christ, Hearn, if you turn this down you can say goodbye to Japan."

William left him sulking in the parlour and went to prepare dinner. Hearn browsed through the book. There were page after page of skilfully delineated beasts and birds, strange orderly landscapes, oddly shaped trees and bursts of spring flowers. There were erotic prints too, drawn with no seeming regard for proportional or physical accuracy: lovers with exaggerated genitalia twisted and contorted into impossible positions. They should have been ridiculous and yet he could not help thinking that these prints had more real art in them than many a Western painting.

He pondered the little figures in the prints walking about in straw raincoats, immense mushroom-shaped hats and straw sandals; bare-limbed peasants deeply tanned by wind and sun; and patient-faced mothers with smiling bald babies on their backs toddling along on high wooden sandals. He wondered if everything in the exotic scenes depicted on these pages was as delicate and exquisite as it seemed. The self-imposed period of isolation was over and Western influence was flooding into Japan. Perhaps this beautiful old world was already disappearing and being replaced by ugly new things, by machines, by technology.

He turned a page and the tiniest, perfectly symmetrical little mountain leapt out at him from behind the great wave that dominated the entire print: Japan's sacred Mount Fuji. There were numerous illustrations of the great mountain in varying sizes, in different seasons and seen from all angles. Whether the mountain was large or small, snow-capped, seen through branches of cherry blossom, vanishing into a cloud, or a mere dot on the horizon, the eye was inexplicably drawn there.

The more he studied this strange world, the more he realised that he had to see it before it vanished. As far as he knew, Western influence had as yet only penetrated the port cities; beyond the ports it seemed the country remained largely unchanged. If he went, he would effectively be stepping not just back in time but into an entirely alien culture. He should go now, before it was too late, before this divine old world was gobbled up by modernity.

He put down the book, went to the kitchen and stood leaning against the doorjamb watching William, who was reheating the previous day's pork and black bean stew.

"How can I thank you?" asked Hearn.

"By going," said William. "Not that I want to be rid of you but..."

For the first time in weeks, Hearn laughed.

On 18th March 1890, armed only with a suitcase, a small travelling bag and Sir William Van Horne's money, Hearn stood beside Weldon on the docks in Vancouver staring at the SS *Abyssinia*. He closed his eyes and remained very still to savour the pleasure he was feeling; the anticipation of an impending journey always filled him with joy. He followed Weldon aboard and they sailed west towards the East, towards Japan.

CHAPTER TWO

Pacific Ocean, 1890

As a young man he had crossed the North Atlantic and explored the South Atlantic but this voyage across the North Pacific was the most tedious he had ever undertaken. Day after day of monotonous grey skies, relieved only by rain, sleet, snow or an insipid sun, kept him in his cabin. There was nothing to be seen, not another ship, not a speck of land, nothing of interest apart from the occasional whale to tempt him on deck.

Weldon was already becoming an irritant. A few days after they set sail he arrived in Hearn's cabin wanting to know if he had written anything yet.

"I can find nothing to write about that might entice anybody to undertake such a hideous journey. It would be a waste of ink to even attempt such a fiction."

"Perhaps these will inspire you," said Weldon.

He laid out some drawings he had done of the twenty year old, iron-hulled steamship. Skilled though they were, they did not inspire Hearn and he resented being urged to work as if he were the underling.

"Very good. Now, if you don't mind, I have things to do."

"I was trying to be helpful."

Weldon turned to leave.

"You can take these with you," said Hearn, indicating the drawings.

Affronted, Weldon scooped up his drawings and left.

Before he left New York, William had given him Basil Hall Chamberlain's *Handbook of Colloquial Japanese* and he used the tiresome time aboard to study. Languages had always come easily to him, but this wasn't a Romance language and the grammar was complex. It was immediately apparent that it was going to be a struggle. To master Japanese he would be required to think backwards, upside down and inside out. His experience of learning European languages would be of no help. The Japanese had borrowed the Chinese writing system and to read required a knowledge of many intricate Chinese characters and strange new letters. The strain on his eye was huge in the dimly lit cabin. Little progress was made.

One day, to relieve cabin fever, he went down to steerage hoping to meet some like-minded people. It was crammed with Chinese passengers. Those who were not sleeping or smoking opium were crouched together in small groups playing fan-tan. He wanted to join them, perhaps smoke some opium, but as soon as they saw him, they stopped playing and flashed hostile glances in his direction. He backed out.

It was cold on deck and, rather than return to his cabin, he peeped in through the porthole of the smoking room. Finding it empty, he went in and made himself comfortable. He had barely lit his pipe when three of the other first-class passengers descended on him. They were businessmen on their way to Japan to exploit the recently opened markets. He had heard enough of them at dinner to know that they were soulless men who saw the world only in terms of profit and loss.

The first man, a giant of a fellow with a cocky deportment, plonked down directly opposite him. The second, tall, lean and snakelike, slithered into the seat on Hearn's right. The third man sat on his left. He was bald but his features were framed with shaggy iron grey whiskers; he was unaware that everywhere he went he annoyed people with his incessant whistling. Filled with their unwelcome presence, the room shrank around him.

"Mr Hearn, we were just talking about you. We were wondering if you are the journalist from Cincinnati?" said the first man.

"Well, I probably am. I doubt there were many journalists named Lafcadio Hearn working in Cincinnati. But that was about fifteen, no, closer to twenty years ago."

"I'm from Cincinnati. I used to read your articles in the *Enquirer*. Very colourful," said Mr Cincinnati, stressing the word 'colourful'.

Hearn tensed; he knew where this was going. In the awkward silence that ensued he could tell that they were enjoying his discomfort.

"Tell me, do you still drink human blood?" asked Mr Cincinnati.

"I assure you, I never drank human blood. I suppose, if you follow Darwin's theory that all living creatures evolved over time from a common ancestry, then the closest I've come to cannibalism was in the West Indies where I ate worms. Cooked while still alive, they were delicious, rather like almonds."

They stared at him, with wary bewilderment.

"I did drink blood from a freshly slaughtered cow once and that is hardly remarkable. Many invalids drink it to improve their health. I had to drink it. How else could I convey the taste and texture to my readers?"

"Well, your articles sure made a strong impression on me. Those Tan Yard Murder Stories were really gruesome," said Mr Cincinnati.

"Jack claims that you once skated on a victim's blood," said the snakelike man, indicating Mr Cincinnati.

"Nonsense, I may have slipped but I assure you I did not skate on anybody's blood."

"But you saw lots of it. You seemed to like it," said Mr Cincinnati.

"I was merely doing my job, reporting on what I saw of the darker side of life."

He immediately regretted having used the word 'darker'.

"You sure knew about that, didn't you?" said Mr Cincinnati.

Hearn did not reply. The men exchanged snide looks.

"And tell me, will you be looking for another wife in Japan, Mr

Hearn?" asked the whistler.

"No, I have no plans in that regard," he said as firmly as he could.

The defensive beast in Hearn raised its head and it was all he could do to restrain himself. His waspish tongue had got him into trouble on many occasions. He would like to have given these pea-brained morons a good tongue lashing, but if he offended them, he could find himself tossed overboard into icy waters and that was not a prospect he relished.

"You'll have to excuse me, gentlemen. I'm feeling rather nauseous. I need some fresh air."

He left quickly and paced the deck wondering if he would ever escape his past. It was thirteen years since he left Cincinnati and sixteen since he married Mattie Foley. Inter-racial marriage was illegal and he had committed the ultimate sin of marrying his mulatto lover. Mattie did not look black – not that he would have cared. Her skin was a rich creamy colour and was in fact a shade lighter than his own, but her unruly corkscrew hair gave her away.

The first time he saw her, she had been scrubbing dishes in the cheap boarding house on Plum Street where he was staying. A run-down mixed neighbourhood, it was all he could afford in his early days in Cincinnati. He had escaped dull conversation with the other boarders in the dining room and on the way to his room he passed the open kitchen door. And there she was, handsome, healthy and, at twenty years old, a year younger than him. Her father was Irish and had sired her with one of his slaves. A few years later little Mattie was given away as a wedding present. Having both suffered abandonment, poverty and hardship, they fell into an easy relationship and soon became lovers.

His reputation as a reporter had been growing. Now well-paid he could have moved to a better part of town, but he stayed with Mattie and eventually proposed to her. It took a while to find somebody willing to marry them, but in June 1874 they exchanged vows in secret. It did not remain a secret for long and within a year *The Cincinnati*

Enquirer's star reporter was fired. Hearn still believed he would have suffered less if he had committed murder or incest. Friends shunned him. Colleagues avoided him. Rumours of the scandal spread about the morally depraved little Irishman. He ignored them all and stood by Mattie but the marriage did not last. In a disturbing echo of his father's ill-advised marriage to his fiery Greek mother, Mattie also turned out to be volatile and disturbed. Once the initial passion had spent itself, he found life impossible with the proud, wilful, and sometimes violent Mattie. One night, after a particularly nasty fight, he turned to his friend, Henry Watkins, for advice.

"She what?" asked Watkins.

"She threatened me with a kitchen knife. She owes money. I didn't have enough to give her to pay her debts and… She'll calm down in a while."

Watkins, or Old Dad as he called him, had remained a loyal friend through everything. He had been the first person to come to his rescue in Cincinnati. Penniless and half-starved, Hearn had turned up at the door of his printing shop on Walnut Street begging for work, any kind of work. Watkins had taken him in and let him sleep on the floor and then set him on a path towards a career in the newspaper business. He was the only person who still called him Patrick, a name he had dropped in an attempt to escape the stigma of being labelled another drunken, destitute Irish immigrant. Watkins, a quiet, civilised, sober man in his early fifties, rooted out a bottle of whisky from his desk and poured them both stiff drinks. He was clearly disturbed by Hearn's story.

"You and Mattie have no children together and legally you aren't married at all. There's nothing to stop you from leaving, Patrick."

"But I love her. I love her more than I'll ever love any woman."

"You're young. What age are you now?"

"Twenty-five. I don't know what to do except… This is embarrassing. I can't stop crying."

The only person he would have admitted this to was Watkins. He knew that the old man would not judge him. He was frank in his views but always kind, and if Hearn had heeded him in the first place he would not have been in the mess he was in.

"You say she's impossible to live with."

"So am I apparently."

"Leave, before things get any worse."

"I can't leave her. She will ruin herself. She's vulnerable, almost like a child."

"And if you stay she will ruin you, if she doesn't kill you first."

"She wouldn't—"

"You don't know that. People are saying very nasty things about you, Patrick."

"Most of it isn't true. Professional jealousy, that's what it is."

"No, that's not the problem. You are aware of the anti-miscegenation laws, aren't you?"

Overcome with despair, Hearn nodded.

"Perhaps you're too young to understand, but the reason people are angry with you is because in marrying Mattie you went against a great national and social principle."

"What should I do?"

"There's no future here for you, I'm afraid. You're already ostracised and as long as you stay in Cincinnati she will have a hold on you."

When he arrived home the following morning Mattie was waiting for him; her eyes were puffed and red from crying. She knelt at his feet and sobbed and begged him not to leave her. She swore it would never happen again, just as she had done many times before. The sex after these rows was always intense. They were perfect together. Until he met her he had believed that no one would ever love him. Growing up he had been convinced that he was someone who did not deserve love. He wanted to believe the soft words she whispered in his ear, but in his heart he knew that Watkins was right. It was time to leave. The violence had been escalating; the gaps between each episode had grown shorter. Perhaps the next time she really would slit his throat.

It should have been easy to walk away but he was afraid he would never be loved like this again. Then the problem solved itself. After a particularly turbulent row, which started with a comment he made about her poor cooking skills, she picked up his dinner, threw it at the wall and left. He still recalled the pain of the break-up; the pain of yet another rejection and by one so low. Though he was not a snob, he did wonder at the time if he had married her because she was beneath him in the social order. She did not look down on him and he had been grateful for that, pathetically grateful.

Their relationship had lasted four years but the fury of white Cincinnati was bitter and endless. In the end he left under a cloud and escaped to New Orleans in the hope of cultivating better company and redeeming himself socially. He did not like thinking about Mattie or about his younger self: blind to all sensible advice, stupidly obstinate and the architect of his own doom. It had been wrong of him to marry her at all, lifting her up only to let her fall lower than ever.

That disastrous relationship taught him that people like himself and Mattie fitted in nowhere. His own existence had been the result of a union between a white officer in an occupying army and a local Greek woman. The discrimination against him had been hurtful but it had been mild compared to what Mattie had suffered. It struck him that one of the most unfortunate outcomes of slavery had been the creation of a mixed race. The white masters and their slaves should have been drawn closer by their children. That had not been the case. And it had been even worse in the West Indies, where mixed race children were hated by blacks and whites alike. They became a wedge, forcing the parent races even further apart.

The smell of smoke wafted, dispelling the salty air and haunting thoughts of Mattie, and turning he saw Weldon approach puffing on his pipe. They both leant on the railings and looked out to sea.

"Captain says we should spot land tomorrow," said Weldon.

"At what time?"

"Around dawn. He said to keep an eye out on the starboard side.

Sorry. No offence meant."

"None taken."

"If you don't mind me asking, how did you lose your eye?"

"An accident during games at school. I got whacked in the eye by the end of a rope. Doctors tried to save it but…"

"Well, no one could say it has hindered your powers of observation. Are you going to join us for dinner?"

"No, I prefer to eat alone."

"It's our last night on board; I thought you might—"

"No, thanks."

Weldon wandered off. Hearn remained on deck thinking about Watkins who was close to seventy now. He was sorry that he had not made time to visit him before his departure. What an ungrateful wretch he was but he had had neither the time, nor the energy, nor the money to make the trip to Cincinnati. And when he finally made his mind up to go it all happened very quickly. As soon as he landed he would write to him. And even as he made this resolution, he was aware that at first he might write every other week, especially if he was lonely, and with time, perhaps only monthly, and then, if he stayed in Japan, only every other year. It was inevitable that old friendships would be forgotten, old faces would become dim as dreams and the fine threads of attachment would eventually yield to the long strain of thousands of miles.

The following day he rose before dawn and stood on deck peering hopefully towards the western horizon. Just after sunrise he caught his first glimpse of Japan. The base of Mount Fuji was concealed by clouds. Its snowy conical tip seemed detached from the earth and floated in the morning sky, up in the air as if suspended on invisible ropes. Of course, he had seen many photographs and woodblock prints of the holy mountain, but this wonderful living landscape was something he could not have imagined. It was divine. As the sun rose the tip of the mountain turned a delicate shade of pink, and he understood instantly the artists' fascination with it. So overcome was he by the sight that his first thought was that at last he had found the country where he would like to die.

CHAPTER THREE

Yokohama, Japan, 1890

As they sailed towards Yokohama he found it hard to believe that at last he was really in the Orient; he had read so much about it, dreamed about it, thought about it, but never seen for himself. It was a perfect spring morning. Wind-waves rolled down from the snow-capped tip of Mount Fuji and cooled the morning air. The light was different here. It was white light with a hint of blue in it, and it surprised him that the most distant objects appeared with amazing sharpness, even to his myopic eye.

The harbour itself was a disappointment. If not for the junks and other curiously-shaped crafts jostling amongst the western cargo ships, he might have been in any European port town. He and Weldon disembarked together and, having arranged to meet for occasional consultations, went their separate ways on the quay. He was glad to be rid of this foolish fellow who was spending his first week at the Grand Hotel, the place to stay in Yokohama for those who could afford it. Hearn jumped into a separate rickshaw and handed the runner a piece of paper with the address of a cheap inn recommended by one of the crew. On seeing the address the runner stared at him with a look of disbelief and let out a squeal of astonishment.

"Grando Hoteru?"

"No, not the Grand Hotel," said Hearn, pointing at the piece of paper. "*Koko*. Here."

Mystified, the runner bowed and took off along the waterfront pulling his fare behind him. Clearly, he had never been asked to take a foreigner to this inn before. As they passed the palatial Grand Hotel, which had been recently built in the Western style as had most of the buildings around the port, he caught a glimpse of Weldon going in through the front door and stifled a hint of resentment. Weldon had no immediate financial worries and was being paid much more than Hearn for his work; this discovery niggled considerably. The fact that he wanted to stay in the Grand Hotel confirmed his view that Weldon lacked imagination. Why travel all this way to live in faux European style? Some minutes later the runner deposited him at a small, traditional inn, far less opulent than the Grand but much more to his liking.

The old lady who ran the inn was not overly delighted to see a foreigner on her doorstep and he caused a commotion when he marched in wearing his shoes. Smiling all the while but muttering what he presumed were profanities, she brought him a pair of house slippers and indicated that he should leave his shoes on a shelf just inside the door. He had only one pair and did not want to lose them, so he tucked them under his arm and followed her. The slippers were too small and kept falling off as he shuffled along behind her through a maze of wooden corridors lined by walls consisting of a series of *shoji*: sliding wooden screens with translucent paper insets. Through the open *shoji* he caught fleeting glimpses of maids, who paused in their work to peer in his direction. They giggled as he passed.

Slippers were going to be a problem. There were slippers for walking around inside the inn, different slippers for his room, different ones for the toilets and for the communal bathing area, for the little garden outside and he could tell by the old lady's tone that to wear the wrong slippers, especially the toilet slippers, in the wrong place would be to incur her wrath.

His room was small but clean. The only furniture was a low table and a flat cushion on a soft floor of fitted straw *tatami* mats. Bedding was hidden away behind a wall of movable panels that slid open to reveal enormous storage space.

His first chore was to take care of business, and to that end he wrote a short note to Professor Basil Hall Chamberlain to announce his arrival and to let him know that he was a keen admirer of his work and would like to meet him. There were regular trains to Tokyo from Yokohama; the journey would take only about two hours and he was prepared to jump aboard a train when Chamberlain summoned. He did not mention that he was hoping the professor would help him find employment. He would broach that subject when they met. There was no rush. Since the adoption of the new constitution, English was now taught in schools and universities and there was a huge demand for native English speaking tutors. He assumed he would have no trouble finding a job. He enclosed Alden's letter of introduction and once it was posted, he hired a rickshaw and headed out into the day.

Leaving the European quarter he suddenly found himself in a place where everything was on a smaller and daintier scale. Everywhere he went people smiled at him as if to wish him well. This was a world where all movement was slow and soft and all voices hushed, a world where land, life and sky were unlike anything he had known elsewhere.

The runner, whose name was Cha, pulled him through narrow, winding streets with no immediately discernible plan of construction or order. All he could see of Cha was the top of his enormous white mushroom-shaped hat and his little brown ankles in their straw sandals as they trotted tirelessly along the dusty streets. Perhaps it was tiredness from the journey – he had not slept well on the ship – but the constant bobbing up and down of his human horse had a hypnotic effect and he found himself in a state of pleasantly odd confusion.

Lively signs cried out from every available surface: from fluttering flags, undulating curtains, doorposts, paper screens and lacquered signboards. The letters were so big as to be easily read from a distance. He wished he could understand them, and determined there and then to apply himself seriously to the language once he had settled in. Each pretty little wooden house, each building they passed had its own unique design. Everywhere he looked the ordinary living and working environment was a balm to his artistic senses. It was as if the book of woodblock prints William had given him in New York had come alive all around him.

He had Cha stop at little shops and was enthralled by the attention to detail and the simple beauty of even the most mundane objects: chopsticks, toothpicks, sweeping brushes, even cooking tools were functional but elegant. Everything he saw he wanted to buy. If he had had money, he could have filled the SS *Abyssinia* ten times over with beautiful objects. Aesthetics aside, he also found it immensely satisfying to be able to stand and look people in the eye. For the first time in his life he was as tall, if not taller, than everyone around him. And it felt damn good.

After meandering aimlessly for a while, he thought he would try out some of the words he had learned on the ship.

"*Tera e iku,*" he called, making a gesture of prayer in the hope that it would get him to a temple.

Cha seemed to understand and speeded up through yet narrower streets cluttered with more little houses and endless shops. It all flew swiftly by as if in a dream. When they reached an immense flight of broad stone steps, Cha stopped and set down the shafts.

"*Otera,*" he said, pointing to the steps.

Hearn hoped he had communicated correctly as he struggled to climb the steep flight of steps, and he was winded but not disappointed when he reached the half-way point and found himself on a broad terrace in front of a strangely carved gateway with its own roof. Gargoyles and grotesque lion heads protruded from the eaves. Dragons and snakes intertwined in a frieze above the open doors of the gate and on the panels of the doors themselves. These beasts did not have the rigidity of sculpture, rather they seemed to writhe and undulate. As he stood before this strange portal, he felt a sensation of both dream and doubt. It seemed vaguely familiar, as if he had been here before, or perhaps the carvings had stirred to life forgotten memories of oriental picture books seen as a child.

He continued on up the steps to the top, where another gateway opened onto a courtyard which was guarded by two huge stone lions. Elegant lanterns dappled the courtyard and on the far side was the temple: a long, low building with a gabled roof of grey-blue tiles. Three wide wooden steps led to the entrance. The walls consisted of nothing more than wood and paper *shoji* screens.

He crossed the courtyard and stood at the temple entrance peering into the dimly lit interior, wondering whether he should go in or not. After the bright sunshine, he could see nothing but faint shafts of golden light in the soft gloom. Seeing him hesitate, an old priest approached, bowed graciously and indicated that he could enter. Copying the priest, he removed his shoes and ventured into the interior, a huge square room filled with the sweet smell of incense. The floor was strewn with giant paper lotus-blossoms with curling leaves which were gilded on the upper surface and painted bright green underneath. They crossed the room and stood before a high lofty altar. There was no Buddha, only a mysterious collection of unfamiliar objects made of burnished metal.

The priest disappeared but came back a few minutes later, bowed and held out a bowl to Hearn. Assuming it was a begging bowl, he dropped a few coins in before realising that it contained tea. Without a word and smiling all the while, the priest bowed and took the bowl away, saving Hearn embarrassment. Moments later he returned bearing a fresh bowl of tea in one hand and Hearn's money in the other. Hearn accepted the tea but not the money.

"Please allow me to make a small offering," he said.

They spoke in hushed voices. Neither of them understood a word the other said, but the priest took the money and placed it on the altar. He indicated with a quiet gesture that Hearn could stay, bowed and slipped silently away. Left alone, he sat on the floor drinking his tea, marvelling at the wonder of the place. Such a simple building, made of little more than wood and paper, instilled a reverence greater than anything he had felt in the opulent cathedrals of the West. He remained very still for a long time, soaking up the solemn silence of the temple and feeling a newfound sense of peace.

He spent the next few weeks hurrying from one Buddhist temple to another, from one Shinto shrine to the next. On one of these trips he met Akira-san, a recent graduate of Tokyo University, who spoke surprisingly good English. With a shock of thick blue-black hair, a smooth beardless face, clear bronze skin and wearing a long wide-sleeved robe, Hearn at first thought he was a girl and waved him away. Unlike their Western counterparts, Japanese women seemed to find Hearn attractive and he had enjoyed the attention for a while but already it was becoming a little tiresome. Akira-san begged to be allowed to accompany him on his outings and translate for him.

"I'm sorry, I can't afford to pay you."

"No, no, I do not want money. I need to practise my English and there are so few opportunities. I am honoured to do it."

He seemed like a pleasant young man, so Hearn agreed. Akira-san was delighted and Hearn got to ask all the questions he had wanted to ask from the moment he landed.

One day, confined to the inn by a turn in the weather, he wrote to his old friend, Watkins.

Yokohama, May, 1890

Dear Old Dad,

Here I am in the land of dreams surrounded by strange Gods I seem to have known and loved before somewhere. I burn incense before them. I pass most of my days in temples and shrines, trying to see into the heart of this mysterious people. In order to do so I will have to blend with them and become part of them. It will not be easy, but I hope to learn the language. In the meantime, a surprisingly erudite young man named Akira translates for me.

Yesterday I visited the Great Buddha in nearby Kamakura. It is over forty feet high. I felt the soul of the East all around me in this extraordinary place. I wandered the surrounding hills in a state of bliss. Nature here is not the nature of the tropics, which is splendid and savage. No, nature here is domesticated. It loves man and makes itself beautiful for him in a quiet grey and blue way. And the trees are believed to have little human souls; they seem to know what people say about them.

Shortly after I arrived I had my first experience of the supreme cliché of Japan: the transient but magnificent cherry blossoms. I have to admit that the spectacle rendered me speechless. I lay on the ground under a giant cherry tree, luxuriating in the delicate fragrance wafting down from the fragile blossoms that filled the overhanging branches and blotted out the sky. I have never seen such a delicate shade of pink and in such gentle profusion as to have an effect that was truly intoxicating. The experience well deserves its reputation. In the middle of this floral paradise, it saddened me to see a sign shouting in English: IT IS FORBIDDEN TO INJURE THE TREES. Clearly other foreign brutes preceded me. I am ashamed to be counted as one of the garlic-eating barbarians.

Of course, I have only just arrived and my views may change but, so far, what I love about Japan is the simple humanity of the country. And there is so much to learn, I could stay here forever. If you do not see me again, I shall be under big trees in some old Buddhist cemetery, six laths above me, inscribed with prayers and a queerly carved monument typifying those five elements into which we are all supposed to melt away.

I trust all is well with you, dear Old Dad. Write to me when you can. Tell me all about yourself. Be sure that I always remember you and that my love goes to you.

L.H.

It continued to rain, and rain torrentially, putting an end to planned trips. The deluge stripped the blossoms from the cherry trees and washed away his feeling of euphoria. He grew tired of the cramped inn, the constant chatter and giggling of maids heard through flimsy walls, the reprimands of the tyrannical old lady who followed him around wiping the floor behind him whenever he wore the wrong slippers. He sat in his room cursing the damp and the morbid, sodden sky outside.

One day during a break between showers he ventured out for a walk. Sea air always cheered him. He saw Weldon near the Grand Hotel and was about to dodge down a side street when he was spotted. Weldon hurried over to him.

"I called to your hotel a few times," said Weldon, after some insincere pleasantries had been exchanged.

"It's not a hotel. It's a traditional inn: a *ryokan*. Architecturally intriguing. A veritable warren of charming rooms and the most extraordinary woodwork I've ever seen. The entire building was constructed without a single nail. It's simply beautiful."

"It smells of cabbage."

"I hadn't noticed. Perhaps your olfactory glands are more finely tuned than mine."

"Well, rather you than me. Didn't you get my messages?" asked Weldon.

"No," lied Hearn.

"Oh. So... How's the writing going?"

"I've written a few letters," said Hearn.

"You know that's not what I mean."

"What do you mean?"

"Articles, Hearn, articles. I need to know what you're writing, so I can supply suitable illustrations."

"You can't expect me to do justice to Japan after just a few days."

"It's been over a month."

"It's not something that can be rushed. I can't write about something in less than the actual time required to live the scenes I am about to describe."

"Well, you'd better get a move on. I'm not going to be here for much longer."

Weldon handed him a small business card.

"That's my new address. Come by later. We can have dinner together. I'll show you the illustrations I've done so far. Perhaps they might concentrate your mind."

Hearn declined the invitation to dinner and left abruptly, crumpling the card in his hand as he walked away. He was furious with Weldon for having the audacity, yet again, to tell him to get working. It annoyed him even further to remember that he would only be paid a pittance, if he got paid at all, and that would only happen if his work got published and there was no guarantee of that. Smouldering with rage, he walked back to his shabby lodgings wishing he had never come. The cost of living in Japan was as high as in New York and money was running out quickly. This was not helped by his visits to the pleasure quarters where the ladies were only too ready to refill his glass and empty his wallet.

The weather did not let up and he plunged into irrational and resentful brooding. Nothing could shake it. Professor Chamberlain replied to his letter saying that he was too busy to meet him but he hoped to when his workload eased. Sensing insults from all sides and blind to indications to the contrary, he became convinced that once again poverty was looming and, almost as if to ensure his own impoverishment, he wrote an angry letter, cursing Alden, cutting all ties with Harper's and telling him in no uncertain terms that all the money in the world could not induce him to contribute a single line to their infernally vulgar magazine.

He fulfilled his obligation to Sir William Van Horne and scribbled a sycophantic essay about the voyage, which he sent directly to him. No more was heard from Van Horne nor from Weldon. He really did not care. He wanted out of there and as quickly as possible. Letters were posted to friends in America asking them, urging them to please find him a suitable position so that he could come back.

The initial delight with all things Japanese had evaporated, and the next few months were harrowing. The modernisation of Yokohama, the speed with which things were changing left him thoroughly disenchanted. His situation was made even more intolerable by the fact that, once he stepped outside of the Westernised areas, he was unable to read or write, or communicate even the simplest things. He was effectively illiterate. On all his previous travels he had had a common language with the local population, English, French, reasonable Spanish, and he had been able to function independently, to talk to people, to workers and to shopkeepers. Through them he would get a feel for a place. Though it had occurred to him before he came, he had not realised just how isolating it would be not to be able to make himself understood, or read signs, or even order food in a restaurant. Half the time he did not know what he was eating. He got endlessly lost. Rambles around the old town invariably ended with him having to show somebody the address of the inn and then being guided home like a lost child. On the days Akira-san was not available, he was truly crippled.

Friends in America failed to find him work; his hot temper and viperous tongue were not easily forgiven or forgotten. He had burnt too many bridges. Desperate to leave but needing money to do so, he reluctantly made himself known in the Western clubs and it was not long before he was offered a position as a private tutor in a Japanese company. His students, businessmen ordered there by their boss, were tired after a long day's work and had no energy left for an English class. Language was Hearn's passion and the slow coaxing of words, the constant need to correct and explain was torture for him.

When an invitation from Chamberlain finally arrived, he travelled to Tokyo to meet him, more out of curiosity than with any great expectations. A servant met him at the station and escorted him through the affluent streets to the professor's stylish old house which was near the university. When the front door opened his heart lifted.

"Is that roast beef I smell?" were his first words to Chamberlain.

"It is indeed. I thought you might be in need of some good old English fare."

Chamberlain was much younger than he expected; in fact Hearn was a few months older than him. He had been in Japan for over seventeen years and was well established and respected. They went straight to lunch and as soon as Hearn tasted the beef he realised how much he missed Western food. Much of Japanese food he found tasteless, the portions were tiny and he never felt satisfied. He was not a man who took a great interest in food but the buttery boiled potatoes served at lunch that day made him realise that, for the first time in his life, he was homesick, but for what home, he did not know.

Conversation flowed and the topic of English teaching came up.

"I'm not sure I'm suited to teaching," said Hearn. "I spend hours painstakingly explaining things to my students, and then I ask them if they understand and they say yes but it subsequently transpires that they haven't understood anything. It's very frustrating."

"Ah, yes, you see, if they said they didn't understand, it would imply that you had not explained properly. In other words it would be a criticism of you, and to criticise a teacher would be considered unspeakably rude."

"How the hell can I teach them if they don't tell me when they don't understand?"

"You'll figure it out."

Hearn had no desire to figure it out.

"Sorry to be so morose. My life seems to be a series of dreams that end in nightmares."

"You'll wake up soon, Hearn. Don't despair. There are aspects of Japan that are sublime."

Hearn noticed two delicately painted dragonflies hovering over stalks of rice on the glossy black lacquered surface of a bowl in the nearby alcove. It was the only piece of art in the room and all the more impressive in its isolation.

"Irregularity," said Chamberlain.

"I beg your pardon?"

"The design."

41

"Oh, of course."

"I find this kind of minimalist, seemingly haphazard design far more pleasing than our Western tendency towards over-ornamentation and symmetry," said Chamberlain.

"Funny you should say that. Anything ugly or commonplace that I've seen here is the direct result of foreign influence. This morning I passed a little shop filled with glorious Buddhist images, and right next door was a shop selling hideous American sewing machines."

"It does seem incongruous until you get used to it. In my early days here I remember thinking everything Japanese was remarkable."

"Yes," said Hearn. "On day one I found myself gazing at a common pair of wooden chopsticks in a paper bag thinking they were extraordinary."

"They probably were. The skills of the artists and artisans here are extraordinary."

"Yet they seem seduced by Western culture."

"That's true. But there's an increasing appreciation amongst the Japanese of their own culture."

"Is there? I haven't seen evidence of it. And now machines enable them to make ugly things to suit vulgar foreign markets."

"Have you been to the new School of Fine Art here in Tokyo?"

"No."

"It focuses on traditional Japanese art rather than Western art."

He could tell by Chamberlain's demeanour that he disapproved.

"Surely that's a good thing," said Hearn.

"I may be being overly pessimistic," said Chamberlain, "but I feel that Japan is looking around at the encroaching foreign powers and growing more and more nervous. The government is actively encouraging not just an appreciation of Japanese culture but they are also nurturing nationalism and an emotional tie to the Emperor. Have you read the new Constitution?"

"I try to remain outside politics. I'm more interested in things weird and wonderful. I leave the subject of the destiny of empires to men with brains."

Chamberlain cast a bemused glance at him.

"Read it. It begins with a declaration of the power of the unbroken and divine Japanese Imperial line."

"Well, they are unique in this regard, and I for one wish they had never opened their doors to the West."

"If they hadn't, the doors would have been broken down. Look at what happened in China."

"I dread to think what it will be like here in fifty or a hundred years' time."

"Perhaps you should leave Yokohama, Hearn. Would you be interested in a position in the Province of Izumo? The government schools in Matsue are in need of an English teacher. Nothing has changed there for hundreds of years."

In truth, in the frame of mind Hearn was in, he wanted nothing more than a ticket back to America, but at the mention of Izumo he had experienced an unexpected hint of excitement. He remembered how delighted he had been to read about this place. It was known as the Province of the Gods. Belief had it that once a year all the gods in Japan, of which there were multitudes, leave their respective homes and go there. Priests light huge bonfires on the beach to welcome them, and a colourful procession leads the gods to their lodgings at the famous Izumo Taisha Shrine. The gods stay there for eight days, hold meetings, drink *sake*, get spectacularly drunk, feast and make decisions about the fate of the people for the following year. Apparently the ceremonies during this period were spectacular and he loved the idea that the gods got drunk. Chamberlain's sombre voice interrupted his fanciful thoughts.

"Have no doubt about it, the Japanese will turn on their white mentors. It's only a matter of time. With no natural resources of its own, Japan will have to expand its territories and I firmly believe that expansionism will eventually lead to war."

"Well, I suppose they have to protect themselves but I hope you are wrong," said Hearn.

"So do I."

After lunch Chamberlain walked him back to the train station. He had enjoyed their exchange. Chamberlain's knowledge of Japan was vastly superior to his and listening to him reminded Hearn of why he had come to Japan. Perhaps Chamberlain was right, it was just Yokohama he needed to leave, not Japan. Outside the station he tried to say goodbye to Chamberlain, but the professor insisted on accompanying him to the platform.

"Now, Hearn, don't forget to write down your first impressions as soon as possible. They are evanescent, you know, they will never come again once they have faded."

"I've been keeping notes," he lied.

"Good. Of all the strange sensations I've had here, none are as charming as those I experienced in my first few months."

"I'll remember that."

"If you like, I will recommend you for that position in Matsue."

"Why not? That would be very kind. Thank you."

"I hope you take it. I'd be interested to hear your observations. It's been a long time since I was there."

They said their goodbyes. Chamberlain waited on the platform and bid him a further farewell by bowing repeatedly to the departing train.

CHAPTER FOUR

Matsue, Japan, 1890

Shortly after his visit with Professor Chamberlain, Hearn was called for an interview in Tokyo, and the Department of Education offered him a job in Matsue. A three-year contract, a good salary and decent terms meant he would have plenty of time to write. He was eager to capture all he had seen so far on paper but until now more pressing concerns, namely finding a way to support himself, had taken most of his time and energy. This job meant immediate escape from Yokohama, and as soon as the contracts were signed he asked Akira-san to accompany him on the journey as guide and translator.

"I'll pay all your expenses and a daily rate for your services."

"I'd be honoured to come with you, Hearn-san."

"Good. I'd like to get going as soon as possible. We'll leave tomorrow morn—"

"Tomorrow?"

"Yes."

"That would be a little difficult," said Akira-san.

"Well, the day after will do."

The young man drew in a long slow breath and turned away.

"Perhaps next week would be a more suitable time to—"

"No. I can't take another day here. If you can't come, I'll find somebody else."

Hearn waited for an answer but none came. Akira-san had promised to make himself available whenever he was needed but now he stood silent, eyes averted, head bowed.

"Well, are you coming or not?"

"Yes, of course. I will make the arrangements."

"Good. We'll leave tomorrow morning."

Their four-hundred-mile journey by train, then by rickshaw on difficult mountain roads and finally by boat began on a hot July day. As they moved further and further away from places, Hearn thought contaminated by Western influence, his spirits began to lift. Once past the towns, they encountered only thatched villages, and the Buddhist temples they passed further west appeared smaller and poorer. Symbols of Shinto, the indigenous religion, were more numerous now in dense cedar and pine forests. Great stone lions and foxes guarded moss-covered rock stairways that led to holy groves, and simple H-shaped gateways towered high on the approach to each village. Shinto seemed to have no rules, no written canon, no threats, no prudish moralising, and this appealed to him immensely. Magnificent in its simplicity, all it seemed to require was that you respect the members of your household and honour your ancestors.

Akira-san told him that every house had a small shrine containing tablets inscribed with the names of the ancestors, and every day offerings of food and water, selected from the family meals, were made. He thought it very moving that the ancestors were not thought of as dead; that they remained among those who loved them; that they were attended to, and spoken to, by the living family members as if they were actually present. It was a far cry from the little he knew of family life where people were barely civil to the living never mind to the dead.

In all the little towns and villages they passed through, people gazed at him in wonder. Apologising for their curiosity with humble bows and winning smiles, they came and touched his clothes and his hair, the softness of which seemed to cause them bewilderment. There was no aggression, no hostility; gentler and kinder faces he had never seen. They stopped one night at a village in an area known for its volcanic springs. He was surprised to find that, primitive though the place was, every house had a communal bathtub with constant, fresh, hot water. Having secured rooms in the local inn, he went straight to the hot tub to soak in the healing water. The old innkeeper came bearing *sake* on a small tray and placed it beside the tub, all the while staring shamelessly at Hearn's private parts and chattering away in Japanese. Hearn was used to people staring at him but this was too intense. He was feeling decidedly uncomfortable until Akira-san arrived and explained that the innkeeper had only seen a European once, many years previously, and the person had long hair of a curious colour and wore a dress reaching the ground. Nobody in the village could tell whether it was a man or a woman. He had been sent by his wife and daughters to satisfy their curiosity as to Hearn's gender.

"And what did he decide?" asked Hearn.

"He said you were a big man," said Akira-san.

Hearn laughed, thinking that was a first. The old man laughed too and then shuffled back into the house to inform the waiting family and neighbours of the news.

In bed that night Hearn felt giddy and at the same time drowsy. Whether it was the effect of the thermal water, the fresh mountain air, the *sake* or a combination of all three, he did not know but a weight had lifted and he fell into a deep sleep.

Each day as they travelled, the country became more and more lovely. Mile after mile the rickshaw jerked across mountain slopes and valleys dense with rice fields, thousands and thousands of tiny rice fields, some no larger than cottage gardens, separated from each other by narrow serpentine dykes. As they travelled along it occurred to him that if the job in Matsue did not work out he would be in serious trouble. With hardly a cent to his name, how would he ever get back to America? Doubts niggled but he did not panic. For some strange reason, he was resigned to allowing whatever happened to happen.

They stopped another night in a remote town, so remote that not even a missionary had been there, and when word got out that a foreigner had arrived, the streets filled with people eager to see him. Never having been scrutinised like this before, and by so many, he escaped into an inn and took refuge in an upstairs room, but he had barely sat down when a stream of people, four and five at a time, put their heads around the door, smiling, bowing and staring at him. Having seen the foreigner, they retired so that others could inspect him. One after another, they arrived and left without a sound. An hour later, there were so many people crowding into the inn, the servant had difficulty bringing dinner to his room. It was becoming tiresome and irritation must have shown because Akira-san got up and closed the *shoji* screens.

Moments later small fingers poked holes through the screens' paper insets. He turned his back on the prying eyes and only then did he notice that the rooms on the upper floors of the houses opposite were packed with people gazing across at him. Young boys and men had even climbed up onto roofs to get a better look. The strange thing was that all this happened in complete silence. It was innocent, but it was weird and made him feel like a ghost, a new arrival in the underworld, surrounded by shapes without voices.

The whole town came out and smiled and bowed as his little party left the next day. Just outside the village they passed a cemetery and judging by the huge number of graves, the dead vastly outnumbered the population of the village. At his request, the runners waited in the rickshaws while he and Akira-san explored the graveyard. His attention was caught by a relatively new headstone amongst the ancient tombs.

"It's the tomb of a sailor lost at sea," said Akira-san. "His body was never found, so instead they buried the flower stalk of life."

"The what?"

"The string," he said, gesturing to his navel.

"Ah, the umbilical cord?"

"Yes, it's buried here. We save them at birth. The name of the infant, the parents, and the time and date of the birth are written on all flower stalks, and they are carefully wrapped and stored in the family cupboard of memories."

"I see."

"He was twenty-three years old."

A perfect, dainty meal, chopsticks and a small cup of tea had been placed on the grave; the tea was still warm. He assumed that this was the work of a loving widow, mother or sister perhaps. The prints of her little sandaled feet were still fresh upon the path. A sudden memory of his own father, who had been buried at sea, caused an unexpected pang. There was no grave to mark his death, no place to go and pay respects or honour his memory. Not that he would have gone. His father had only ever been a fleeting figure, someone cool and aloof, who came in and out of his early childhood years at long intervals. He had abandoned him and Hearn felt no filial duty towards him.

Hearn could understand why he had remarried but what he could not understand, or forgive, was that when he sailed away to India with his new wife and her two daughters, he left his son behind. It was little solace to the young Hearn when he was informed that they were on their way back when he contracted malaria and died aboard ship. Had his father made it home, would he have wanted him then? He doubted it, but he would never know for sure.

The sight of the meal on the tomb of the lost sailor moved him deeply. He wondered what it would be like to be so loved, to have a family who looked after you and cared for you in life and even after death. Old memories overwhelmed him. He felt sick and hollow inside.

Nobody, it seemed, had any right to expect happiness in this world unless gifted with great physical strength and force of will. Little phantoms of men, like himself, were tossed about like feathers in the wind, and in this grim frame of mind he climbed back onto his rickshaw. It took the runners, going at a brisk pace, a full fifteen minutes to pass the cemetery and as they rolled along he looked out at the legions of tombs, monuments to all who had ever lived in this remote place, and he thought how insignificant individuals were, how futile it was to even try to leave a mark behind. In time the silent witnesses would crumble. Many of the tombs had already been worn into shapeless lumps, their carved inscriptions washed away by the rain.

They were nearing the end of the overland journey and it was dark when they reached the port town of Yonago. From a distance it looked like a small electrified city, lit up and shining in the night, but as they approached he saw that these were not electric lights. Blazing pine torches were fixed in the ground outside most houses; beautifully painted lanterns, decorated with a peculiar fringe of paper streamers, glowed outside others. Akira-san could see him looking around quizzically.

"It's for the Festival of the Dead," Akira-san explained. " We call it *Bon*. It's held every July."

Hearn had been so preoccupied with getting to Matsue that he had forgotten all about this intriguing festival.

"The lanterns and torches outside each house guide the spirits of the ancestors home. They're hungry and thirsty after the long journey back from the other world."

"And so am I," said Hearn, who had not managed to shake off his morbid mood.

They had been travelling all day with hardly a break and he was exhausted, not just from the journey or from the heat, but also from the relentless humidity which left him drained. The poor diet and skimpy meals with barely a pick of meat did not help either. He was not overly concerned about his lack of energy, it was nothing that a fine big steak would not fix, but he realised that there was little hope of that here; he had not seen a single cow on the entire journey.

"When did the festival begin?" asked Hearn.

"Yesterday," said Akira-san.

"So there'll be more celebrations tomorrow?"

"Yes, the last day is special."

Though curious, the idea of wandering around an unknown town at midnight did not appeal to Hearn particularly as Akira-san had told him that Yonago could be a little rough. Once they had located their accommodation and eaten, he retired to bed.

Next morning, the third and final day of *Bon*, they set out to explore. The temples were decorated with flowers and sprigs of sacred plants. Where real lotus flowers were not available, colourful paper ones were used. It was a poor town and he was surprised to see generous offerings of rice, noodles, vegetables, watermelons, peaches, plums, sweet cakes and all kinds of expensive treats spread out on the altars.

"The temple offerings are for hungry ghosts who have no living relatives or friends left to feed them," said Akira-san. "We call them *gaki*. The priests look after them."

"That's very kind."

"It's not just kindness, Hearn-san. If *gaki* aren't fed, they cause trouble."

"How?"

"They enter into living bodies and suck the warmth and nourishment from them. It happened to my father once. He was cold and shivering one minute and then feverish the next. And he shouted at my mother. It went on for days until *gaki* went away. I remember it well because he never normally raises his voice."

"I see."

"We believe that people who argue are possessed by *gaki*."

How convenient it would be, thought Hearn, to be able to attribute one's unsavoury behaviour to demonic possession rather than to simple badness.

"The dead suffer if they are forgotten, Hearn-san. So offerings to the ancestors are made in every house. It's our duty and we undertake it happily. Our children and grandchildren will do the same for us, especially during *Bon*."

Hearn had a sudden memory of Akira-san quietly suggesting that they delay the journey.

"Why didn't you explain about this before we left Yokohama?"

Akira-san did not answer and avoided his gaze.

"Shouldn't you be at home making the offerings?"

"Never mind," said Akira-san with a smile. "Mother is doing it."

"If you had said you had family duties, we could have waited."

"It's not a problem."

Hearn made a mental note to be more attentive to this mild-mannered young man. Professor Chamberlain had told him that the Japanese speak in oblique subtleties, and it was up to the listener to gauge what was really meant by the tone or by the accompanying gesture, rather than the actual words. He had ignored Akira-san's reticence to depart and selfishly imposed his own agenda. The young man had meekly complied with his wishes and had probably upset his family by being absent for this important family occasion. Feeling like an insensitive oaf, he left Akira-san at the temple to give him time alone to pray.

The town was thronged with families out for the day and with long processions of men, women and children of all ages dancing. The cemeteries were also full of people pouring purifying water over tombstones, praying, making offerings of food and burning incense for the souls of the ancestors. Flowers were placed before each grave and lanterns hung outside every tomb. Despite the solemnity of the occasion, the atmosphere was joyful and, at the same time, respectful. He kept his head down and with his black hair, and dressed as he was in *yukata*, the simple cotton robe that the hotel supplied to all guests, he was able to observe the festival rituals without attracting much attention.

At dinner that evening he heard measured hand clapping somewhere nearby. It was soft and at long intervals, and at still longer intervals came a deep low boom: the sound of a great drum, a temple drum.

"It's the Dance of Souls," said Akira-san. "You should see it. It's not like the dances in the cities. It's the dance of ancient times. Customs haven't changed here for centuries."

Once the meal was finished they ventured out. The night was still and clear. A huge white moon cast strange shadows on the tilted eaves and horned gables of the little houses. Following the crowds, they found themselves in a temple courtyard and at its centre was a high bamboo frame supporting an enormous two-sided drum. Still as statues, two semi-naked men bearing batons in each hand stood poised on either side of the drum. Sweat glistened on their bronzed limbs as they beat a rhythm in perfectly synchronised, choreographed movements.

Out of the shadows a procession of dancers filed into the moonlit courtyard; figures lightly poised like birds, first one foot, then the other, sandaled feet all gliding together, pliant bodies swaying, white hands sinuously moving as if weaving spells. Hearn was enchanted, bewitched by the primordial beat of the drum, the ghostly movement of the dancers' hands, the rhythmic gliding of feet and the fluttering of the marvellous long sleeves of their *kimono*. The women were apparitional, soundless, velvety as the flitting of great tropical bats, and they danced for the souls who had risen from the nearby graves where the white lanterns hung. They danced for their fathers and their fathers' fathers, and he was certain that the souls of unknown generations gazed with joy upon this magical scene.

Later that night, after the living had done all they could for the dead, the souls of the ancestors were sent back to the unseen world in a strangely moving farewell ceremony that took place on the beach. Hundreds of families arrived with little boats made of closely woven barley straw. The boats were no more than two feet high and each one was filled with flowers, food, tiny lanterns and written messages of faith and love. As each frail craft, with lanterns glowing at the prow and incense burning at the stern, was launched into the sea, the families bowed their heads, joined their hands and prayed. He did not know what they were praying for, he heard only, at moments, the soft sibilant sound made by gently drawing the breath through the lips, which among the Japanese was a token of the humblest desire to please.

He stood on the shore watching this tender rite and became aware of something dimly stirring in his heart, like an ancient memory blended in some strange way with his own knowledge of an older world where household gods were also the beloved dead. It was the sweetest, most mysterious sensation. The ghostly visitors drifted away on the tide in their little boats. The sea shimmered with hundreds of faint flickering lights and, as he watched, he heard a murmuring of voices, like the murmur of a far off city. He could not help thinking that it was the indistinguishable speech of souls on this glittering highway for the dead.

The festival was over and he expected to leave the following morning, but over breakfast Akira-san seemed nervous as he informed him that they must wait at least one more day in Yonago. He was used to Hearn's demands and braced himself for the childish burst of temper that usually erupted when plans went awry. To his surprise, Hearn remained calm.

"Why must we wait?"

"The boatmen won't sail until the Ships of Souls are gone," said Akira-san.

"You mean, the little boats?"

"Yes, the spirits of the dead are on them and they might still be out there."

"I see. Are there no fishermen about who would—?"

"Nobody will go out on the water. You might laugh, Hearn-san, but if we sail now ghosts could fill our boat and sink it and the demons of the deep would pull us down and eat our entrails."

"Why might I laugh?" said Hearn, trying not to show his delight at the discovery of this wonderful superstition.

"A Western missionary told me that such beliefs were childish nonsense."

"I'm not a Christian, Akira-san. I'm deeply interested in such beliefs."

"The innkeeper told me that a body was washed up on the shore here a few years ago. It had no visible injuries but was hollow and light like a dried-out gourd."

"That settles it," said Hearn. "We'll wait."

Akira-san was relieved. Hearn went back to his room and wrote about all that had happened on the journey. He was especially pleased to write about the Japanese beliefs in ghosts, a phenomenon he had not doubted since those terrifying nights locked in his bedroom in his great-aunt's house in Dublin all those years ago, all those miles away. The memories lingered with him and still had the power to unsettle him. Ghosts, which he had been aware of as a child and whose existence had been vehemently denied by the adults, were believed in and readily accepted, honoured even, in Japan. Ghosts, spirits, souls: the words were interchangeable and unremarkable. He wrote all that day and through the night until the first rays of morning light filtered into his room. Just before noon Akira-san woke him and told him that it was now safe to travel.

They sailed to Matsue, a city situated on a strip of land between the Sea of Japan and the vast Lake Shinji. Two rivers and numerous canals, crossed by curious little hump-backed bridges, ran through it and, just as Chamberlain had said, the Pro-Western changes enforced by the Meiji government had not touched this city. To his joy, there was neither an English sign nor another white face to be seen. He was the only foreigner in the province and he was aware of the irony of the situation: he was the very thing that he loathed seeing in Japan but he justified his presence by telling himself that he was there to observe and record, not to change things.

They set out to acquaint themselves with the lie of the land. The district of the merchants and shopkeepers formed the heart of this pristine city; the houses were modest, close together and two-storeys high. To the south was the temple district and in the surrounding hills to the north were large, single-storey houses surrounded by expansive gardens. These had been the homes of the warrior class – before the abolition of the Shogunate some twenty years earlier – when the city had been a military stronghold. Most of the *samurai* houses were clustered around Matsue Castle, a vast and sinister iron-grey shape that seemed to grow out of the ground. Topped with two colossal bronze fish arching their curved bodies skyward, and resembling a sinister *samurai* helmet, it was a magnificent monstrosity.

"It's one of the oldest castles in Japan," said Akira-san as they climbed the three hundred feet up to the top of the castle. "The innkeeper told me that a local maiden was interred alive under the walls when it was built as a sacrifice to the gods."

"And who was this maiden?" asked Hearn.

"Nothing is known of her except that she was beautiful and fond of dancing. A law was passed forbidding maidens to dance in the streets because when they did, the ground would shudder and the great castle would quiver from top to bottom."

It was an amusing legend and made the steep climb seem less arduous. By the time they reached the top they were both breathless. Akira-san did not like heights and he stayed inside. Hearn stepped out and stood on the ramparts looking down. The whole city could be seen at a single glance. People walking the roads below appeared no larger than flies. He felt like a soaring hawk inspecting some new unplundered terrain. This is the place. This will do, he thought, this will do very nicely indeed.

CHAPTER FIVE

Winter, Matsue, Japan, 1890

The little house he rented in Matsue had seemed ideal. It had a garden right at the point where the Ohashi river opened out onto Lake Shinji. On summer mornings he woke to the peal of the great Tokoji temple bell echoing across the water, announcing the arrival of dawn. He would slide open the *shoji* screens and watch the local people with little blue towels tucked into their belts descending the stone steps on the opposite bank of the river. Having washed their faces and hands and rinsed out their mouths in the traditional Shinto purification ritual, they then turned their faces to the rising sun, clapped their hands four times and prayed, giving thanks for the sweet light that made the world beautiful. Such simple gratitude never failed to move him. And in the balmy evenings he sat gazing out over the lake, watching the tones and colours change like the shades of fine shot silk billowing in a gentle breeze.

Access to information was considerably curtailed when Akira-san left and went back to Yokohama but he managed. His Japanese was improving and he had written quite a number of essays about small things that other writers might ignore: animals, insects, flowers, shadows, graveyards, strange customs and any odd thing that he might hear about or notice during his daily routine. He thought of these essays as tiny glimpses into the enchanting life of Matsue and, when he had a large enough collection, he would send them out for publication.

One thing caused him some disquiet. The more he came to understand and appreciate Japan, the more he questioned his role there. At first he told himself that he was only there to observe and record, and that was true. But he could not deny the fact that, as an English teacher, he himself was a form of contamination. He was helping to groom the next generation for interaction with the West and so he was, in no small way, contributing to the dissolution of this pure and unique culture. It sat uneasily with him. He consoled himself by saying that if he did not do it somebody else would, perhaps somebody less sympathetic to Japan than he was. The doors to the outside world had been opened and would never close again.

Since taking up his post at the school he had been showered with gifts: food, *sake*, a little wooden pillow, Japanese clothes, wooden sandals, and all kinds of things to make his life comfortable. But the strangest gift of all was presented to him by the daughter of the Governor of Izumo, who thought that the foreign teacher might be lonely. It was a caged insect: a grass lark. At first he was baffled by the insect, which he needed a magnifying glass to see. It was about the size of a mosquito with a pair of antennae much longer than its own body. He brought it home and that evening at sunset the room filled with delicate ghostly music of indescribable sweetness. As the darkness deepened, the sound became sweeter and sweeter, sometimes swelling until the whole house seemed to vibrate with elfish resonance, sometimes thinning down into the faintest imaginable thread of a voice. All night long the tiny insect sang and it did not cease until the temple bell proclaimed dawn.

The days were full. His duties at the school were not difficult and the boys were all wonderfully docile and patient. Once they realised that he did not consider them savages as their previous teacher had, they were most receptive. Teaching schoolboys turned out to be much more agreeable than he had expected. A fellow teacher, Nishida-san, spoke reasonable English, and he prepared the lessons in advance so that Hearn's lack of Japanese made for no difficulty in the classroom.

Nishida-san had a plain, broad face that belied his thin body and he oozed eagerness to please, so much so that at first Hearn thought him a little simple. Nishida-san may have been slow in his responses but he was far from simple; he was a deep thinker who thought everything through thoroughly before speaking.

Stress became a thing of the past, and every night Hearn went home looking forward to the song of the grass lark. Loud or low, it kept up a penetrating sound that was strangely soothing. He assumed that the song it sang was a love song; it was calling out for a mate. Breeding and selling of insects was a lucrative industry, and he was about to buy a female, but he was warned that if the grass lark mated it would die.

Night after night he listened to the creature's plaintive, unanswered trilling. It touched him like a reproach and became a torment of conscience and of wonder. How was it that the grass lark knew this mating song? He had been told that it was hatched from an egg in a clay jar in the shop of an insect merchant and had only ever lived in a cage, as had its parents and all the generations that had gone before it. It had never known life in the fields and yet it sang the song of its species as faultlessly as if it understood the significance of every note. It was a song of organic memory, a deep dim memory of former lives when it trilled at night from the dewy grasses of the hills.

The poor little grass lark continued to sing his heart out for the bride who would never come; it had forgotten about the resulting death and only remembered the need for love. He began to think that perhaps humans' search for love was also a phantom of organic memory. The living present had very little to do with it. He himself had stumbled blindly into love, to his own detriment. Still, it seemed cruel to deny the grass lark its basic instinct and he was about to release it when he realised that it would not find a mate; it was late

59

in the season and they were probably all dead. The little creature was only alive because of the relative warmth of the room. If he set it free, it would not survive a single night. Even if he let it go in the daytime, it would soon be devoured by ants, or centipedes or the ghastly earth spiders that prowled the garden.

Winter came and the *shoji* screens were no defence against the plummeting temperature. The grass lark died and he was irrationally heartbroken. His custom of feeding it every day – the tiniest sliver of cucumber – and thinking about its needs and wants had created an attachment, which he only became conscious of when the relationship ended. It was absurd; life seemed suddenly empty and all because of an insect half the size of a grain of barley.

The first snowstorm piled five feet of snow around his flimsy house. The lake froze. The city, the fields and the mountains were smothered with snow. Severe winds chilled him to the bone, and his one little *hibachi* stove provided only an illusion of heat. He caught pneumonia and was forced to spend weeks in bed, shaking, feverish and coughing up blood. Concerned well-wishers visited daily bearing warming broths, curious medicinal remedies and charcoal for the *hibachi*. It was his first serious setback since his arrival in Matsue and with it came a check to his enthusiasm about his great Japanese project.

"I believe I would be warmer living in a cattle barn. Another winter like this will put me underground."

He drank the warm *sake* his colleague, and now friend, Nishida-san had brought.

"So much snow. Most unusual."

"I never saw a heavier snowfall, not even in Canada."

"Soon it will melt and you will be well again."

He could see that Nishida-san was embarrassed, almost ashamed, as if he was to blame for the climate and for Hearn's illness. He put on a cheerful face to placate his friend.

"You've all been astonishingly kind to me. Thank you, Nishida-san. If not for you, I don't know what I'd do."

Some weeks later, when he was back at work, Nishida-san surprised him with a peculiar solution to the ongoing problem of Hearn's inability to keep warm.

"You should marry, Hearn-san."

"What? Marry because I am cold?"

"Yes."

He searched his friend's face to see if he was teasing. He was not.

"That wouldn't be a good reason to marry."

They were sitting in the chilly teachers' room drinking tea. His desk was next to Nishida-san's and on each desk was a small *hibachi* made of glazed blue and white stoneware. In an attempt to warm himself, Hearn held his hands close to the few lumps of glowing charcoal in the bed of ashes in his *hibachi*. Nishida-san looked at him with concern.

"You really do need a wife, Hearn-san. Somebody to look after you, to keep you warm at night, to cook and clean for you and keep your clothes in good repair."

"That sounds like a form of slavery."

"Oh, no, it would be an honour for any Japanese woman to serve you."

"Nonsense. Besides, I couldn't make such a commitment. I'll only be here for a few years and then I'm going to retire to the West Indies."

"But until then you should have a wife."

"Even if I agreed, who would have me? I'm an old man."

"You're not young but I know someone who might marry you."

The woman he had in mind was twenty-two year old Koizumi Setsuko, the only daughter of a proud *samurai* family with good breeding and steel in the blood. Despite her aristocratic roots, with the abolition of the *samurai* class, her family had fallen from a position of privilege to abject poverty. Their only income, and it was paltry, came from the mother who took in needlework and from Setsuko, who had been reduced to taking a job as a humble servant.

"I'm a romantic. I couldn't possibly—"

"This is not romance, Hearn-san. It's practical. You must think about it."

"My dear friend, to live forever in one woman's company would kill a man with boredom."

"It need not be forever. Marriage with a foreign man would not be considered permanent and could be easily ended if you decided to leave."

"No, I couldn't bear to be tied down."

"Oh, but this woman is quiet and dutiful. You will hardly notice her but you will notice the comforts she will bring you. And she will let you come and go as you please."

"Is it possible that such a woman exists?" said Hearn, who had often dreamed of having a quiet wife, who would leave him in peace to do his work.

At home that evening he slid open the *shoji* screens and sat on the floor looking out at the chilly night, thinking about Nishida-san's proposal. In the distance, paper lanterns hung along the far side of the lake like a long line of shimmering fireflies. Across the river, the broad *shoji* screens of hundreds of dwellings were suffused with the soft yellow radiance of invisible lamps. In these lighted spaces he could see slender moving shadows, the silhouettes of graceful women. He silently prayed that glass would never be adopted in Japan as it would put an end to these delicious shadows. He listened to the voices of the city until the great bell of Tokoji temple rolled its soft thunder across the dark and he thought how pleasant it would be to have a graceful Japanese woman moving silently about in the shadows of his own house.

Overall, Hearn found the Japanese women charming but many of them were nervous in his company and they giggled a lot behind cupped hands. It was a habit that irritated him. But Nishida-san had piqued his curiosity and, the following day, he broached the subject with him.

"This woman you were talking about—"

"Koizumi Setsuko-san?"

"Yes. She's not a giggler, is she? I couldn't tolerate that."

"She is definitely not a giggler. She has little to laugh about. If you were to marry her, you would be doing the family a great honour, and I should alert you to the possibility that her family would have to come and live with you."

"How many of them are there?"

"Her father died of consumption when she was young. She lives with her mother and her grandfather. There is also an elderly maid. They can't afford to pay her but she has stayed with them through everything."

"I'm not sure I want a wife, never mind a mother-in-law."

"Setsuko-san and her mother are both very refined. The old man is charming. I think you'd like them."

A few more miserable nights shivering in his icebox of a house decided Hearn. He would meet this Koizumi Setsuko. Nishida-san, the self-ordained matchmaker, arranged the meeting. Setsuko was quiet and respectful and, as Nishida-san had been at lengths to point out, at twenty-two, she was neither young enough, nor pretty enough, nor rich enough to be choosy. Though almost twice her age and a foreigner, as a teacher and a writer – both professions held in high esteem in Japan – Hearn was a good catch. And whereas her family were struggling to survive, he was well paid and could easily provide for them. After some initial small talk she informed him, through Nishida-san who was interpreting, that she had been married before.

"I thought you should know. After my husband deserted me I had the marriage dissolved and I was registered back into the Koizumi family."

"Are there children from the marriage?"

"No."

"May I ask, what became of him?"

Hearn posed this question somewhat tentatively; he did not want to marry this woman only to have his head lopped off by some disgruntled former husband.

"I don't know," she said. "Perhaps when he married me he thought my family were still prosperous, though I made it clear to him that we weren't. When he realised just how poor we were, he ran away."

"The swine."

"It was a difficult time for many *samurai* families. Like all the other former warriors, my father had to find a new way to make a living. He set up a weaving factory, but he had no business sense and he couldn't compete with foreign imports."

"As we are being open, I should tell you that I was also married," said Hearn. "Well, I considered myself married, though legally, the marriage was not recognised. We went our separate ways many years ago."

"Did you have children?"

"No."

"So we are both free to marry," she said.

"Yes, but I must warn you that my intention is to complete my teaching contract and then retire to the West Indies."

"Thank you. I understand," she said and bowed.

He went home that night and got drunk. What was he thinking? After his disastrous marriage to Mattie, he had sworn he would never marry again. He could still see her, beautiful, sensuous Mattie with her glorious golden skin and fiery black eyes. He also remembered how they had fought with the wild passion of young people in love who believed their every trifling thought and action to be of universal importance. He must have been mad. He was mad. Madly in love, in lust, besotted, and by marrying her he had brought so much trouble upon himself.

But it would be different this time. He was not entering into this marriage in the mindless height of youthful passion. This was not a love marriage. It was an arranged marriage: a marriage of mutual convenience. He liked this frank and honest woman, and he was satisfied that she knew what she was doing. They were both entering into the marriage contract with a clear understanding of the terms. It would suit them both. This time his eyes were not clouded by romantic and impossibly unrealistic expectations and, given the ease with which the marriage could be dissolved, he decided he had nothing to lose.

Two weeks later he watched his bride glide slowly towards him. She was weighed down by layers of *kimono* and spectacular hair ornamentation that was so heavy she could barely hold her head up. Her face had been painted white. It was the face of an alabaster statue, motionless, expressionless. And where the mouth should have been, there were tiny red lips, cherubic in shape. They bore no relation to Setsuko's lips. All signs of the person underneath had been masked; human nature had been tamed and controlled. Her movements were prescribed and she would not deviate from the expected form. This woman could not be further from his spontaneous, passionate Mattie. And he was glad of it.

He felt elegant and strangely at ease in the traditional Japanese clothes he had agreed to wear for the marriage ceremony: *haori*, a short jacket and *hakama*, wide pleated trousers that looked like a skirt. They hung perfectly on his lean body and did not restrict movement like Western clothes did. In fact they felt so comfortable he thought he might continue to wear them. It will be easy to be agreeable, he thought, as he stood to meet Setsuko. She was at his side now. As he had been advised by Nishida-san, he did not look at her or show any sign of affection. Neither did she look at him; she kept her eyes on the floor and the bridal couple bowed, as one, to her family.

Chapter Six

Matsue, Japan, 1891

In order to accommodate Setsuko's mother, grandfather and the maid, they moved to a bigger house. The former residence of a high ranking *samurai*, it had spacious rooms and substantial gardens. Setsuko had found the house and arranged the move. He left for work one morning and when it was time for him to go home there was a rickshaw waiting to pick him up outside the school. The family met him at the gate and bowed as they called out the traditional greeting to welcome a family member home.

"*Okaerinasai.*"

"*Tadaima,*" he replied, meaning: I am home.

And he felt deliciously at home until he got inside and discovered that Setsuko's grandfather, Oji-san, had taken the best room in the house. It was the room Hearn had planned to use as his study. A keen gardener, the old man chose it because it overlooked a special part of the garden that contained no large plants or trees but was paved with pebbles. In the centre of this area there was a miniature lake, containing a tiny island with tiny mountains and dwarf pines, azaleas and peach trees, some of which were more than a hundred years old but scarcely more than a foot high. Seen from the room, it had the appearance of a distant landscape, with a real island in the centre of a lake. It was a brilliantly conceived optical illusion in what was effectively a small pond. Hearn had looked forward to gazing out on it while he worked.

"What's going on here?" he asked his wife, indicating Oji-san's possessions, which had been arranged in the room. "This room is to be my study."

She looked nervously from the floor to the garden where Oji-san was tidying away weeds.

"Come," she said.

She shuffled away with tiny urgent steps. He followed her to another room where his things had been unpacked and laid out just as they had been in the old house.

"This room is lovely and mine is right next door," she said.

"No, I want the other one."

He went back to the other room and began to gather up Oji-san's few possessions. She followed, calling after him in a quiet, restrained voice.

"Oji-san picked this room for himself."

She stood in the doorway, bowed her head and stared at her feet.

"There are plenty of other rooms for him to choose from."

"But he chose this one."

"Who is going to pay the rent? Who is going to pay the bills? I am. Therefore I get to have first choice. I'll talk to him and—?"

"No, please, you mustn't say anything to him. He's the head of the family. It's his right. Please don't insult him by making him take a lesser room."

"I have no intention of insulting him."

"If you ask him to move, he will be insulted."

It was the first time she had disagreed with him. She sank to her knees and bowed deeply, and when she straightened up he could see that she was distressed.

"Perhaps it is different in your country but here, it is not about who pays, Danna-sama," she said, using the respectful term for him as her husband. "It is not about money. It is about respect."

He looked out at Oji-san who was happily humming as he weeded the garden. Simply dressed in the quiet subdued colours of the aged, he had a wondrously gentle countenance, with a long white beard and a head as shiny as an ivory ball. Hearn felt a ripple of shame run through his body at the idea that he might upset this lovely old man.

"Very well. The other room will do."

Setsuko breathed an almost imperceptible sigh of relief.

~

Though he missed the expansive views from his first house, he grew to love his new home. It was on a quiet leafy street, beside the castle moat. Every day, no matter at what time he came home, he would find a hot bath waiting for him, fresh robes laid out and dinner ready. He had never been so clean. The bathtub was not for washing in, ablutions were done before immersing oneself in the hot water, it was for heating the body and for relaxation. Once he got used to the almost scalding temperature, he found it wonderfully restorative. Afterwards, even on the coldest days, he could walk around the garden in nothing but a light cotton *yukata* with steam rising from his body.

Hanako, the maid, was a tiny old woman whose hair was in constant disarray. Her movements were unsure, jittery. Whenever she met him in a corridor she would bow repeatedly and back away mumbling something incomprehensible in a high-pitched, nervous voice. She came into his room one day to clean and, dismayed to find him there, she dropped her sweeping broom.

"It's alright, Hanako-san," he said. "Come in, come in."

She seemed panic stricken at every word he uttered and remained frozen on the spot. Her eyes darted warily from the floor to him and back again.

"Please carry on."

She began to tremble. Setsuko was passing by and she said something to Hanako, who scurried away.

"I'm afraid she doesn't understand you, Danna-sama."

"Is my pronunciation that bad?"

"No, it's just that you're a foreigner and she assumes you're speaking English. Even if your Japanese was perfect, she still wouldn't understand. I'm sorry if she disturbed you."

"Never mind, I was just about to leave."

She picked up the broom.

"She's been with the family all her life," she said, feeling a need to explain the presence of this highly-strung person in the otherwise tranquil house. "She has nobody."

From then on, he did Hanako the courtesy of not speaking to her and she gradually became less tense around him.

~

Spring came. Each day after returning from school and changing from his teacher's uniform into the infinitely more comfortable Japanese clothes, he found compensation for the weariness of five hours' teaching in the simple pleasure of sitting on the shaded veranda overlooking the gardens. The mossy garden walls topped with thick, sloping tiles seemed to shut out even the slightest murmur of city life. All he could hear was birdsong, the call of cicada or, at long lazy intervals, the solitary splash of a diving frog.

None of the garden creatures seemed to be afraid of him. The little frogs resting on lotus leaves scarcely shrank from his touch. Lizards sunned themselves within easy reach of his hand. Water snakes glided across his shadow without fear. Bands of cicada serenaded him from the plum branch just above his head. An insolent praying mantis posed on his knee, and in the golden twilight hours the plaintive call of the yamabato dove floated across to him from the castle grounds.

The garden walls secluded him from much more than just the city. They sheltered him from inevitable progress. He knew that soon tall fair-haired men with beards would come with armies of Japanese labourers and they would construct a railroad which would cut through the rice fields and mulberry groves. It was happening all over Japan. Lines of telegraph poles would be planted parallel to the railroad and trains would come, roaring and smoking, making the ground quake as they passed ancient temples, and causing the Buddhas in the cemeteries to tremble on their stone lotus flowers.

But within his walls dwelt the all reposing peace of nature and the dreams of ancient times. The four gardens that surrounded his house were gardens of long ago. The future would know them only as creations of a forgotten art whose charm no genius could reproduce. It saddened him to think that it would all eventually vanish. Already many of the neighbouring gardens, some larger and more beautiful than his, had been converted into rice fields or bamboo groves, and the city would soon swell and change and grow commonplace and demand that these indulgent gardens be sacrificed to the building of factories and mills. The peaceful, ancient way of life was doomed. Impermanency was the nature of things. Honoured to be able to witness it, he often thought back to his unhappy beginnings in Yokohama and how, had he had money, he might easily have given up, fled back to America and missed this magical world.

Once they got over the teething stages and the household learned that under no circumstances was he to be disturbed when he was in his room, and that noisy chores should be done any time other than when he was working, things settled into a pleasant routine. Setsuko was a skilled communicator; he had no difficulty understanding her Japanese and this was because she always spoke slowly and clearly, and used simple vocabulary. She was endlessly patient and made no demands or complaints even when he was late home or when he drank too much. There was not a word of criticism, not even when he stayed out all night; the lovely ladies in the pleasure quarters were, on occasion, hard to resist. She knew where he had been and she said nothing. It was of no interest to her. In fact she expected it as, it seemed, many Japanese wives did. What she would have minded was any threat to her economic stability or to her status as wife. As there was no threat to that, she was content to cook and clean and manage the household finances, and she did so with great diligence.

He had little interaction with his mother-in-law, Oka-san, who had been traumatised by the family's descent into poverty. She was fifty years of age though she looked much older. Wary of her daughter's foreign husband, she seldom left her room. He saw her one morning, a frail little woman, hunched over a piece of needlework. Beside her on the floor was a large pile of *kimono*. When he came back late that afternoon, she was still sewing.

"Your mother has many *kimono*," he said to Setsuko when she brought him his dinner.

"No, she has only one good one which she keeps for special occasions."

"But I saw—"

"They're not hers. She sews. It's her job."

"It's not necessary for her to work. I make more than enough for all of us."

"She is proud. She wants to contribute."

"Please tell her to stop. You look after the household budget, Setsu. Give her money, whatever she needs."

The bundles of *kimono* stopped arriving at the house. Oka-san grew stronger and began to come out of her room more. She knew he needed silence to work but if he was not writing, she sometimes sang while she pottered about. Learning, one day, that she used to play the *shamisen*, he bought her one. This small gesture endeared him to her greatly. An instrument rather like a lute, it sounded like a banjo and he liked to hear the clear resonant sounds floating out from her room. Though the dominant mood was one of melancholy, she managed to convey a vast range of emotions on this simple three-stringed instrument.

Lying in bed, one sleepless night, he asked Setsuko about her mother, and learned that when she was a child, her father committed ritual suicide after a disagreement with his lord.

"Ah, the *samurai* code of honour."

"She has had much sadness in her life. When she was fifteen, her family arranged for her to marry a handsome young *samurai*. She was happy with the arrangement but he wasn't. On their wedding night, she found her new husband with his lover in the garden; he had slit her throat and then killed himself."

"I've read of such things but I still find it baffling."

"It was an honourable solution for him. Soon after that, she married my father but the family fortunes failed and he died."

Setsuko explained how her mother had been raised to be a creature of elegance and refinement. Widowed at a young age, she had no idea how to make a living or how to care for others.

"She learned to sew but that brought in almost nothing. She tried to hide it from me but I know that sometimes she had to beg to keep food on the table. We were struggling... And then you came along."

In the stillness of the night it occurred to Hearn that perhaps all of Oka-san's pain was channelled into her strangely haunting music.

~

A few months into his marriage he arrived home to find a desk and a Western chair standing incongruously in his study. Setsuko had had them made for him. It had troubled her to see him kneeling on the floor, hunched over the low table with his good eye close to the text in an effort to decipher words. The desk was taller than a normal one. When he sat at it, the top of the desk was just above his chest, and he did not have to stoop over the pages he was working on. Though he lived for the most part like the rest of the family, seated on cushions on the *tatami* matted floor, the desk and chair were more comfortable for him and he was grateful to her for this thoughtful present.

Lots of visitors came and went: colleagues, students, friends who would come and stay for dinner and afterwards tell stories or sing old songs for him. He learned a silly little song about a *tanuki*, a type of raccoon dog, with enormous testicles which swung back and forth even when there was no wind, and any rendition of it would elicit great merriment. When there were guests, Setsuko preferred to stay in the background and only occasionally came in to serve food or to bring a refill of *sake*. One night he was a little drunk and he watched her pouring drinks for him and Nishida-san and he thought how elegant her movements were and how lucky he was to have her for a wife. He put his arms around her and kissed her cheek.

"Isn't she wonderful," he said to Nishida-san. "I can never thank you enough for introducing us."

He felt her stiffen in his arms and to his surprise, she politely, but quickly, left.

"Did I say something wrong?"

Nishida-san sucked in air through clenched teeth; Hearn knew that this gesture signified a reluctance to answer.

"What did I do wrong, Nishida-san?"

"Oh, nothing really."

"Oh, come on, you're my only friend. How can I learn if nobody tells me when I put my foot in it? I will always remain the ignorant foreigner."

"It's just that… We never talk about our own family members. We never praise them to others. And to display affection in public is… Well, it's considered improper."

"This is not public. I'm at home."

"But I'm a guest and Setsuko-san was embarrassed."

"Why?"

"Think about visits you have made to other Japanese homes. You were at the governor's house. Did you see his wife?"

"No. Oh, I did see her, briefly, when I was leaving."

"And I expect that she was refined, courteous, exquisite."

"She was."

"But the governor never spoke of her. Of the relationship between the governor and his wife, you know nothing."

"I suppose not."

"Family life is sacred. The home is a sanctuary. It's considered improper to show what happens there."

After that night he was careful not to embarrass Setsuko again when guests came. And they continued to come. Sometimes they would bring odd objects for him to look at, antiques that they thought he would find curious. Inspiration came from all sides and everything he learned he wrote down. Life had never been so pleasant. In fact it occurred to him more than once that he should go and meet some horribly disagreeable foreigners so as to have his pleasure checked a little. The indulgence was not healthy. He was much too happy. And sometimes he wished somebody would do him wrong so that he would not miss them when he left, which was what he still planned to do as soon as he had saved enough money to buy a little house in Saint Pierre.

~

Setsuko seldom initiated a conversation unless it was concerning a domestic matter, but she always seemed pleased whenever he addressed her. As she quietly tidied away after dinner one night, he asked her what she thought about his habit of shutting himself up in his room night after night.

"Before I sleep, in the quiet of the night, I like to hear the scratch of your pen on paper. I am comforted to know that you are writing. You are happiest when you are writing."

It was true. All other work was just a means to an end. He wondered should he mention to her that, charming as his students were, he was getting bored teaching English. He decided not to say anything. Any hint that he was thinking of giving up his job would cause her alarm. She saw that his *sake* cup was empty and refilled it. Her movements were precise, gentle and courteous; just by being, she made him feel good about himself.

"Thank you," he said.

"May I ask a question?"

"Of course."

"Why do you write on yellow paper?" she asked, eyeing the great stack of yellow writing paper he ordered in bulk.

"Because yellow is the sacred, cosmic colour," he said.

The real reason was that yellow was easier on the eye, and his poor tired eye, his faulty window to the world, needed all the help it could get.

A small smile lit up her face. He knew that she did not understand much of what he said. His Japanese was basic and half the time she did not know whether he was speaking Japanese or English. He would begin his sentences in Japanese and then, impatient to communicate, switch to English. She listened attentively and pretended to understand in order to encourage him in his efforts. Though she wanted to learn English, he forbade it because he believed that language prescribed behaviour and he was afraid that knowledge of English might spoil her gentle nature.

His own behaviour had become more considerate of late. When he spoke in Japanese, he could not muster the scathing wit or eloquent pomposity that rolled readily off his tongue in English. In reaction to the contempt with which he was often regarded in the West, whether because of his deformed eye, his small stature, or his swarthy skin, he had developed the habit of battling all perceived slights with withering put-downs. There was no need for such combative language in Matsue as people were endlessly kind and respectful to him. He had become something of a celebrity and hardly a week passed but there was something in the newspaper about the learned foreigner in their midst.

Setsuko had cleared away the dinner dishes and was kneeling at the *shoji* screen about to leave when, on impulse, he invited her to join him for a drink. She did not show any surprise at this unusual request. She bowed, left and came back a few moments later carrying a small *sake* cup and knelt beside him. He poured her a drink. In the five months of their marriage, they had never sat down alone like this for the purpose of sociability. Their only conversations had been about practicalities. He expected little or no intellectual stimulation from her and, so far, she had stayed obligingly outside the realm of thought. Now that she was here beside him, at his impetuous invitation which he was already regretting, he found himself obliged to make small talk. He loathed small talk.

"Is there to be no relief from this endless heat?"

"Not until September. Sorry."

"The weather is not your fault, Setsu. There is no need to apologise. You must think me a cranky old man. All winter I longed to be warm, and now I crave a cooling breeze, even a hint of one. "

"Shall I tell you a ghost story?" she asked.

He was puzzled by this non sequitur.

"It might help."

"What do you mean?"

"In summer we tell each other ghost stories. A good one will make you feel cold."

He scoffed at the idea.

"Do you know the story of Earless Hoichi?"

"No."

"It's a very old story. One of my favourites. Shall I read it to you?"

"Why not."

She hurried off and returned with a tatty old scroll and read him the story of Earless Hoichi, a musician, who was tricked into playing music for the ghosts of the dead warriors who haunted the cemetery near the temple where he lived. Hoichi was blind. He did not know that his audience were ferocious demons and that he was in grave danger; one wrong note and they would rip him to pieces. When the temple monks discovered his predicament, they were diligent in their efforts to make him invisible so that the demons would go away. They wrote prayers all over his body, on his arms, legs, toes, even the soles of his feet were painted with holy words. Though she read slowly for Hearn's benefit, after a few minutes he interrupted her.

"Tell it to me in your own words, Setsu. Formal written language is difficult for me to understand."

"Oh, sorry, I—"

"No need to be sorry. Now, tell it again from the start if you don't mind."

He refilled their drinks. Pleased that he was eager to hear the story, she began again, hesitant at first, but growing in confidence and becoming more and more animated as she spoke.

"The following night, Hoichi waited for the demons to come. Even though he believed they couldn't see him because he was protected by the holy writing on his body, he was terrified. He heard their heavy footsteps approaching and he trembled as they came closer."

Suddenly she extinguished the light and left the room without a sound. He was alone in the dark. As a child it had filled him with fear and it still did. He heard the bamboo rustle outside. Through the translucent *shoji* screens he saw the silhouette of the bamboo moving as if someone, or something, had disturbed it. The light in the garden lantern flickered and faded and he heard heavy footsteps draw closer. A chill ran down his spine. A deep booming voice growled in the night.

"Hoichi, Hoichi, where are you?"

He reeled back, startled by the ferocity of Setsuko's voice.

"Look, there he is," roared a demonic voice. "I can see his ears."

Wet hands grabbed Hearn's ears and he jerked back in shock. He was covered in goose pimples and he laughed out loud when he realised that he was cold. She relit the lamp and sat beside him.

"So, the monks forgot to write on his ears," he said once he had regained his composure.

"Yes, they forgot," she said. "And the demons caught him by the ears and ripped them off but he escaped and survived."

"It's a good story?"

"And you are no longer hot."

He nodded. She was quietly pleased. He asked her to tell the story again and whenever something struck him as particularly interesting, he made a note of it.

"Poor Hoichi," he said.

"No, no, not poor Hoichi. News of his ordeal spread and people came from far and wide to hear him play and he became wealthy."

"A ghost story with a happy ending, that's most unusual. Thank you, Setsu. You're a wonderful storyteller."

Embarrassed by this compliment, she bowed her head.

"I only told the story as I heard it myself as a child. It is quite ordinary. There are many such tales. You could make them special. Perhaps your students would translate them for you. It might make your time at school more interesting."

He had not said anything about his time at the school, and again it occurred to him that there was much more to this woman than he had given her credit for. It was a good idea. He would use his time teaching English to learn the old stories; stories as yet unknown in the Western world.

They went to bed but he did not sleep. Moonlight seeped through the *shoji* screens lending a soft golden glow to the room until a passing cloud plunged the room into darkness. The house was so quiet, all he could hear was the steady beat of his own heart and he thought of blind Hoichi trembling at the approach of the demons. The oppressive summer heat no longer bothered him and he began to enhance the story and to embellish it. In the middle of the night he decided to get up and write down his thoughts while they were fresh in his mind. He slid the *shoji* screen open as quietly as he could so as not to wake Setsuko.

"You should sleep, Danna-sama," she whispered as he stepped outside.

"I can't. I know I shouldn't write at this ungodly hour but if I don't, I'll forget what I want to say. Go back to sleep," he said gently as he slid the screen closed.

It was dawn before he finished working on the story of Earless Hoichi and then, driven by his conscience, he wrote a long-overdue letter to his old friend, Watkins.

Matsue, June, 1891

Dear Old Dad,

Life here is a joy. Everyone is kind, gentle and good-natured about everything. Of course, this does not apply to the missionaries, who have no reason to like me as one had to be discharged from his teaching position to make room for me. I teach my pupils to respect their own faith and the gods of their fathers and not to listen to proselytising. I rarely meet a Westerner. The only white people who get this far are the occasional despicable missionaries intent on making a convert.

I am safe and well and suitably employed. My salary is generous so I am able to afford one of the nicest houses in town, to have several servants, to give dinners, and to dress my little wife nicely. Yes, I am married again. Her name is Setsuko, I call her Setsu, and she is delightful. This marriage, like my previous one, is in legal limbo. It was a small ceremony attended by her family and one or two friends, but it has no legal status until it is registered. If we register it, Setsuko would lose her Japanese citizenship and all rights to inherit or own property, which in the long run would prove disastrous for her if things do not work out between us. For now, I am deliriously content.

You asked in your letter when I might return to America. Right now I couldn't go even if I wanted to. I seem to spend money as fast as I earn it. Apart from that, there is Setsuko to consider. I fear that she would be very unhappy away from her people and her gods.

I am making progress with my writing on Japan. This country is so strange that it is impossible for anyone who has never lived here to understand the enormous difference between the thoughts and feelings of the Japanese and our own. So, no, I will not be back any time soon, but I promise that before I retire to my beloved Saint Pierre I will come and annoy you for a while.

For now, I am content to stay here. You could always visit me of course. There is much I would like to show you and that you would enjoy here. The Orient is more fascinating than you may suppose.

Here, the people really do eat lotuses. They form a common part of a diet that has taken me considerable getting used to. But you never know, it may well be that the lure of a juicy steak and some plum pudding might coax me back to you yet. Please think about coming and write soon.

With affection,
L.H

CHAPTER SEVEN

Matsue, Japan, 1891

One thing that took a lot of getting used to in Matsue was the lack of privacy. There was no such thing. There were no secrets. Everything he, or anyone, did was known to everybody. Life was astoundingly frank. The moral effect was, in his opinion, extremely good, though the missionaries, who lied endlessly about Japan, tended to disagree with him and he sometimes had robust exchanges with them in the letters' section of *The Japan Mail*, an English language newspaper to which he subscribed.

It was hardly surprising that there was no privacy, given that nothing but light paper screens divided people's lives; screens through which anyone with a finger could poke a hole, and it was not considered outrageous to do so unless the screen was decorated with an elaborate painting. Nobody knocked before entering a room; there was nothing to knock on. Neither locks nor bolts were used by day and, when weather permitted, the front and sometimes the sides of houses were removed, and the interior laid open to the light, to the air and to the public gaze. Not even the rich closed their front gates by day.

In this world of paper walls and openness nobody seemed ashamed or afraid. Whatever was done, was done more or less in public. Neither vices nor virtues could be hidden. The idea of living unobserved was unimaginable. Hearn concluded that, because all matters were open to the inspection of the community, no one tried to inflate his own standing by belittling his neighbour. Such attempts would have been in vain in a community where nothing could be concealed and where, he had learned, affectation was regarded as a mild form of insanity.

Even in a secluded house like his, popular custom had it that there was no need to shut the door, or lock oneself up, except perhaps at night. In his district, no serious crimes had occurred for hundreds of years and the newly built prisons of the Meiji government stood empty. In such an atmosphere he found that it was impossible to remain either nervous or impatient, or to be ill-natured, or to conceal anything. His life, like all others, was an open book and, although naturally reclusive, he found himself taking part in society in a way in which he had never done before. Through an interpreter, he began to give lectures and make speeches in front of large groups of people, and these were duly printed in magazines and newspapers. Public speaking used to be an ordeal for him, but one look at all the placid, smiling Japanese faces reassured his shrinking soul at once.

His Japanese was improving and it amused him to eavesdrop on people – who were unaware that he could understand Japanese – talking candidly about him. The most common observation they made was about his nose: how it protruded compared to their neat little flat ones. They described his as a 'tall nose'. He heard one man comment that Hearn need never worry about the future because, 'with a nose like that, he could bore his way through the world.'

More and more, Hearn began to enjoy the freedom that a lack of personal history brought to him in Japan, where nothing was known about his past. In the West when people talked about him they had seldom been kind. The half-Greek gypsy boy with sallow skin and dark eyes had been viewed with suspicion in Ireland. At school in England his classmates mocked him for being a Paddy; scared, sickly and noticeably foreign, and with no parents to kick up a fuss, he had been a perfect target for bullies. As a student in France, they had assumed he was English and he had been hated there too. During his twenty years in America he had been looked down on for being poor, for being drunk and debauched, for the company he kept and, worst of all, for his scandalous marriage to Mattie. At this stage in his life he did not care what people said or thought about him, but he found the Japanese extraordinarily non-judgmental. He assumed that it was because, having had no experience of foreigners, they did not know what to expect of him.

Once it was established that he was not a missionary set on converting them, he was exalted to an almost godly status by most, but a small minority were less hospitable. He had gone on a trip to Otsuka – a primitive village full of dark energy and bad manners – to see the dancing during the Festival of The Dead. A year had passed since seeing it for the first time in Yonago, and he wanted to see it again as he had heard that the dance differed from place to place. It was disappointing. The dance there bore no resemblance to the elegant performance he had witnessed in Yonago.

At some point during the ceremony, he was spotted and people shouted and hurled sand and mud at him. The abuse was mild, more like the taunts of naughty children. A foreign mob would have thrown stones, which they were careful not to do in spite of the fact that there were no police around. Embarrassed by this insulting behaviour, Setsuko and Nishida-san whisked him away. Hearn was a little taken aback as he had never seen such rough Japanese and the encounter gave him the first decidedly disagreeable feeling of being unwelcome, of being an outsider. A horrible thought struck him: no matter how long he stayed in Japan, he would always be an outsider. Even if his Japanese became fluent, he would still stand out. Everywhere he went, people would always stare at him. Even simple acts, like walking down a street, or going to a shop to buy something, could not be achieved without attracting unwanted attention.

The following morning they left and made their way to Tamatsukuri, the oldest hot spring resort in Japan, famous as a bathing place for the gods. The water there was said to have remarkable restorative powers and if you bathed once, your skin would become young. Bathe twice and your illnesses would be cured. Eager to immerse himself in the healing water, he changed into *yukata* and went to bathe while the others went shopping for souvenirs.

He had never thought much about personal hygiene; it had always been a perfunctory act carried out before dressing when necessary, but in Japan washing was almost a sacred ritual. Naked men and women, young and old, all bathed together in public bathhouses. Bodies were scoured diligently with rough cloths and private parts were scrubbed before immersion in the communal bathtubs.

The baths at the inn where they were staying were impressive. There were hot tubs, cold tubs, thermal tubs, and outside rock pools by the river overflowing with steaming water. On entry to the bathing area, clothes were left in wicker baskets and people wandered from one tub to another in a state of soporific delight. Nobody seemed to notice anybody else. But they noticed him and stared with wide-eyed curiosity, making no effort to hide the fact that they were talking about him. Normally, he would have ignored them but he was still a little disgruntled after the unpleasantness of Otsuka. Naked, he stood up in the middle of the hot tub and addressed the room in Japanese.

"Why are you staring at me? I'm just a human being. Nothing special. Just an ordinary human being."

The entire bathhouse erupted in laughter and, mortified, he left. He was glad that neither Setsuko nor Nishida-san were there to witness his humiliation. He did not like being gawked at like an animal in a zoo, being laughed at, or being the focus of prying eyes. Most people stared at him in an innocent, friendly way but it was the few hostile ones that he dwelt on and that reinforced his long-held belief that he was somehow inferior.

Setsuko went to bed early that evening, leaving him with Nishida-san, who had noticed that Hearn was unusually quiet at dinner.

"I'm sorry about Otsuka," he said. "I shouldn't have brought you there."

"That didn't bother me too much but this afternoon…"

He told Nishida-san what had happened in the bathhouse.

"Tell me what you said," said Nishida-san.

"I said, I am just a human—"

"No, tell me in Japanese."

Hearn repeated what he had said in Japanese and Nishida-san burst out laughing.

"What's so funny?"

"You didn't say, 'I am just a human being.' You said, 'I'm a carrot. I'm just a carrot.' It's an easy mistake to make. *Ninjin* is a carrot. *Ningen* is a person."

Hearn remembered that when he got out of the tub his skin was bright red after the scalding heat of the water and he realised that carrots in Japan came in different colours. There were bright red ones, as red as he had been after the heat of the water. No wonder they laughed. On another occasion he might have been amused but not that night. His defence against tormentors had always been his superior knowledge and quick wit. In English he could silence or intimidate most people with his snappy retorts but his intellect counted for nothing here. He could not string a decent sentence together.

On the way home the next day, he had an overwhelming desire to see the sea and so they detoured to the coast north of Matsue. It was a day of high surf. Young men and boys appeared on the beach carrying planks of wood. They swam far out to sea and came back riding the crests of the waves on their planks. Despite Setsuko's protests, he joined in. They were surprised at how quickly he mastered the technique. The afternoon playing in the waves with these good natured young people restored his spirits.

Boyhood summers spent on Tramore beach had been the highlight of his childhood. Concerned for his safety, Aunt Sarah had instructed a local boatman to teach him to swim. His teaching methods had not been gentle. With the terrified boy perched on his shoulders, the weathered old man would wade out into the sea until the water rose up to his neck, and then he would throw him in and watch him struggle. The first few times he had to be pulled out almost at once, but after that the boatman showed less mercy and helped only when he saw that the boy was in danger. He soon learned that if he paddled with his hands he would stay afloat. By the end of the summer he was able to lift his slender arms above the surface in swift curves and glide with ease across the water. He learned not to fear the sea, how to ride a swell, how to face a breaker and how to dive.

Later on, when he lived in the tropics, he had been grateful to his somewhat brutal swimming teacher. After even the most sultry night, when the air seemed to burn and mosquitoes filled his room with incessant buzzing, come dawn he would run along the soft sand and plunge into the water. Once submerged, drowsiness, weariness and feverish feelings were instantly dispelled, and he would abandon himself to the healing caresses of the sea.

In Martinique he had learned to read the signs of the heavens. By observing the skies and by listening, he learned how to predict wild weather. He watched for scudding and bridging of clouds, sharpening and darkening of the sea line and halos about the moon, and he became alert at the shriek of gulls flashing towards land in level flight out of a transparent white sky.

He missed Martinique, its air sweet with the scent of cinnamon and mangoes and coconut milk. He missed the tremendous sunsets, the great palms and the sea with its ceaseless play of silver light and flashing of little fish. He loved listening to the liquid babble of the women as they passed by beneath his balcony in brightly coloured dresses that they tied up in the front to enable them to walk with ease. Some of them were very black, others beautiful shades of gold and bronze; they looked as if they had just stepped from the walls of ancient Pompeii.

He particularly missed his languid life in Saint Pierre, which he thought of as a kind of tropical New Orleans. Many of the houses were painted yellow and they gave a lemon tint to the narrow palm-lined streets that twisted and turned down to the harbour. Starting each day with a long swim, he would then write for a couple of hours. When work was done he would sit on his balcony, smoke his pipe and gaze out across the red tiled roofs at streets steeped in sunshine, electrically white, in a radiance so powerful that it lent, even to the pavements, the glitter of silver ore. Apart from the sometimes excruciating afternoon heat, he loved the place and he was determined that one day he would go back; he would abandon everything to live again in the land where summer never dies.

Setsuko laid a gentle hand on his arm. How long had she been beside him as he stood at the water's edge, staring out across the sea, he wondered.

"Your mind is far away, Danna-sama."

"It is. I love the sea. I read somewhere that if you want to learn to pray, go to the sea."

"Is your heart also far away? Do you wish to go home to your people?"

He hesitated.

"I have no home."

"We have a saying here: *sumeba miyako*. It means, wherever you live becomes home."

"I wonder if that is true?"

A small wave washed across their bare feet.

"Somebody told me once that waves are caused by the tears of women?"

Used to her subtlety, he wondered if this was her way of telling him that she would be broken-hearted if he left. He would like to have reassured her that he had no such plans but it would have been a lie. Instead he said:

"What about the tears of men?"

"I have never seen a man cry."

"I cry sometimes."

"Yes, I have heard you in the night. I hope you are not unhappy."

"Sometimes when work is going badly I despair. They are tears of frustration. But have you not also heard me laugh? That's when I'm inspired."

"Yes, I have heard you cry as if the world were ending and I have also heard you laugh and roar most fiercely. I was worried, so I asked Nishida-san if he had married me to a mad man."

He glanced at her with amusement.

"What did he say?"

"He asked if you were kind to me. I said you were. Then he said I must put up with your strange ways. He said you are an artist and I must be patient."

"Thank you for being patient, my dear little Setsu."

She bowed ever so slightly and then turned to indicate the runners waiting by the rickshaws.

"Mother will worry if we don't get home before dark."

They gathered up their belongings, boarded the rickshaws and the little group headed for Matsue. Between the blue sea on the left and the billowing green on the right, there was a long, sinister, grey line: another sprawling cemetery. Knowing his penchant for graveyards, Nishida-san glanced back at him to see if he wanted to stop. He shook his head. Given the happy day they had had, he was feeling oddly morose. Setsuko saying her mother would worry if they did not get home soon had set his thoughts on a familiar downward spiral.

As the rickshaws bumped along in the evening sunshine, he wondered had his mother ever worried about him after she left him with Aunt Sarah; he was only four years old at the time. She must have had a difficult time in Dublin. Moving from the freedom of a Greek island to the stifling constraints of that damp, dreary city would have been torture for a woman used to being outdoors in the sunshine. She spoke barely any English and would have had to endure endless hours in stuffy drawing rooms, listening to the dull, incomprehensible voices of his father's snooty Protestant family. He knew enough about them to know that they would have looked down their noses at his mother, a foreigner of dubious social class and a Catholic to boot. Her presence in the house must have been trying for everybody.

All her life she had taken siestas, but in Dublin sleeping in the afternoon was considered lazy. Though she had spells of deep depression and bouts of hysteria, once she even tried to throw herself from a window, he knew nothing of her fragile state, of her frayed nerves and mental aberrations. Sometimes she came to him in dreams, bending over him, smiling, caressing him, speaking soft words to him, sometimes gently chiding, but always with a kiss.

His mother, he could forgive for abandoning him but he could not forgive his father. Perhaps he should have been more understanding. Like his own marriage to Mattie, his parents' marriage had been fraught and the legality of theirs had also been questionable. This effectively made him illegitimate, a subject about which he had been extremely sensitive as a young man. Labelling a child a bastard was hardly Christian. He knew it was nonsense and yet no amount of rational thinking could dislodge the innate sense of shame he felt, or shake him out of bouts of morbid self-pity.

Near Matsue the road became smoother. Setsuko leaned against him, rested her head on his shoulder and closed her eyes. He wondered what she was thinking. If she was also tortured by her troubled life, it never showed on her face. She never scowled at the world the way he did or inflicted her bad moods on others. Such unselfishness was admirable. He doubted he would ever be capable of such self-control. She snored sweetly and he felt a warmth towards her that surprised him. He liked this strong, astute woman, more than liked her, and it occurred to him that the relationship was becoming much more than just 'an arrangement'.

Chapter Eight

Matsue, Japan, 1891

Setsuko's suggestion that his students translate old folk tales had worked out well. He was delighted to get so many. Some were just a few lines on scraps of paper, some were long and detailed and came in simple schoolboy translations, others came with exquisitely illustrated scrolls, and it was thrilling to see these beautiful artefacts which he knew no Westerner had ever laid eyes on. The themes were universal and similar stories could be found in the West, but in Japanese tales, failure to keep one's promise or to behave correctly resulted in a punishment much more terrifying than any meted out in their Western counterparts.

The upside of a childhood spent in a state of perpetual fear was that he was able to mine that terror mercilessly in his writing. He took his students' basic tales and began transforming them; ghosts, ghouls, magic, the supernatural, anything at all macabre he was able to write about with ease. He had had considerable success with his book, *Some Chinese Ghosts*, which had been published some years earlier, and his work on voodoo and black magic, written while in New Orleans, had also been well received. With this in mind, he selected a number of ghost stories. Some of them were quite flimsy but he could enhance them while keeping their unique flavour and tone, which, he believed, Western readers would find intriguing.

One day, while working on a tale about ghostly retribution, the *shoji* screen slid open. Setsuko bowed but did not enter.

"Sorry to interrupt but… The well—"

"Oh, yes. I forgot. Give me a few minutes."

She was about to close the screen when he called her in and asked her advice about the piece he was working on. She enjoyed being consulted and made herself comfortable beside him. He translated his English language version of the story into Japanese for her.

It was about a *samurai* who promised his dying wife that he would never marry again but less than a year after her death he remarried. The new wife moved into the house but from the start she felt uneasy in a way that she could not explain, vaguely afraid without knowing why. She began to have nightmares about the deceased first wife, and she became so frightened that whenever her husband went out, guards had to be placed outside her locked bedroom to keep watch. Returning home late one evening, he was alarmed to see that the guards were asleep and could not be woken. He unlocked the bedroom door and found his young wife's headless body lying in a pool of blood. The head had been ripped off.

"Not chopped off, as you'd expect, but ripped off," said Setsuko. "Excellent. Tell me again about the killing."

"The dead wife's fleshless fingers gripped at the new wife's bleeding head and tore and mangled it, just as the claws of a yellow crab cling fast to a fallen fruit."

"Yes. I can see it. It's wonderful."

"I'm not sure about the ending though," he said. "Perhaps the dead wife should have taken her revenge on the husband. He broke his promise. Surely he's the one who should have been punished."

"That's not the way a woman feels," she said. "It's a perfect ending."

She said it with such definitive coolness that he reminded himself never to cross her. He had come to realise that under the submissive sweetness of this gentle woman there existed surprising toughness. Centuries of the highest social culture had wrapped her character with soft coverings of courtesy, delicacy and patience, but beneath these charming outer layers there remained a core of steel. Cross her wantonly and there would be no pardon. Her delight at the ending of the story confirmed this. It was at once disturbing and at the same time reassuring to know that he need never worry about her. If wanderlust overcame him, he could up and away. Unlike with Mattie, whom he had been afraid to leave in case she fell apart, no matter what happened, Setsuko would survive. She was strong and resilient and knowing this was strangely liberating for him. Ironically, it drew him closer to her.

"Now, please come, the cleaners are finished and you must draw the first bucket of water from the well."

She stood up.

"Can't you get one of the cleaners to—?"

"It has to be done by the man of the house."

"Well, Oji-san could—"

"He's not feeling well. He's asleep and I don't want to disturb him."

"Why can't you—?"

"I'm a woman. The god of the well would be angry and the water would always be muddy if I do it. It has to be you," she said.

To ensure that he did not forget, he wrote down the words 'god of the well' before he followed her out. He loved all these quaint superstitions. It seemed there were gods everywhere: in animate and inanimate objects, in rivers, in rocks and mountains, in wells, in trees, in everything. In the most unlikely places, if he saw an ornately woven rope draped around a rock or a tree, it meant that it was considered sacred. He had never before come across such reverence for nature.

Some weeks earlier, a letter had appeared in *The Japan Mail* from a missionary claiming that Japan was a godless country. Hearn took great pleasure in responding, with what at first seemed like a conciliatory letter, telling the missionary that he was correct. However, Hearn went on to say that he was correct but for only eight days of the year when the gods were on vacation and most of the country was indeed godless. But if the missionary cared to travel to Izumo during that time, he would find multitudes of gods, eating and drinking their holy heads off with their colleagues as any self-respecting gods should be. And he finished by saying that perhaps the said sanctimonious missionary should take a holiday himself, preferably somewhere far away, and leave the good people of Japan in peace.

Light was fading as Hearn and Setsuko crossed to the north eastern corner of the garden. Formerly a bamboo grove, the area around the well was now a wasteland of weeds, grasses and wildflowers. It was the least attractive part of the garden and was hidden from sight behind an intricate bamboo fence. There was seldom any need for him to go there as ice cold water flowed from the well into the house through an ingenious aqueduct of bamboo pipes. She handed him the bucket and he lowered it down into the deep dark well.

"I didn't realise that there were two small silver carp in there until I saw the cleaners take them out this morning," he said.

"Yes, they live there. They're taken out and put in a tub of water while the well is cleaned and refilled."

He pulled up the full bucket. She reached for it but he insisted on carrying it. They headed back to the house together.

"I'll never be able to drink that water again without thinking of those two little fish, circling around in darkness and continuously startled by the descent of splashing buckets," he said.

As they approached the side of the house he stopped and put down the bucket beside a stone lantern with a thick covering of dark green moss. He breathed in the scent of nearby flowers sweetly discernible on every waft of tepid air. All around them the ground was covered with a soft undulating carpet of moss. This luxuriant ground was not for walking on; it had to be crossed on large irregularly shaped stepping stones.

"I sometimes feel like those little fish," he said. "Circling in darkness and endlessly surprised by the unexpected."

She looked up and met his gaze.

"One day you might want to escape the darkness," she said.

"Or I might leap into the shiny bucket and be lifted up to who knows where?"

She gave a hint of a smile.

"You have been unexpected, little Setsu, an unexpected joy."

It was true. He had fallen in love with his wife. How could he not love this woman whose only aim was to please him? There were no hysterics, no petty meanness, no bad moods, or if she had such feelings, she kept them to herself. She demanded nothing of him and accepted whatever attention he chose to give her. Yet, there was nothing servile about her. She moved around him with grace and elegance. She was his ideal woman.

He had no illusions about her being in love with him. She had married him out of duty, out of love and loyalty to her family. It had been a totally selfless act: she had sacrificed herself to save them from destitution, and he respected her immensely for it. If she felt physical revulsion towards him, a strange, half-blind foreigner twice her age, she never let it show. Over spring and summer she had warmed to him. Perhaps she had been relieved to discover that he was not an ogre, who would force himself on her and demand his conjugal rights whether she liked it or not. He had waited to consummate the marriage until she had invited him to do so. This was not unduly frustrating for him; the ladies in the pleasure quarters were more than accommodating when need arose. However, once Setsuko took him into her *futon*, his trips to town ended.

Initially they had slept in separate rooms but now, bar the nights he fell asleep at his desk, he joined her at whatever time he put down his pen, usually at dawn. He would slip quietly into her room, lie beside her and watch her sleeping with her head on the little wooden pillow that allowed her to sleep without her hair arrangement being disturbed. He had tried the wooden pillow but found it torturous. On hot summer nights he sometimes used a small tubular wicker pillow; there was more give in it, and it allowed cooling air to circulate under his neck. It pleased him to see her smooth golden skin beside his just before he closed his eyes. Life seemed perfect.

~

He had written to Chamberlain and kept him up to date on his activities, and the professor had replied by sending him one of his own translations of the legend of Urashima. He thought it might interest Hearn because of its similarity to the old Irish folk tale of *Oisín in the Land of Eternal Youth*. The details varied but the essence of the two stories was the same: the hero meets a beautiful woman and goes with her to an enchanted land. After many years of health and happiness, he longs to go home and see his family once more. Pleas not to go fall on deaf ears; he cannot be persuaded to stay. In the Japanese story, the wife gives her husband a little lacquered box tied with a silk cord, and she warns him that if he opens it he will never be able to return. In the Irish story, the husband is warned that if he dismounts from his horse he will meet a similar fate.

When Urashima arrives home he, like Oisín, finds the world changed. Hundreds of years have passed and his family and friends are long dead. Feeling himself under some strange illusion, and wanting to dispel the illusion, Urashima opens the box. A cold spectral vapour rises from the box and forms a great cloud which floats away over the sea. In an instant, Urashima's hair turns white, his limbs wither, his strength ebbs, and he sinks down lifeless on the sand, crushed by the weight of four hundred years. The same thing happens to Oisín when he dismounts.

He thought about these stories and wondered how two such similar stories could evolve in two radically different cultures on opposite sides of the world. He also wondered why, in neither case, was there any mention of the poor bereaved women. The return of the cloud would have alerted Urashima's wife to what had happened. There was no mention of Oisin's distraught widow either. All the pity was focused on the foolish men who had destroyed their own happiness. Having lived charmed lives in lands of opulence and luxury for centuries, and then to die a quick death, hardly seemed something meriting pity. For him, there was far more power in tales where characters, having disobeyed the gods, were not allowed to die quickly and relatively comfortably, but were forced to remain alive to learn the true depths of sorrow and loss. These endings seemed a truer reflection of life as he knew it.

When Hearn was at home he liked to wander outside or sit on the veranda, smoke his pipe and look out at the garden. Through his monocular, he could study the miniscule wild life: the insects and frogs of which there were a few varieties. His favourite was the tree frog, a pretty little creature, exquisitely green. Over the summer he had noted eleven varieties of butterflies and lots of *semi*, Japanese crickets. Setsuko had told him there were seven kinds of *semi*, but he had only spotted four and they were mostly gone now. And of course, there were the dragonflies. The spectrally slender Emperor dragonfly was the most beautiful. It gleamed with indescribable metallic colours. The fish in the pond also intrigued him. They were tame and put their heads up to beg for food whenever his shadow fell across the water.

On rainy days he especially enjoyed watching the lotus plants. The great cup-shaped leaves, swaying high above the pond, caught raindrops and held them until the rainwater in the leaf reached a certain level, then the stem would bend and empty the water into the pond with a loud splash. Relieved of its burden, the plant would straighten up and the process would start over again.

Hoping for rain, he looked up at the sky. Clouds were floating by and he thought again of Urashima and Oisín and realised that the stories were not about pity for the men who had lost everything. Rather, they were stories that allowed one self-pity, and that was their enduring appeal. Self-pity, and regret for youth, vitality and happiness lost forever. He had been feeling restless of late. Mostly he thought of Saint Pierre, and its tropical charm was growing in his heart and mind. He wondered would he, like the sad heroes of these stories, someday leave this land of strange wonders, and then regret it forever.

A three-foot-long snake came out of the foliage and slid across a large paving stone, moving in the direction of the pond. When he spotted it he retrieved some dried fish from his pocket, squatted down in front of it and fed it.

"Why do you feed the snake?"

He turned to see Oji-san standing behind him. The old man was almost deaf and conversation involved a lot of shouting.

"So that it won't eat the frogs," said Hearn.

"The crows and the pikes eat most of them. And the weasel, have you seen him?

Hearn nodded.

"He's a glutton for frogs. Come sit with me."

It was an unusual request. Oji-san usually kept to himself. He shuffled away and kneeled comfortably on a flat cushion on the raised veranda. Unable to kneel for more than a few minutes, Hearn sat beside him on the polished wooden boards with his legs dangling over the edge to the ground.

"Feeding snakes! I never saw such a thing. Your students are lucky to have such a kind teacher."

"Did you not have kind teachers?" asked Hearn.

"There were no public schools when I was a boy. I attended a special school for the sons of *samurai*. We were treated well but the peasant boys in the *terakoya* schools were not so lucky. If they did not obey, they were held down and beaten with bamboo. We were fortunate. We spent our days learning Chinese language and literature. The wisdom of the Chinese sages is eternal. Do you study it in your country?"

"No, ordinary people don't. Perhaps a few scholars might."

"All men should learn loyalty and honour. It's what makes a man."

They sat together in silence for a short while. It was as beautiful as any summer day could be, but the falling leaves and the absence of *semi* were evidence that autumn had come.

"I miss the *semi*," said Hearn

"Do you like them?" asked Oji-san.

"Yes, we have no such insect in the west. We have something similar, a cicada, but it doesn't sing as nicely."

"I don't like them. The buggers keep me awake at night. We have a saying: human joy and youth is as brief as the song of the *semi*. It lasts a season, and then it's gone."

"Perhaps you prefer dragonflies?" said Hearn. "They flash all around but make no sound."

"Everybody loves dragonflies. When I was a young man I had long hair and it was tied up in a knot in the shape of a *yamma-tombo*, a very large dragonfly," said Oji-san. "Hard to believe, isn't it?"

He laughed and rubbed his bald head.

Looking at Oji-san kneeling on the cushion, it was hard to imagine this seemingly frail old man as a strong young warrior. He was eighty-six and still had his swords. In the sheltered folds of the garden, he sometimes practised drawing his sword, cutting and blocking invisible attacks in highly stylised moves. Hearing him cry out one day, and thinking he had fallen and was in pain, Hearn had rushed out to help him but stopped short when he saw Oji-san chopping up imaginary enemies. With each cut he let out a deep guttural roar, and after each cut he flicked the phantom victim's blood from his sword with great aplomb and then replaced it in the scabbard. Hearn backed away without being seen, thinking it odd that this fierce man, who had no doubt chopped off a few heads in his day, had spent the morning arranging flowers.

In the first months in the new house he learned that Oji-san loved nature as, it seemed, did all Japanese. He could not recall ever having had a conversation with a man in the West about flowers. It was a regular occurrence at his school for male colleagues to comment on and discuss what flowers were in bloom; the plum and the cherry were the most anticipated and appreciated.

Oji-san regularly patrolled the garden searching for the optimum bud or blossom. He once explained how the natural charm of a flower depended on its setting, its mounting, its relation to leaf and stem. Hearn often saw him carefully selecting a single graceful branch and hours later, when he passed his room, the old man would be still painstakingly trimming and placing it with the daintiest manipulation. To complete an arrangement, he often placed a white or pale blue screen behind it and a lantern nearby to enhance the exquisite shadows cast by the blossoms. Hearn had come to love these delicate works of art. Flowers were arranged by all the family and displayed in alcoves in each room, but Oji-san's creations were the most beautiful. Hearn began to see in nature much that had remained invisible to him before; he was learning about aspects of life and beauties of form to which he had been utterly blind.

"See that tree over there," said Oji-san, pointing to a tree with glossy bronze leaves.

"The laurel tree?"

"Yes. An old leaf won't fall off before a new one growing behind it has developed well. It symbolizes the hope that the father will not die before the son has become vigorous and able to succeed him as head of the family."

Oji-san did not look at him as he spoke. He kept his eyes firmly on the laurel. Hearn knew what he was getting at but was too polite to raise the subject directly. His only son had died, so his hope for the future of the bloodline lay with him and Setsuko.

"We have no plans to have children, Oji-san. We haven't spoken about it."

Oji-san hinted at his disapproval with a low, barely audible grunt.

A black dragonfly appeared and hovered around the old man before coming to rest on his knee with its long dazzling body poised delicately and its fine wings spread out ready for flight. Oji-san bowed to the insect and greeted it.

"I've never seen a black dragonfly before," said Hearn.

"He was probably once blue. The colour rubs off during mating, leaving black patches. By the look of him he was fond of the ladies."

"Really?"

Hearn wondered if he was serious.

"I had a great time when I was young but now…" said Oji-san with an amused glance in Hearn's direction. "I can't even find it anymore."

Oji-san laughed. Hearn found himself laughing too. The dragonfly propelled itself into the air and flitted around Oji-san.

"I love to watch them darting about," said Oji-san. "They're so fast sometimes you can hardly see them. But they can see you. They can see all around them."

"Lucky them. I can hardly see in one direction," said Hearn.

"They're not so lucky. They only get to fly around in this lovely world for a short period. So they make the most of it. They live most of their lives underwater and, when they're ready to change, they stick their heads up out of the water and remain very still while they adapt to breathing air. It takes them a while to get used to their new surroundings. Then they shed their old skin and fly away leaving the watery past behind."

Hearn had learned how to listen carefully and he knew that this was Oji-san's way of telling him to move on, forget the West, settle down and have children.

"I understand," said Hearn.

"Good."

The dragonfly flew away.

"Farewell," said Oji-san, bowing ever so slightly to the departing insect. "See you again soon."

The old man remained very still, staring off into the distance.

"No man dies so utterly as the man without children," said Oji-san and then he let out a long weary sigh.

Five days later Oji-san died peacefully in his sleep. He had bequeathed all his earthly possessions, his swords and his suit of armour, to Setsuko to pass on to her sons.

After the cremation, Setsuko and her mother searched through the ashes for a little bone called *Hotoke-san*, Lord Buddha. The future of the deceased could be predicted by the shape of this bone. It was important that they find it. If Oji-san's next life was destined to be one of happiness, the bone would look like a small image of Buddha. But if it was ugly or shapeless, the next birth would be an unhappy one. They found the bone in the area near the throat and it had the most auspicious shape, taking the form of *San Tai*, Three Buddhas. This was a guarantee of great happiness for the departed soul and it afforded the family considerable consolation for the loss of their beloved Oji-san.

Chapter Nine

Matsue, Japan, 1891

In one of his early letters to Chamberlain he had described the bitter winter in Matsue and told him that he had been seriously ill. He mentioned it more to praise the community for the way they had rallied around him, rather than to complain. So it surprised him when the offer of a job on the southern island of Kyushu arrived in the post. Chamberlain had come up trumps yet again. The salary was almost double what he was getting now and if he accepted the offer, he would be financially secure for the next five years, have plenty of time to write and, most importantly of all, he would not have to endure another freezing winter in Matsue. The climate in Kyushu was mild, it seldom snowed and, having discussed the matter, Setsuko and her mother agreed to go with him. The director of the school had seen what the previous winter had done to Hearn, and sad as he was to lose him, he released him from his contract and encouraged him to go.

His colleagues organised a banquet in his honour and presented him with a pair of three-foot-high vases decorated with exotic birds and flowering trees. They dated back to feudal times and were rare and valuable items. One of his brightest students, Kosuga Asakichi, stood up and gave a short speech in English. He blushed all the way through it, the same way he blushed in class when he made a mistake or when he was praised.

"You are the best and the kindest teacher, and we are very sad you are leaving us. Please mind your health. Good luck in Kyushu. Before you go please accept this gift, *Sensei*. It is the symbol of the soul of the *samurai*. It is just a small gift to show appreciation."

Asakichi bowed deeply and held out a magnificent old sword in an ornate crimson lacquered scabbard. Accepting it, Hearn was overcome with emotion and had to fight hard to keep back the tears. Though he received many parting gifts, this one overwhelmed him. It had been given with generosity, kindness and loyalty and it represented everything he had come to learn and love about his students.

A few days before his departure an outbreak of cholera closed all the schools. He went to say goodbye to Nishida-san, who had been ill for some time and had been unable to attend the banquet. Never having been in his house before, he was surprised at how small it was. Hearn wondered if the Japanese teachers begrudged him the huge foreigner's salary that allowed him to live in relative splendour. They worked harder and were paid much less than he was – but he had seen no evidence of resentment, if it existed.

One of Nishida-san's daughters brought warm *sake* and some light food on small decorative plates: slivers of grilled mackerel, pickles and rice balls. She placed them delicately on the table without making a sound. About to comment on her effortless grace, Hearn remembered that it would be inappropriate and stopped himself. After some brief pleasantries, she left the men alone to talk.

"You look terrible, Nishida-san. Would you not move to a healthier place? To Tamatsukuri maybe. The hot springs would do you good."

"There's cholera there too, I hear. No, I'm fine here. I'm well looked after."

"I'm sorry you missed the banquet," said Hearn, shaking his head in bewilderment. "All I had hoped for was some goodwill towards me. I didn't expect to see such generosity and displays of affection. I mean, I was only doing my duty."

"You did much more than that, Hearn-san. The students adore you."

Embarrassed, Hearn changed the subject.

"Have you been to Kyushu?"

"Yes, I was there once. What can I say about it? It's the most conservative part of Japan."

"In what way?"

"The ancient *samurai* spirit there is stronger than ever; its reputation is famous. Wealthy people send their sons to Kyushu to be imbued with a spirit that demands severe simplicity in life and habits."

"Has it changed much in recent years?"

"Kyushu hasn't been slow in adopting Western ideas."

"Oh no."

"Progress is not always a bad thing, Hearn. They have railroads and improved methods of agriculture far more advanced than anything here. At the same time, it's the place least inclined to imitate Western manners."

"And did you visit Kumamoto? That's where I'll be based."

"Yes, I did. National sentiment is strong there. Stronger than even in Tokyo. Indeed, they boast about it. But I should warn you, they have little else to boast about."

Nishida-san refilled their *sake* cups and laid the empty flask down on its side. His daughter must have discreetly peeped in and seen it; she appeared a few minutes later with a refill.

"It's such a pity you're leaving. I'll miss you. And the students are heartbroken. They're planning a big send off."

"Oh, no. They mustn't do that. They mustn't risk exposure. You must send a word. Tell them not to come."

"I wouldn't like to try and stop them," said Nishida-san with a merry but short-lived laugh that seemed to cause him pain.

Nishida-san was obviously tired, so Hearn said farewell to his dearest friend, who had hugely enriched his time in Matsue. He tried to stop Nishida-san from seeing him to the front door but he insisted.

"You must forgive me. I won't be able to come and wave you off."

"I won't forgive you if you do."

Nishida-san smiled and stood at the door bowing until Hearn was out of sight.

Rather than go directly home, Hearn hired a rickshaw and asked the runner to take him on a last nostalgic lap of the city. He had noticed a fleeting furrowing of Nishida-san's brow when he asked him about Kyushu, and he wondered what he meant when he said that Kumamoto city had little to boast about. He berated himself for not having researched the location properly; he had only considered the benign weather.

Gloomy thoughts were dispelled when the rickshaw rolled across the long white bridge with its iron pillars and he remembered the opening ceremony that had taken place earlier in the year, and how the first people to cross a new bridge had to be the happiest people in the community. He remembered asking Setsuko how they selected them.

"They had to be married for more than fifty years and they had to have no fewer than six living children."

"Six children! I'll never qualify."

"Let's wait and see," she said, letting her arm brush against his.

It was the slightest contact but it thrilled him more than any hand holding or embrace could have done. Together, they watched the proud patriarchs cross the bridge first, followed by their venerable wives, the grown-up children, the grandchildren and the great-grandchildren amidst a great clamour of rejoicing, fireworks and cannon fire. It had been a wonderful night.

Once over the bridge they turned into the narrow Street of Fishermen where the houses were so old they seemed to grow from the ground. He loved the sombre ashen tones of the woodwork and the furry browns of the thatched roofs. They passed along the opulent Street of Merchants, through the vast and curious quarter of the temples, through the pleasure quarters he used to visit; he smiled at the memory of long lusty nights there. The runner slowed, glanced back at him and asked if he wanted to stop.

"No, thank you. I'm done with all that."

They passed theatres and the wrestling ring where matches were held on long summer evenings and where, shortly after his arrival, Nishida-san had brought him to see a sword demonstration. Ignoring the Meiji government ban, the governor of the province had organised it and many former *samurai* had come in full armour to show their remarkable skills. Though he did not know him at the time, Oji-san had been one of the proud old warriors who had taken part.

Impending departure heightened his senses and as they passed through the city he realised that what was once wonderful had become commonplace. Now, he was seeing everything again as if for the very first time, and it delighted him just as it had when he arrived fifteen months earlier. Everything seemed more magical, more precious. Everything seemed to shine.

The runner left him at his front gate, refused to take any money and bowed deeply before disappearing into the night. Everybody knew he was leaving. Tears threatened, and instead of going directly into the house, he went for a ramble around the castle moat and into his favourite shrine: Jozan, the great Inari Shrine. He passed it every day on his way to school and seldom went by without dropping in to visit the fox gods.

It was late, there was nobody at the shrine and it felt particularly eerie. Hundreds of primitive moss-covered stone foxes looked down on him from their tall plinths with an air of knowing mockery. He imagined they were leering, sneering, listening with cocked ears, watching the ebb and flow of centuries and sniggering slyly at mankind. He sat on a stone ledge to savour this world of ancient gods and in the darkness he felt his fragile form fade; a ghost already gone.

Though Nishida-san had let it be known that Hearn had requested that people not venture out to see him off because of the cholera outbreak, an hour after sunrise on the morning of his departure some two hundred students and teachers assembled before his gate to escort him and his family to the steamer. The procession skirted the castle and then wove its way through the labyrinth of higgledy-piggledy streets.

As they approached the wharf, he saw a huge crowd waiting for him: more students, their parents and relatives, friends and acquaintances, merchants from whom he had purchased little things, the well-cleaners, even the firemen who had hosed down his roof and the surrounding trees during particularly dry spells. Nishida-san's father was there also with a farewell letter and a small present from his sick son, and the governor of the province had sent his secretary with a courteous message. Overwhelmed, he shook endless heartfelt hands and bowed and bowed until he finally climbed aboard the steamer to cheers and cries of *manzai, manzai*: ten thousand years to you. Not wanting to be parted from him, his favourite pupils followed him onto the steamer and insisted on accompanying him to the next port.

It was a lovely late October morning, sharp with the first chills of winter; the cold was the only thing in Matsue that he would not miss. As the steamer pulled away from the wharf, the water churned and his heart sank under a rush of vivid memories – the kind that always crowded in on him the instant after parting from a beloved place or person. His last look was of the Ohashi River, the old houses crowding close to the banks and beyond the city the great grey castle towering over grand shaggy pines. And beyond that again, long nebulous bands of mist made the far off hills appear to hang in the air. Setsuko came on deck and stood beside him.

"Are you sad?" she asked.

"Yes. I'll miss the morning family gathering at the threshold to wish me a happy day."

"We will have another threshold to gather at and wish you a happy day."

"I'll miss the garden and the lotus flowers."

"We will find another house with a pond."

"I'll miss the cooing doves."

"I'm sure there will be birds in Kyushu. Come inside, you'll catch a chill."

"I will, in a moment."

She left him there and gazing back towards Matsue it occurred to him that he had never enjoyed such an unbroken experience of human goodness before. In his time there, no one had said a single ungenerous word to him. He had never even had his patience tried. It was remarkable.

Soon, only faint blue water, faint blue mists, faint blues and greens and greys of peaks looming in the distance were visible. The spectral delicacy was so lovely, he could not help thinking that Izumo, the Province of the Gods, was indeed a land where sky and earth so strangely intermingled that what was real could not be distinguished from illusion.

CHAPTER TEN

Kumamoto, Japan, 1891

Large areas of Kumamoto, a vast, unsightly city, had been burnt to the ground fourteen years earlier during a rebellion. To Hearn, it looked like a wilderness of flimsy shelters erected in haste almost before the soil had ceased to smoke. Even the great warrior Kato Kiyomasa's magnificent castle, with its outward sloping walls that not even a mouse could climb, stood in ruins. There were no quaint streets, no great temples and no wonderful gardens.

After a few lengthy rambles he discovered that there were no remarkable places to visit, no sights to see and few amusements. He supposed this was the very reason the school was thought to be well-located; there were no distractions for the students who came from all over Japan to study and to learn the famous 'Kyushu spirit'.

The vulgar splendour of the school had surprised him. It was vast and sprawling and not at all to his taste or in keeping with the Spartan design evident elsewhere in Kumamoto. He kept getting lost. From some classrooms it took him ten minutes to walk to the staff room. Not that there was any incentive to go there as camaraderie among the teachers, all twenty-eight of them, was almost non-existent. Some of them spoke passable English, others spoke French, but none of them made any effort to speak to him. He missed friendly Nishida-san, who had shown him the ropes in Matsue and made him feel welcome. He missed those kind eyes and wise advice.

Travels out of the city were also disappointing and after a few short trips, Setsuko let him explore alone. Mostly he wound his way through a perpetual sameness of rice fields, vegetable farms, tiny thatched hamlets and interminable ranges of uninteresting hills: a vast green monotony. There were no compensations for the jolting of the rickshaw; no gems at the end of a tiresome journey. Occasionally he would nod off and doze into reverie with the wind in his face, only to be wakened by a violent jolt. He would return home aching and despondent and sit at his desk staring at a blank page, wondering how he would endure the same dull landscape and the deplorable absence of anything even mildly interesting for five whole years.

On working days he took to eating his lunch in the cemetery beside the school; it was peaceful, closer to his classroom than the staff room and more inviting. This peculiar luncheon venue probably did not do much to enhance the reputation of the strange foreigner but he did not care. He liked to sit in the sun and gaze across at Mount Aso. A constant stream of smoke rose from the mountain and sometimes scattered ash fell on the city. It reminded him of Mount Pele on Martinique. He had climbed it once; an arduous ascent, mile after mile, tripping over slimy tropical roots and he had fallen many times. At the top he had been rewarded with a swim in its crater lake where he could hear faint volcanic rumblings deep in the heart of the mountain.

He was not sure how he felt about the Kumamoto students and, from their impassive demeanour, it was impossible to gauge how they felt about him. They were much older than his students in Matsue had been and, whereas they might once have been amiable little boys, they had developed into earnest, taciturn young men. It was understandable that there was little joy amongst them given their workload. They were expected to master written Chinese, a labour he felt to be the equivalent of learning six European languages all at once. On top of that, English and German, or English and French, were also compulsory. He thought it insane that they were forced to learn languages that few of them were ever likely to benefit from. Even the best of them had little hope of getting to the Imperial University until at least the age of twenty-three.

When the students were not in class they were forced to don military uniforms and drill for hours. It seemed to Hearn that some of them, particularly the ones from the wealthier families, enjoyed testing how much physical hardship they could endure. And if there were a national crisis, he had no doubt that the student body, all four hundred of them, would instantly transform into an army of iron soldiery. These young men were exhausted. There was no trace of the affectionate familiarity that he had experienced in Matsue; relationships began and ended with the militaristic bugle call with which classes were assembled and dismissed.

The house provided for him by the school was utilitarian and that was the most flattering thing he could say about it. It was small, dark, and had a tiny neglected garden that overlooked other ugly houses. Setsuko went house-hunting and soon found them something better, not quite as elegant as their Matsue house, but more than adequate. In the evenings he stepped out of the harsh Kumamoto life into the soft courteous world of Matsue's old ways. When he was pleased, which was seldom enough, the house laughed with him. When he was downhearted, the house was silent. Home was his haven.

One chilly December day, he abandoned the cemetery and ate his lunch in the staff room where he overheard a conversation between two other teachers. Despite evidence to the contrary, the idea that a foreigner could understand Japanese seemed to be beyond their comprehension, and they carried on as if he was not there, every now and then sneaking sly lizard glances in his direction.

"First sign of a north wind and he dumps his ghostly lunch companions."

"Foreigners are soft."

"What's he eating? A cow?"

Muted chuckles.

"No. Same as us: rice and leftovers from last night's dinner."

"He's quite skilled with chopsticks."

"That's true."

"I wonder has he heard yet."

Hearn's ears pricked up but he showed no sign of interest.

"I doubt it."

"I wonder what he'll do."

"Go back to America, I suppose."

"What about you?"

"I don't know. If we close down, it'll be hard to get another job here."

Alarmed, he went to the director's office immediately after the lunch break to ask if it was true that the school was closing down. While not overly friendly, Kano-san, the school director, told him that the government was cutting back on education and had already closed down three schools. Theirs was on the list for closure, but he had no idea if or when it might happen. The prospect of sudden unemployment was a blow. He had responsibility to Setsuko, to her mother and to old Hanako.

On arriving home, he paused at the gate to watch two old men, the hired gardeners, plant a single sapling. Having fixed it in the ground, they stepped back to study it. Oka-san joined them, a discussion followed and the sapling was taken up and replanted in a slightly different position. He slipped quietly into the house, where he found Setsuko sitting in the middle of the main room with pieces of Oji-san's armour spread out all around her.

"Oji-san said I must check for insects regularly so that it doesn't get damaged."

Wondering if he should tell her about the possible closure of the school, he sat beside her on the *tatami* floor and picked up one of the sleeves. Made from a complex combination of bamboo, cloth and tiny iron and leather scales, and bound together with silk cords, it was surprisingly light and malleable. The demonic helmet was designed to instil fear and had clearly been modelled on the horned heads of the live beetles he had seen for sale in insect shops. Some of these ferocious looking creatures were three or four inches long and they were the favourite pets of young boys, who liked to pit them against each other in battle. Better not to trouble her with bad news until it was confirmed.

"It's hard to believe this once fitted Oji-san," he said.

"Mother said he used to be twice the size but I don't remember him like that. He was always just little old Oji-san to me."

"I miss him."

"There's no need to miss him. Oji-san is here with us."

It was strange to hear her talking about Oji-san this way. For her, his spirit was still with them. Every morning she, or her mother, would set a little cup of tea for Oji-san in front of the family shrine which housed a little tablet with his name on it alongside the names of other deceased family members. Later in the day one of them would bring him a token offering of boiled rice. It was a ritual never overlooked. They regularly refreshed the flowers in the shrine vases, said silent prayers, or sometimes talked out loud to Oji-san and to the other ancestors.

"How long will Oji-san be here?"

"For a hundred years," she said.

"Is that all?"

"Yes. Even in the temples, prayers and offerings are made only for a hundred years."

"What happens then? Do the dead cease to care for remembrance or do they fade out at last? Is there a dying of souls?"

"No, there's no dying of souls but after one hundred years they are no longer with us. Some say they are born again. Others say they become gods. But reverence is still made to them on certain days."

"Like during the Festival of the Dead."

"Yes. My father said that he could see the souls of his grandparents. They were small dim shapes, dark like old bronze. They couldn't speak but they made little moaning sounds. Of course, they didn't eat but they liked to inhale the warm vapours of the offerings of daily food set before them. He said that every year they became smaller and more vague."

"Did you see them?"

"No. But sometimes I think I see my dear father. I feel his presence. I remember the last time I saw him alive."

"When was that?"

"Just before he died. I was six years old. It was a winter's day. The wind was blowing hard around the roof and in the bare trees outside. Quails were whistling in the distance making melancholy sounds. I gave him a sweet orange. He smiled and tasted it. It was the last time I saw him smile."

"What a sad but lovely memory."

"That was seventeen years ago. It seems like a moment. And soon winter will come again. The same winds will blow. The quails will utter the same sad cries. Nothing changes. I still talk to him."

Outside in the garden, the two old men continued to plant and replant the sapling, and Hearn thought how pleasant it would be to believe that the people we loved would always be with us, that the soul did not die with the body and that the essence of the person remained. He had no such certainty. And until now he had had nobody he cared about apart from Watkins. He silently berated himself for not having written to the old man for some months.

Setsuko inspected the armour and, when satisfied that there was no infestation, she wrapped each piece in folds of cotton cloth. Her wrapping skills were a geometric wonder. There were no bumps or creases or loose bits sticking out. Totally engrossed in her task, she replaced them systematically in special wooden storage boxes, heavy things first, lighter things on top. Such contentment in simple living was unknown to him.

He wondered what it would have been like to grow up in a family with parents and grandparents and ancestors to remember fondly and honour. Of course, Aunt Sarah had been good to him; but he had always felt that he had been more of an irritant to her than a joy. Boarding school meant he saw little of her, and there had been no communication from her after Molyneux shipped him off to America. Assuming that Aunt Sarah believed herself to be well rid of him, and ignoring the fact that neither she, nor anybody else, had any idea where he was, he had wallowed in self-pity and made no effort to contact them. Perhaps he himself was to blame for his own isolation, a thought that did not sit well with the belief that he had been hard done by. He quickly dismissed it.

Though feeling alone for much of his life, a few months before he left for Japan he received a letter from a man claiming to be his brother. This was the first he had heard of a sibling and he was rightly sceptical. A brief correspondence proved that James Daniel Hearn was indeed his full blood brother. When Hearn's mother abandoned him and left Dublin, she had been pregnant and gave birth to James a few months after she arrived back home in Greece. The marriage was over and she was unable to care for James, so she sent him to Dublin to be reared. James and he had been brought up only a few miles from one another. Why he had not been told he had a younger brother he could not understand.

James, keen to meet him, offered to pay his expenses if he would come to Michigan. He declined the invitation on the grounds that he was busy preparing for Japan but this was a lie as he had not yet found funding for the trip. James was persistent and came to New York. Strapped for cash, Hearn could not resist the offer of a good meal at The Fraunces Tavern where James had taken a room. Arriving early, he sat at a window overlooking Pearl Street and when he saw a tall, fair-haired man come striding up the road, he knew it was James. The resemblance to their father was striking. Watching James approach, he experienced a surge of intense emotion. It lasted just for a moment but it unsettled him. He had not expected to feel anything.

James came in, all smiles and bonhomie. They shook hands

formally.

"This is strange," said Hearn.

"It's long overdue, Patrick. I'm delighted to meet my famous brother at last."

Hearing this stranger address him with familiarity by his long-discarded childhood name rankled. James did not notice. He was hale and hearty and full of innocent optimism and, judging from his sturdy frame and rosy cheeks, life had been good to him. Over lunch he explained how fond he was of the family in Dublin and how he was in regular touch with them. The Protestant Hearns had taken him in, educated him and even set him up in business. With family money, he had been able to buy a farm, and now he was happily settled with a wife and children. He was the epitome of a conservative, clean-living Anglo Irish Protestant. In a nutshell, James was everything he was not.

"Just think, we overlapped in Dublin for quite a few years and they never thought to introduce us," said James.

"And all because of a few statues."

"What do you mean?"

"Well, what's the difference between Catholics and Protestants? They effectively believe the same thing and yet they judge each other and hate each other for no substantial reason. Your guardians were probably afraid that if you mixed with me, you'd come home reciting the Hail Mary."

"I take it you're not a practising Catholic any longer then, Patrick."

"If you had had the extreme misfortune of a Catholic education, a system chiefly consisting of keeping the pupils in ignorance, you'd understand why I don't believe in any form of religion,"

"Lucky for me I escaped that fate," said James.

"Lucky for you, you escaped that faith."

James did not laugh.

"You heard about your aunt's death, I presume?" said James.

"No. When did she die?"

"Not long after you left for America."

"Left for America? It wasn't a jolly adventure, James. I was banished."

"I'm sure she didn't know about that. I mean, she was ninety-one, was ill and had been for quite some time. All that trouble with the bankruptcy affected her terribly."

"I imagine it did," said Hearn.

"Of course, I never met her myself. The families didn't mix."

Hearn knew all about the falling out between the Protestant Hearns and Aunt Sarah, who had converted to Catholicism when she married. It was clear to him now that he, a dark-skinned little gypsy boy, had been a mortification to the respectable Protestant Hearns and they had fobbed him off on childless Aunt Sarah who had, in their eyes, already disgraced herself by marrying a Catholic. They did not want a picaninny in the family but they had no trouble fostering blonde, blue-eyed James.

"Molyneux was very good to your aunt."

"So well he might have been," said Hearn, irritated by the mention of Henry Molyneux Hearn.

"He and his wife cared for her until the end. They didn't have to."

"It was the least they could do," said Hearn. "If that fellow hadn't taken it upon himself to be her financial advisor, I would have been a very wealthy man. Instead, thanks to him I ended up stranded here with nothing and no way home. I was destitute, a beggar, I almost starved to death. Now, perhaps you'll understand my lack of curiosity about the family."

"I'm sorry. I didn't know," said James.

"Well, now you do."

"Surely you could have written to let them know where you were."

"I did. I wrote to Aunt Sarah and got no reply."

"Perhaps she had already moved to England to live with the Molyneuxs."

"Perhaps."

"Anyway, Patrick, here we are now, united at last."

James tucked into his meal and cleaned his plate. Good as it was, Hearn could not enjoy his beefsteak. Why had he agreed to this meeting? What else had he expected to talk about except the painful past? Pouring himself another glass of wine, he tried to banish the sense of resentment and illogical dislike he was feeling for his irritatingly cheerful brother.

"Tell me about our mother," said James.

"I hardly knew her. I tried to get in touch with her on a number of occasions but I had no luck."

"Perhaps she didn't want to be found," said James. "I also tried to contact her. I wrote to her family but heard nothing back."

"Of course they didn't reply. They're illiterate peasants and they probably couldn't read your letters even if they received them. Why would you expect a response from the people who tried to murder our father?"

"What?"

"They stabbed him, the thugs. If father's fellow officers hadn't arrived on the scene and intervened, we wouldn't be here."

James seemed shocked. Hearn wondered if he was more shocked at the attempted murder or at the idea of having such delinquent relatives.

"Who told you that?" asked James.

"A small boy hiding under the dinner table can glean quite a lot of unsavoury information."

"I think you are misinformed, Patrick. The Cassimati family were not peasants and they were not illiterate. Mother was home schooled. She had no English but she spoke a few languages."

"Well, that's news to me."

"They were a respectable family and I assume they were outraged when she became pregnant out of wedlock," said James. "It brought disgrace on the family. They didn't set out to murder father. I heard it was a row that got out of hand."

"Huh!"

Hearn was feeling deeply uncomfortable. Could this be right? Or had James been fed a sanitized version of the story?

"Well, we'll never know now," said James. "Sadly, I don't remember her at all. May she rest in peace."

On hearing this, Hearn turned pale.

"Oh," said James. "Sorry, I thought you knew."

"No. When—?"

"Must be seven, no, eight years ago now. Yes, eight years. She died in 1882. Sorry, I assumed—"

"How could I have known? I told you, I haven't heard from the family since I left."

James fell silent. It was too much for Hearn to take in. When the waiter came to take their plates away, he made his excuses and prepared to leave.

"Please don't go, Patrick? We have so much to talk about. Do you know that you have three half-sisters?"

Stunned, Hearn sank back into his seat.

"Elizabeth Sarah Maude, Minnie Charlotte and Posey Gertrude, who for some reason is known as Lillah. They're lovely and they're eager to meet you."

Oblivious to Hearn's distraught state, James prattled on. It seemed the three girls were the progeny of his father's second marriage and had been born in India. They were all in their thirties, respectably married with children and living in England. As well as being on good terms with the three half-sisters, James also received regular letters from their two step-sisters. Hearn had been aware of the existence of the step-sisters. He remembered them from the day his father took him to the park with Alicia, the woman who subsequently became his second wife. When they went to collect her, two angelic little girls with curly blonde hair like their mother's had been standing on the steps outside the front door of the family house. They had stared at him and he had stared back from the barouche; for some unknown reason, this image remained clear in his mind.

Guilt about his mother tormented Hearn. He had always thought he would go to Greece and find her but he had kept putting it off and now it was too late. Over the course of the meal, he had learned about her death and had gone from being alone in the world to having six siblings, in-laws and countless nieces and nephews; it was difficult to absorb. Always bemoaning the fact that he had no family, now suddenly, he had all these relatives. He should have been pleased but he was not. Where were they when he was young and vulnerable, unknown and impoverished?

James produced a formal photograph of the family mounted in a small leather case. The straight noses, the high foreheads he recognised but he could not think of them as family. They may have looked like him but he had no shared history with them – there were no emotional ties. Dark thoughts swamped him, nothing specific, just a feeling of despondency.

"How about some pudding, Patrick? "

Hearn had noticed plum pudding on the menu. It was his favourite dessert, but he had lost his appetite.

"No, thank you. I have an appointment. I'm afraid I must go," he said, smiling anxiously.

"Well, now that we've met, I hope we'll have plenty more occasions to get to know each other better. You should come up to us, to the farm. It's very peaceful. You could write there."

"Thank you. Perhaps when I come back from Japan."

"I look forward to it."

"Yes, indeed."

"In the meantime, we can write to each other," said James. "You have my address. You will write from Japan, won't you?"

"Of course."

The bill arrived; he allowed James to intercept it and hurried away to his non-existent appointment.

Once outside, he stopped and attempted to calm emotions bolting out of control. Could James be right? Had he got everything wrong? Should he have made an effort to keep in contact with the family? He had thought about it many times but nostalgia always gave way to the idea that they would reject him. Why give them the opportunity to shun him again? No words expressed the inexplicable pain he was feeling. No one thing, no one event stuck out in his mind as the cause of these powerful emotions; it was an accumulation of feelings and faint memories that blurred and dimmed even as the distress increased.

Tears now came when he thought about his mother. He knew that she had returned to Dublin looking for him at one point, but the family had refused to tell her where he was. Aunt Sarah's former maid, Catherine, had confided this to him in London before he left for America. Presumably, she had come looking for both her sons. Once settled in Cincinnati, he had written to Aunt Sarah asking how he might contact his mother but had received no reply. He should not have given up; the other side of the family might have helped. Whether she was a peasant or not made no difference to him. He loved her and believed that whatever good there was in him came from her, not from his father. How could he love that rigid, grim-faced man? His mother's eyes were the dark eyes of a wild deer and when he looked in a mirror her eyes looked back at him. She had made him and had given him all that makes a man noble, not the strength of power and calculation, but a heart and the ability to love.

In the months that followed the meeting with James, there were letters and invitations from his new-found family. They seemed like nice people though somewhat dull. Like James, they had led cosseted, privileged lives and he wondered if he met them, what they would talk about. Unable to cope with the chore of answering the same questions over and over again, he chose his half-sister, Minnie Charlotte, as the person with whom he would correspond. She could share his letters with the rest of the family but even that became onerous as replying to her meant writing endlessly about himself, which was tiresome.

Unable to see the point of corresponding with people whom he would more than likely never meet, he cut ties forever when he left Yokohama. He told Minnie Charlotte that he would forward his address in Matsue but he never did.

The sound of hands clapping brought him back to the present. Outside, it seemed that the gardeners had found the right spot and Oka-san was satisfied that the little tree fitted perfectly into the overall plan of the garden. He watched them shifting, transferring, removing and replacing newly purchased shrubs and bushes just as he changed and rearranged words to give a sentence the most delicate, or the most forceful, expression possible.

Setsuko tidied away Oji-san's armour. Quite unconsciously, he pulled his knees up to his chin and wrapping his arms around them, tried to forget James and the family he had turned his back on. The Koizumis were more of a family to him now than his own blood relatives had ever been. But if he suddenly dropped dead, he wondered if they would mourn his passing? Would they write his name on a tablet and put it in the family shrine? Would they place little cups of tea on his grave and invite his soul back to visit during the Festival of the Dead? He was surprised at how much he hoped they would, given that he had known them for less than two years. Was that enough to be counted as family? Feeling his wife's inquiring eyes on him, he rubbed his arms as if for warmth.

"It's colder here than I thought it would be but at least there's no snow," he said, feigning cheerfulness.

Setsuko closed the box containing Oji-san's gauntlets.

"I've ordered a Western stove for you," she said and watched his face, expecting a pleased reaction.

He remained sullen.

"It's being sent from Yokohama and will arrive any day now. You can light a fire in your study. I've arranged to have a chimney put into the wall."

"That's very thoughtful, Setsu, but surely the heat will merely fly out through the *shoji* screens."

"The paper panels can be replaced with glass."

"Oh, but I would miss the lovely shapes and shadows glimpsed through the translucent paper," he said.

"Maybe we can have paper and glass."

There was no point in trying to dissuade her. The arrangements had already been made but such expense was reckless given their situation.

"That would be nice, Setsu. Thank you."

"I'm just being selfish. I don't want you to get sick again. I'd have to nurse you and that would be tedious."

He could see from the slight grin on her face that she was teasing him.

"What would I do without you?" he said.

"Perhaps you will be able to write again when you are warm. I'd love to read your books. Maybe someday you might write one in Japanese."

"No, I don't think so. My Japanese will never be good enough. I can't read it, so I'll never master it. Anyway, I have enough trouble with English."

~

One week later the chimney was complete, a cast iron stove had been installed and glass panels had been inserted into the reinforced screens. The workmen had left the translucent paper in place, so the screens still looked the same but his study was snug. Unfortunately, no new ideas came. The book he had written in Matsue, *Glimpses of an Unfamiliar Japan*, was finished. It was a collection of essays documenting all the strange and wonderful things he had discovered there; while he believed the book would be interesting to foreign readers, he felt that he had merely touched on Japan at a superficial level. He had not delved into the inner emotional life of the people. Reticent by nature, he decided he would have to make more of an effort to engage with his colleagues, his students and people he encountered.

Reading the essays made him nostalgic for all the things he had left behind in Matsue. Sad and unable to muster the enthusiasm to polish the writing to a level that he deemed acceptable for publication, and thinking that perhaps he was being too self-critical, he sent it off as it was and then instantly regretted it.

As the months passed rumours about the impending closure of the school died down. He initiated conversations and discovered how well-informed his colleagues were about the world beyond Japan, about Western aesthetics and the occidental emotional character in general. They were educated and many of them had travelled abroad. When he talked to them about Western art or thought, they listened politely. It was clear that they knew what he was talking about, but his utmost eloquence elicited scarcely more than a few brief comments. If he had had similar exchanges with Westerners, he would have assumed their inadequate responses to be proof of mental incapacity. It would have been a mistake to make such a judgment about his colleagues. He recalled a conversation he had had with Weldon shortly after their arrival in Yokohama. They were having a beer in a small bar down at the harbour.

"They really are a race of children. I can get no sense out of any of them."

"How can you say that, Weldon? You don't speak Japanese and you make no effort to."

"You don't have to speak to them. Look around. All they're interested in are material things, mass producing gaudy trinkets and—"

"Yes, but... Have you not visited the temples? Have you not seen their exquisite art?"

Even before he came to Japan, Hearn had been astonished by the ability of Japanese artists to reproduce with a few simple brush strokes not only the peculiarities of a creature's shape but also the characteristics of its motion. Be it only a spider in a wind-shaken web, a dragonfly riding a sunbeam, or a pair of crabs running along a beach, the pictures were alive – intensely alive – and corresponding Western art looked dead in comparison.

"You have Japan-itis, Hearn, as do most Europeans and Americans. Anything to do with Japan sells right now. It's just a fashion. It won't last but while it does let's make some money."

"You're an artist, Weldon. Are you telling me you don't appreciate—?"

"I'm just not as impressed as you are. Some of their art is positively comical."

"I'm beginning to wonder which of us it is who's almost blind," said Hearn.

"Maybe that explains it?"

"To hell with you, Weldon."

"Well, answer me this: if their culture is so wonderful, why are they mindlessly copying the West?"

There was no point in engaging with Weldon any longer. Having discovered on the journey over that he had come merely to make money, it was a waste of time to try to make him appreciate the astonishing beauty all around him if he could not see it for himself.

"Well," said Weldon. "Why are they copying us?"

"I can't answer that. We've only been here a week and while I see evidence of Westernisation... I just hope they can retain all that is fine in their own culture."

"They're children I tell you, all smiley and stupid. Christ, I can't wait to get back to the civilised world."

What Weldon had failed to understand, and what Hearn was beginning to realise, was that a smiling, agreeable face was a rule of life in Japan. Cultivated from childhood as a duty, the smile was instinctive. They believed that to express one's own personal anger, pain or sorrow was rarely useful and always unkind. It was considered rude to appear serious or unhappy, as it would make others anxious.

Even if their hearts were breaking, they would speak of it with a smile, and when matters were very distressing, the smile might change to a low soft laugh. The laugh was politeness carried to the utmost point of self-abnegation.

Weldon misunderstood all of this and, as for his assertion that the Japanese were stupid, he could not have been more wrong. Many of the less-educated classes and many business people seemed to be caught up in servile imitation of Western ways, but the more educated classes, the people Hearn spoke to who had travelled and studied abroad, seemed resistant to Western influence. They may have admired Western material and technological superiority but their admiration did not extend to Western morals. In fact the more these erudite people learned about Western society, the less impressed they seemed to be. If so, they kept their critical thoughts to themselves. He had come to believe that their lack of condemnation of Western ways was due to an ingrained abhorrence of being rude. Apart from his wife, the only Japanese person he had met who he could rely on to be candid was Nishida-san, and unfortunately he was miles away.

No inspiration came. Every afternoon he sat at his desk and forced himself to record conversations he had had, or heard, at school that morning, and his thoughts on and interpretations of daily events. It was pure grind. He did it in the vague hope that it might result in something of value. What worried him most was that he felt nothing for what he was writing. He wanted to discover something that would stir him profoundly, but his knowledge of Japan was now sufficient so as to prevent illusion.

He encouraged Setsuko to tell him anything interesting that might happen to her during the course of her day.

"What kind of thing?" she asked.

"Anything at all, anything queer or curious that you think might interest or amuse me, anything touching or noble that you might happen to see. A bit of kindness by the roadside for example. A line or two might inspire a whole story."

"But I seldom leave the house."

"Well, go out more."

"Where would I go?"

"Wander the streets, visit shops. Buy me little presents. They don't have to be expensive."

She seemed bewildered by his request.

"For example, I heard Hanako scream earlier, and then you were both laughing. What was that about?"

"It was nothing. She almost stood on the *hikigaeru*."

"*Hiki…?*"

"It's a big toad. He's an uncouth goggle-eyed thing that lives in the garden."

"Oh, yes, I've seen him."

"He comes in everyday to be fed."

"Really?"

"She'd have been very upset if she'd stood on him. She loves frogs. Have you not seen her collection of small green ones in the cage behind the kitchen? They have such a sweet sound. She likes to pet them. Lots of people keep pet frogs."

"And does she pet the hikigaeru also?"

"No, he's too ugly. But he's considered a lucky omen and he can suck all the mosquitoes out a room by simply drawing in a breath."

Encouraged by his laughter she continued.

"There's a legend about a giant *hikigaeru* who, when he sucked in his breath, drew not just insects but men into his mouth."

"That's exactly what I mean, Setsu. That's the kind of thing I'm looking for."

After that conversation she told him all kinds of gossip and trivial bits and pieces about her day, and he duly recorded her stories and anecdotes in his notebooks. She went to bookshops and markets and sought out hanging scrolls and old books she thought he might like. His spoken Japanese had improved, but his written Japanese had not progressed past some basic letters. The tiny, complex writing system caused him eyestrain, so he had given up trying to read. Instead, Setsuko read the books, summarised them and told him the stories to ensure that he had a constant flow of fresh material.

There was one thing he found intensely irritating that she could do nothing to remedy. His study was at the back of the house, and beyond the high fence enclosing the garden, the thatched roofs of some very small houses could be seen. A troubling noise was coming from one of the houses. The sound was faint at first but grew more audible as the weeks passed. It continued all day and through the night. Even with glass in the closed *shoji* screens, he could hear the man – he was sure it was a man – softly groaning in pain. What had started as a mild irritant soon became a monster, distracting him from work with which he was already struggling. The moans grew louder and longer as if every breath caused agony. It was impossible to ignore. One night he banged down his pen, got up from his desk and stomped about the room in a fury. Having heard the disturbance, Setsuko appeared, carrying his smoking box.

"Somebody is very sick," she said.

"I think it would be better for all concerned if that somebody were dead."

She flashed him a look of reproach and made three quick sudden gestures with both hands as if to negate the effect of his brutal words. She placed his smoking box beside his desk; it had been cleaned out and replenished. He sat beside her and filled his pipe.

"It is torturous. He might as well be here in the room with me. I can't work and I keep asking myself how it can be possible for a human being making those sounds to endure much longer."

"Perhaps you should move to the front of the house. He can't be heard there."

"Maybe they can't afford a doctor. I'll go around and see the family. We might be able to help in some way."

He could tell from her expression that she knew this was not prompted by kindness.

"Let me first send Hanako to inquire," she said as she moved to leave.

"Very well."

Twenty minutes later she returned.

"The Watanabe family are miserably poor but a doctor comes regularly. The elder son has been ill for years; he's only thirty-four but it seems nothing can be done for him."

She did not linger, and he knew by her uncharacteristically curt tone that she was displeased with him. He smoked his pipe and fumed. It was a positive relief to him later that evening when the moaning was drowned out by the beating of a little Buddhist drum and the chanting of a small crowd.

"*Namu myo ho renge kyo.*"

The words proclaimed devotion to the Mystic Law of the Lotus Sutra and the purpose of repeated chanting was to reduce suffering. Akira-san had explained that Buddhists believed the chanting banished negative karma and reduced karmic punishments from previous and present lifetimes. The voices were solemn and low, the pace steady and slow. It induced a peaceful hypnosis and somewhat eased his troubled mind.

The chanting and the beating of the drum continued for several hours. With every pause in the chanting, the groans of the man could be heard. It grew worse and then it suddenly stopped, and he heard a passionate burst of weeping. Setsuko's voice startled him; he had not heard her enter the room.

"Somebody is dead," she said in an unusually cool voice.

"Send them the money for the funeral expenses."

"You are very kind," she said without looking at him.

"No, I'm not kind. I am smitten by conscience for my earlier lack of compassion."

Placated, she bowed and was about to leave when he added,

"Oh, and tell Hanako to send our condolences and if possible to find out whatever she can about the deceased."

"I will go myself."

She nodded and left. He could not help suspecting some kind of tragedy, and a Japanese tragedy was always interesting.

Sure enough, Setsuko came back sometime later with an intriguing story. The Watanabe family consisted of four: father and mother, both old and feeble, and their two sons, Taizo and Koji. It was Taizo who had died. The younger son, Koji, a rickshaw runner, was the sole breadwinner. Having no vehicle of his own, he hired one and, though strong and swift, he earned very little; there was too much competition for the business to be profitable. It taxed all Koji's power to support the family and he could not have done it without unfailing self-denial. Apparently, he never indulged himself, not even to the extent of a cup of *sake*, and he remained unmarried, living only for his filial and fraternal duty.

Taizo had been a fishmonger and many years earlier he had fallen in love with a servant girl at an inn. They pledged themselves to one another but difficulties arose in the way of their marriage. The girl was pretty and had attracted the attention of a man of some means, who asked for her hand in marriage. She disliked him, but her parents decided in his favour as he was the wealthier of the two suitors. In despair the lovers decided to kill themselves.

They met one night, renewed their pledge, drank some *sake* and bade farewell to the world. Taizo killed his sweetheart with one clean cut and then immediately slit his own throat. Unfortunately for him, he was found before he expired. The police arrived with a military surgeon from the garrison, who saved his life. He was nursed back to health and after some months of convalescence he was put on trial for murder.

What sentence was passed was unclear, but after a term of imprisonment he was allowed to return to his family. People shunned him; he had made *joshi*, a suicide pact, with his beloved, and he had committed the unforgiveable sin of surviving. Only his family remained loyal to him.

Once back in the family home, the wound in his throat began to cause him pain. Though treated, a slow cancerous growth began to spread from it. People said that the hand of his murdered sweetheart opened the wound at night, undoing all that was done by the doctors during the day. At night the pain increased, becoming unbearable at the precise hour they had attempted to carry out the suicide pact. He lingered on for seven years in ever-increasing agony. Somehow the family managed to pay for medicine, for doctors, for more nourishing food than they allowed themselves. They prolonged by all possible means the life that was their shame, their poverty, their burden. And now death had taken the burden away and they wept.

When Setsuko finished she got up and left without a sound. Hearn sat still. The room was quiet at last but the silence seemed imbued with sadness. Every now and then the melancholy weeping of the bereaved family floated across the back garden to him. They loved the man they had made so many sacrifices for. He wondered if perhaps we love most the people and things that cause us the most pain.

Chapter Eleven

Kumamoto, Japan, 1892

The episode with the dying neighbour got him thinking about love. Did Setsuko love him? There were no overt displays of affection, not to him, nor to her family either. Whatever affection she might feel had not been visible to him at first. Whatever displeasure she felt was kept equally under control. That was not to say she was devoid of feelings. Hearn knew she suffered, that she experienced joy and anger just like any Western person; she just did not show those feelings. The signs were subtle but he was learning to read them.

Endearing terms such as my darling, my love, my dear, did not exist in her vocabulary. Her affection for him was neither spoken of nor could he hear it in her tone of voice; but he saw it in acts of courtesy and kindness. She looked after all his domestic needs, helped him with his work, seemed to believe in him and brought out the best in him. Hers was a nurturing love. During the daytime she cared for him, almost the way a mother cares for a child. At night, behind closed screens, she became his lover.

When they first met he had not been physically attracted to her, but as he got to know her that changed. He respected her, he was grateful to her and his love for her had grown; she was endlessly thoughtful and good to him. At times he felt he did not deserve her. She had a pure heart, a pure soul, and over time she had become beautiful to him in every way. And he was beginning to think that she had come to love him too. They had been married for over a year and a half now and he was certain that love was not something she had fallen into or would fall out of; their relationship was not subject to vagaries or whim, and that would not change. He was her husband and she would remain a dutiful wife. And there was great security in knowing this.

The greatest novels he had read explored passionate love and it now occurred to him that said passion would seem morally repugnant to the Japanese. This was hinted at in the classroom on more than one occasion. His students could not understand why there was so much about love and marriage in English novels, or why foreigners had so much trouble getting married. To them, marriage was a simple, natural duty and their parents made arrangements at the appropriate time. That foreigners should have so much trouble getting married was puzzling enough to them, but that distinguished authors should write about such matters, and that their work was vastly admired, seemed infinitely more bewildering. Romance, Western style, seemed all selfish indulgence to them.

Of course, love was written about in Japanese literature. He knew from experience that they were not at all prudish about passionate love, lust, or infatuation inspired by mere physical attraction, but the women in such tales were seldom the daughters of refined families, and that sort of love did not lead to marriage. There was no happy ever after for besotted lovers in Japan if the parents did not approve. They might commit ritual suicide, or they might elope, but they would never be forgiven for dishonouring their parents. They would never be welcomed back into the bosom of the family. Marriage was a duty, arranged by families for practical, economic reasons, just as his own marriage to Setsuko had been. Of course, these kinds of arrangements existed to some degree in the West, but in Japan love and marriage were entirely separate matters and to refuse to do one's duty and marry as directed by your parents was unthinkable. What would they have made of his marriage to Mattie?

In the stories Setsuko told him, the typical heroine tended to be a perfect mother, a pious daughter willing to sacrifice all for duty, or a loyal wife who followed her husband into battle, fought by his side and saved his life at the cost of her own. There were no sentimental, love-sick maidens dying, or making others die, for love. Of course, dangerous beauties and charmers of men existed in Japanese tales; but from Setsuko he learned that respectable women were never put on display, wooing was out of the question and, in civilised circles, compliments to another man's wife or daughter were considered an outrageous impertinence.

He wondered how many times he had put his foot in it on social occasions. He recalled with shame telling the Governor of Izumo Province that his wife was very beautiful – she was. He had paid numerous compliments to other deserving wives and daughters and wondered if he had been forgiven for this perceived rudeness because he was a foreigner, an outsider, a *gaijin*? Ignorance was expected of *gaijin*.

The only other person who had ever drawn his attention to proper etiquette, or corrected him when he erred, was Nishida-san. He remembered that before he introduced him to Setsuko he had advised him to refrain from kissing, embracing or holding hands in public.

"She would be ashamed if you were to show affection in such a way," said Nishida-san.

"But why?"

They had been in his little snow-covered house down by the lake in Matsue. It was freezing and he was in bed with yet another nasty dose of influenza, so Nishida-san had brought him noodles and some herbal remedies. He told Hearn that, from his reading of Western literature, he had been astonished at how large a place the subject of kisses, caresses and embraces occupied in poetry and prose fiction. Such gestures did not exist in Japanese literature. They were not considered to be tokens of affection.

"Public displays of affection are seen as proof of moral weakness.

Such behaviour is considered ill-bred whether you are a peasant or a noble lord. It is... How can I put it? It is seen as a selfish, egotistical display of happiness: look at me, I am happy. Flaunting one's personal happiness is considered vulgar. Now sit up and eat."

Hearn obeyed. Nishida-san could see that he was puzzled and while Hearn heated his icy hands on the warm noodle bowl and sipped the nourishing fishy broth, Nishida-san explained that Japan was a group-oriented society. Families, fellow students, colleagues formed into groups with a strict code of duty and loyalty. It was important to ensure harmonious relationships within the group to which you belonged; this requirement automatically implied a restriction on freedom of ideas and behaviour. There was no room for the individual.

"The nail that sticks out will be hammered down," he said. "It's an old saying that summarises the national feeling towards individualism."

Hearn learned that to pursue one's own goals or happiness at the expense of the group was considered reprehensible. Personal desires had to be subordinated to the demands of the group. Offenders were ostracised and to be ostracised from the group, especially from the family, was the greatest shame and dishonour you could incur.

"So nothing matters except duty to the family?" said Hearn.

"Correct."

"What if you have no parents? What if you are an orphan?"

"You must still do your duty, strive for the common good. You must do your duty to your community, to your country, to the Emperor."

"So one's own personal happiness doesn't matter at all?"

"Exactly. Every man is born selfish, Hearn-san, but to freely indulge this selfishness is to be no better than an animal."

"The nail that sticks out will be hammered down," said Hearn, repeating Nishida-san's words. "Then I must stick out like a sore thumb."

"Yes, but you are an outsider. You are *gaijin*. The rules don't apply to you."

"You mean that my behaviour is of no consequence."

"Yes, it is of no consequence."

"Because I'm considered a barbarian."

"Let's just say that you are different."

"What if I marry Setsuko? May I kiss her then?"

"Not in front of others. If you become a member of the Koizumi family, your behaviour will matter to them."

"But I will still be an outsider."

"Yes. You will still be *gaijin*. I'm sure they will make allowances for you and your wife will guide you. In the meantime, if you want to show affection to her, or to her family, be kind and thoughtful."

"So no matter how long I stay here, I will always be considered an outsider. That's depressing."

"You could chop off that big nose of yours. If you had a little flat one like ours, you might blend in."

Nishida-san always managed to make him laugh.

"I will keep that in mind."

Nishida-san had topped up the charcoal in the *hibachi* and left him feeling a little better, a little warmer, but considerably more bewildered about his then impending marriage.

~

Hearn paced up and down the school parade yard, puffing on his pipe, thinking warm thoughts about Nishida-san until the bugle call signalled the start of his next class. The nineteen-year-old literature students were studying Sir Thomas Mallory's *Morte d'Arthur*. When they came to the passage where the hero leaves his dying brother to go and rescue a damsel in distress, the puzzlement in the classroom was palpable. He encouraged them to express their opinions, and they were surprisingly vociferous in their condemnation of the story.

"It is a horrible story, *Sensei*. What kind of man would abandon his dying brother merely to rescue a stranger?" asked a perplexed young man in the front row. "Family comes first."

"She was a damsel in distress," said Hearn.

All around the room he was met with disapproving, puzzled expressions. He attempted to explain to them about knightly idealism but it was beyond their understanding.

"Perhaps he was driven by passion?" suggested another student.

"No, you forget I told you he did not know the girl. He was not in love with her. He was a knight in shining armour, a hero doing his duty for a defenceless maiden."

"To abandon one's brother in order to save a stranger goes against our understanding of correct behaviour," added another bewildered student.

That was the general consensus: family came first. Other classical Western stories and myths he had attempted to explain had been met with equal incomprehension and sometimes barely disguised disgust. Western heroes did not impress them. They considered heroism a matter of course: something belonging to manhood and inseparable from it.

The ancient Greek tale of Admetus had incited an earlier class to particular dismay. On the day that Admetus was fated to die, the gods agreed to pardon him if he could find someone to die in his place. Admetus asked his aged parents. They refused. When no volunteers were found, Admetus' wife went to the Underworld for him. The class saw this as a story of cowardice, disloyalty and immorality. They could barely contain their loathing for Admetus and eagerly voiced their disdain.

"Too good a wife for so shameless a man. But she was noble and virtuous."

"If King Admetus had been worthy, his father would have happily died for him."

"King Admetus was afraid to die."

"What a hateful coward."

"His subjects were disloyal."

"Yes, they were. The moment they heard of their king's danger,

137

they should have rushed to the palace and humbly begged that they might be allowed to die in his stead."

"But what if he were a tyrant?" said Hearn.

"No matter how cowardly or cruel a king might be, it is the duty of his subjects to die for him."

"Who does not love life, *Sensei*?" said a normally silent student. "Who does not dislike the thought of dying? But no brave man should so much as think about his life when duty requires him to give it."

The students put no value on their own lives, and Hearn knew that they would willingly forfeit them if need arose. He wondered if he would be capable of such selflessness; he doubted it.

Looking around the classroom at this group of intelligent, thoughtful young men, he realised that it was not just love in Western society that bewildered his students, but Western behaviour in general. He wondered if Westerners and the Japanese would ever understand each other, or even be able to agree on anything. He used to think that Japanese people agreed with him when they failed to argue with him, but he had been wrong; they just allowed him his mistaken thoughts. They either indulged the stupid, uncivilised *gaijin*, or, too embarrassed to argue as to disagree would be rude, they smiled and nodded. Orientals and Occidentals were miles apart.

When the class ended he remained in the empty classroom and thought, that's it, in a nutshell. It all came down to motivation. In the West, selfish motives prevailed. In Japan, unselfish motives prevailed. The former led inevitably to disorder and disturbance; the latter, when altruism strove for the common good, led to peace and prosperity. He had already seen how serious Japanese thinkers did not confuse Western technological advancement with ethical superiority; they were well aware of the moral weakness of the boastful West. It seemed inevitable to him that, just as the Roman Empire had collapsed, greed and self-aggrandisement would eventually cause the West to implode.

With all the talk of selfless behaviour and duty, he realised as he walked home that day that it must have been difficult for the

Koizumis to put up with his uncontrolled bursts of temper and bad moods, which it had not occurred to him to try and conceal. Setsuko never reacted to his tantrums. She did not feed his anger by arguing back. She observed him quietly, almost the way one would observe an animal in the zoo, intrigued, appalled perhaps, and then she would apologise even though she had done nothing wrong. Now, such exchanges made him feel ashamed.

More and more he was aware of his own childish inadequacies and the uncivilised nature of his behaviour and, not wanting to diminish himself in his family's eyes, he did his best to rein in his temper. It was becoming a little easier, he was learning the rules and for the most part he had it under control, except in instances relating to his work. When he was writing, the house had to be silent; disturbances of any kind angered him. Unhelpful criticism, or a negative letter from a friend or publisher, could also send him into a rage.

On reading the proofs of the book he had written in Matsue, *Glimpses of an Unfamiliar Japan*, he exploded. Just as Henry Alden had done, the new publisher, Houghton Mifflin, had taken huge liberties with his work. The changes by omission, punctuation, reordering of paragraphs, and the condensing of whole sections of text rendering it colourless, seemed to strip the writing of all personality. Furious, he wrote back telling the publisher in the foulest language to go to hell. He had not painstakingly written this book in order for the publisher to treat it anyway they liked. He called Setsuko and told her to post the letter immediately.

A few days later, when he had calmed down, he looked at the proofs again and thought that perhaps he had overreacted. The changes were not as numerous as they had seemed. He regretted his initial rash reaction. The insulting letter he had sent would, more than likely, result in another potential source of income being cut off, and he could not afford that given the precarious state of the school. He must have been smouldering silently for some time because Setsuko appeared. If she could hear his pen scratching away on paper, she would not disturb him, but if there was no evidence of activity for any length of time, she would check on him on the pretext of bringing in his smoking box or something small to eat or drink. She noticed his forlorn state.

"It's not a very pleasant day," she said.

"No."

"Something is troubling you, Danna-sama."

"Oh, never mind. It's too late to do anything about it. I just wish I hadn't sent that letter to Houghton Mifflin."

"You did seem upset at the time."

"I was. But I shouldn't have written it."

"Then it is good that I didn't post it."

He was surprised but relieved to hear it.

"Unless you tell me something is urgent, I keep your letters in a drawer and wait at least a week before posting them."

How well she knew him. If literature reflected life, then Setsuko was a true Japanese heroine. Though happy that his dutiful wife would always look after him and never desert him, he could not say with all honesty that he did not think about leaving her. The beautiful illusions of Japan, the strange charm that had come with his first entrance into its magical atmosphere, had stayed with him a long time but had finally faded. In Kumamoto he had learned to see the country without its glamour and he mourned for the sensations of the past. But they were gone and, as Chamberlain had warned him, would never return.

Since they met in Tokyo, he had been in constant communication with the professor, and he had proved a valuable contact, critic, friend and promoter of his work. Hearn's initial tendency had been to defer to him but of late, in their exchange of letters, he felt that he could hold his own. Thanks in part to Chamberlain, and as a result of published lectures and articles, he was being taken seriously as a Japanologist, and he had been referenced in a number of academic papers by other authorities on Japan. This knowledge did little to raise his flagging spirit. His sense of isolation was further compounded after a brief visit from Chamberlain, who was travelling in the area.

"You're looking well, Hearn. Much better than the last time I saw you. When was it?"

"Three years ago. I'd just arrived and was walking around wide-eyed, oohing and aahing at everything I saw."

"Ah, yes, I remember now. Just before you left for Matsue."

"I should have stayed there. Kumamoto is... There's a strange dark energy here."

"Do I sense disillusionment?"

"I'm afraid so. I can't write. Well, I've scribbled a few miserable notes. Nothing substantial. I've seen roughness and aggression here, drunkenness and men beating their wives, and to think that I called them all angels."

"Ah, but you were cosseted in Matsue. In the major cities, the gentle old world clashes daily with the hard impulses of New Japan."

"I see it here every day. Oh, it's so good to speak English again."

"Surely you have opportunities to speak English at school."

"The students engage with me during class times but only a few talk to me outside the classroom. They're so different from my Matsue students. They still write to me, you know."

"What about the teachers? Surely they—"

"I'm trying but... I'm not popular. I think some of them would like to get rid of me."

"Why do you think that?"

"They're in league with the missionaries, who I expect are doing their best to blacken my name."

Chamberlain had read the on-going exchange between Hearn and the missionaries in the newspapers.

"But what do you expect when you say that you don't believe in God or in Christ," said Chamberlain. "I saw where you argued that Jesus was not a grand character in your eyes, even as a myth, and that you abhor Christianity, which you consider to be antagonistic to art, to nature, to passion and to justice."

"Oh, you read that one, did you?"

"I read them all. They create quite a stir. Were you always a pagan?"

"No, I was once a Catholic, an Irish Catholic, at least my guardian tried to make me one. It didn't work. She only succeeded in making me think of all priests as monsters and hypocrites, of nuns as goblins in black robes and of religion as epidemic insanity."

"You certainly don't spare them."

"Why should I?"

"They have influence. A little restraint on your part—"

"I will fight them till I drop," said Hearn with a quiet anger in his voice. "As far as I'm concerned, Christianity consists of conventional dreariness and ugliness, dirty austerities, long faces, Jesuitry and the infamous distortion of people's minds. They would destroy all that is beautiful in Japan."

Reports boasting of hosts of conversions infuriated Hearn. Between the Protestant sects and the Catholic sects they claimed to have converted over a hundred thousand people. Hardly a great achievement, he thought, as it left thirty-nine million, nine hundred thousand unconverted souls in Japan. Conventions, and very malignant ones, forbade the unfavourable criticism of these reports but in his opinion, an opinion he felt obliged to express, the figures were not altogether trustworthy. He knew that amongst the poor there were many ready to profess conversion for the sake of obtaining financial assistance or employment. Many boys pretended to become Christians in order to obtain instruction in a foreign language and then openly, gladly returned to their ancient gods.

"The missionaries do good work, Hearn. In times of floods, famine, earthquakes or chol—"

"Oh yes, and then we hear a sudden announcement of numerous conversions. I doubt the sincerity of the converted and the morality of the methods."

"There is some truth in what you say but better keep it to yourself.

The missionaries can be vindictive."

"I know that. I think there's some kind of intrigue going on between them and the school and the Department of Education. Perhaps I'm being paranoid?"

"Perhaps. Perhaps not. It's not wise to anger them."

"Probably not but—"

"It's the mutinous Irish in you coming out," said Chamberlain.

"They make my blood boil. The atmosphere in school is terrible. I'd leave tomorrow if I could find somebody to take my place."

Setsuko arrived, bringing tea and rice cakes. Exchanging pleasantries with the professor, Hearn could just about catch the gist of what they were saying in *keigo*, honorific Japanese, a level of language beyond his ability. It was not the pronunciation that was different; *keigo* had a separate vocabulary, which varied according to the status of the person speaking and to whom they were addressing. He thought it an ingenious control mechanism, which left nobody in doubt as to their place in the world. Chamberlain had mastered *keigo*, and as he spoke, this sophisticated form of the language infused every inch of his being; he became Japanese in manner, posture and gesture. There was much restrained smiling, subtle nodding, polite bowing and sucking of air through pursed lips. He could see that his wife was impressed by Chamberlain's linguistic skills. She did not linger and Chamberlain did not pass any comments about her when she left.

"You were saying, you would like to leave Kumamoto. I can't say I'm surprised."

"Yes. More and more I dream of Saint Pierre. It's paradise, Chamberlain. Have you been to Martinique?"

"No. I had planned to travel the world, but I came here shortly after university and never left."

"I can see how that could happen."

"It sneaks up on you. Suddenly, twenty years have passed and you are old. It all seems to happen in an instant."

"It's not going to happen to me. I've saved some money. Well, I haven't, my wife has. I was never any good at that kind of thing. I'm more and more convinced that that's where we need to be."

A brief look from Chamberlain, his raised eyebrows told Hearn what he already knew: he could not ask Setsuko to go with him.

"And is Setsuko-san willing to—?"

"We haven't discussed it."

"I see. But I can't blame you for wanting to leave. From what I've seen, Kumamoto is a barren place."

"It is."

"What about Kobe or Tokyo? Move there. At least you'd have Europeans to talk to. You wouldn't be so bereft of like-minded company."

"No, I think I'm finished with Japan."

"That would be a great pity, Hearn. I suspect your best work is yet to come."

Chamberlain's visit was all too short and left him feeling even more alone. He had made no friends in Kumamoto, not one. The dialect was different and he could barely understand them or make himself understood. The more miserable he became, the more he thought of Saint Pierre; this sleepy city had fascinated more sensible men than himself, causing them to abandon ambition, popular esteem, friends and society and settle there for the rest of their days in dreamy contentment. Images of it hovered tantalisingly in his mind's eye as he made his way through the grim streets of Kumamoto to school and back again.

But responsibility weighed heavily on him as he dreamt of leaving. Setsuko, with Hearn's permission, had been sending money to a struggling aunt and uncle in Matsue. Rather than take the money and contribute nothing, they and Manyemon, an old man who had also worked for the family in the past, had arrived in Kumamoto and taken up residence with them. Living under his roof now was his wife, her mother, an aunt, an uncle and the two servants, Hanako and Manyemon. On the school salary, he could well afford to keep them and their presence made Setsuko and her mother happy. It was no intrusion into his life; there was plenty of room. The house was gleaming, the garden flourishing and everything was kept in good repair. He hardly ever saw them as they, like Oka-san and Hanako, kept to their side of the house.

Any thoughts he had of escape were further complicated when he learned that Setsuko was pregnant. The news brought joy to the family, but he was thoroughly daunted at the prospect of fatherhood. Not wanting to abandon a child as his father had done, he resigned himself to staying put. With no friends to talk to, he spoke of his predicament only to the silent tombstones in the cemetery.

CHAPTER TWELVE

Kumamoto, Japan, 1893

Autumn had come: the Period of Great Light. The sun's glow had suddenly become whiter, the shadows sharper and all outlines clear as the edges of splintered glass. The mosses, parched by the summer heat, had revived in wonderful patches and bands of bright green that covered all the bare spaces of the black volcanic soil.

One fine October day, Hearn found himself ascending a succession of tiny stepped fields. On reaching the ridge of the hill, there was a cemetery far more ancient than the one beside the school. It was no longer in use and the local people now buried their dead in a more secluded spot. Harmless thin black snakes wriggled across the path as he climbed, and huge grasshoppers the colour of parched leaves whirred away from his shadow. Just before he reached the broken steps that led to the cemetery gate, the path vanished.

He turned and looked back at the school far below. It looked like a miniature modern town with its long rectangular blocks of utilitarian buildings. These stone and red-bricked buildings would not have looked out of place in London or Philadelphia but they seemed decidedly at odds with the surrounding landscape of terraced fields and the figures working in them.

In one particular tiny patch of hedged-in land, a farmer and his ox ploughed the soil with an ancient plough. His wife helped; the hoe she used looked as old as the plough. They worked with a strange earnestness, as if they knew that labour is the price of life. Hearn had seen this man before in coloured prints, on hanging scrolls, on screens of great antiquity but here he was before him now. His father and his fathers had worn that straw hat, straw coat and straw sandals, and his sons and his sons' sons would do the same. It seemed to Hearn that they were not separate individuals, fathers and sons were as one, and with this perpetual renewal the peasant was content.

As he rambled about the cemetery, he was in no way content. Setsuko would give birth soon and he was filled with anxiety. The previous night he had dreamt that phantom shapes, ugly nameless creatures, entered the house and the floors groaned under their awful weight. He could not see them clearly but he felt their presence just as he had forty years ago, as a frightened child in his bedroom in Dublin. They were coming for him and he wanted to escape but he could not move, or cry out, or do anything; he was helpless in the face of imminent horror. He woke with a start, drenched in sweat, to find the whole house shaking: it was an earthquake. He did not like earthquakes but he had got used to them. The tremors went on for too long and after a minute, without any call or rallying, the entire household hurried outside and huddled together in the bamboo until the earth settled.

The thought of being a father terrified him. If, as commonly believed, a child follows the ways of his father, inherits his strengths and weaknesses, he wondered had he inherited his father's weakness? Would he prove a failure to his child? That he might inflict such unhappiness on anybody filled him with despair.

A small shapeless stone statue caught his attention: it was *Jizo*, the Buddha who cares for the souls of little children. He had seen these statues everywhere, in temples and graveyards but also in public places. Shortly after their marriage Setsuko had brought him by boat to visit a very famous *Jizo* in a dusky cave by the sea north of Matsue. It was said that each night the ghosts of little children piled up small heaps of pebbles and rocks before the statue. They left fresh prints of tiny feet in the sand, faint but perceptible by day. As was the custom, Setsuko brought a gift of small straw sandals and left them inside the grotto so that the infant ghosts would not wound their feet on the sharp rocks.

Leaning closer, he scraped away the thick layer of moss on the statue and discovered a face with the charm of a sleeping child. There was a curious beauty in the immature features and sweetness in the lines of the lids and lips. Deeply moved, he added a stone to the little pile of mossy stones piled around *Jizo*'s feet and said a prayer to this tender god. He prayed that his child would be healthy and that it would be born with two good eyes and he wished with all his heart that he would not let his child down.

Kumamoto, November, 1893

Dear Watkins,

Last night my son, Leopold Kazuo Koizumi, was born. I could not speak when I saw him; he is perfect and to me he seems the most strangely beautiful creature on this earth. He is a strong boy and he has large black eyes. His mother's features are curiously blended with mine and he looks more Japanese than Western even though he has my nose. The physician says, from the form of his little bones, he will be tall. Lucky boy.

My son will wear sandals and dress like a Japanese and become a good little Buddhist. He will not have to go to church or listen to stupid sermons or be perpetually tormented by absurd conventions. I will give him my whole life, my time, my strength, my care. I will give him everything I can before going to the grave.

The strangest and strongest sensation of my life was hearing for the first time the thin cry of my own child. For a moment I had the strange feeling of being double; but there was something more, something impossible to analyse. Perhaps I felt an echo in my heart of all the sensations felt by all the fathers and mothers in the world at similar instants in the past. It was a tender but ghostly feeling.

I believe now that no man can possibly know what life means, what the world means, what anything means, until he has a child and loves it. And then the whole universe changes and nothing will ever again seem exactly as it seemed before.

With affection,
L.H.

The arrival of Kazuo put paid to any thoughts of leaving. Now, he was content to look on adoringly while the women of the house fussed over the treasured child. Kazuo could almost have passed for a Japanese boy but after a few weeks his eyes turned blue; in them Hearn saw his father's eyes. He pampered the boy with an excessive abundance of toys and silk garments. A fancy perambulator was ordered from Yokohama; such a contraption had never been seen before in Kumamoto and it became a talking point of the neighbourhood. Walking around the garden with his son in his arms, he felt at peace with the world. He knew that he was loved, and that no one would ever love him more than those around him now. This was a precious consideration and the thought that at some point he would need to resume his travels, if only for a while, made him uneasy. Why would he even think of leaving? He had come to realise that the Japanese were the best people in the world. It was a torment to him to think what would become of the family if he did leave, or if he died.

~

The following July, leaving for work on one of those sweltering mornings, he was met at the front door by a group of children asking for donations for the local festival of *Jizo*. He gladly contributed, now being particularly fond of this gentle god, the protector of children, who, he liked to think, had answered his prayers and given him a fine healthy son with two perfect eyes.

149

After dinner that night he ventured out to see the festival with Setsuko and Oka-san, the doting grandmother, who insisted on carrying nine-month-old baby Kazuo. Perched before their front gate they found an enormous dragonfly. More than three feet long, Hearn was startled by how realistic it looked and moved closer to examine it. He discovered that the long body was a pine branch wrapped with coloured paper, the wings were four fire shovels, and the gleaming head was a little teapot. An ingeniously placed candle cast extraordinary shadows on the wall behind it. It was simply wonderful.

"The children made it for you to thank you for your donation," said Oka-san.

"You are too generous, Danna-sama. You give so much."

"It was a worthy cause," he replied.

"It's lucky you have a sensible wife to mind your money or you would give it all away," said Oka-san.

"Or spend it on Kazuo," said Setsuko.

"But it gives me pleasure," he said.

The narrow streets were busier than usual. Families were out for the evening; children, parents, grandparents, all clacking along in *geta*, those wooden sandals with three-inches-high soles, held on only by a single strap between the toes. To Hearn's continued astonishment, children ran about in them and, miraculously, they never tripped. Their *geta* never fell off. It was a lovely musical sound, the pattering of *geta*, like pebbles shifting under a receding wave.

Near the local shrine they passed rows of vendors selling souvenirs, toys and sweet treats. The shrine had been decorated with flowers, lanterns lit up the night and offerings of food and drink had been set out before the little *Jizo* statues. Fresh baby bibs had been put around their necks, perhaps by grieving parents in the hope that *Jizo* would protect their departed children in the other world. A platform had been erected and children dressed in brightly coloured *yukata* danced on it, their pretty speckled sleeves fluttering in the warm breeze.

Oka-san wandered off, lovingly chatting away to her grandson, and he took the opportunity of time alone with his wife to broach a subject that had been on his mind for some time. As things stood, Kazuo was illegitimate. Hearn remembered how shocked he had been to learn that if they registered their marriage, Setsuko and Kazuo would be considered foreigners and would have no right to own or inherit property. Royalties were still coming in from his earlier books. *Glimpses of an Unfamiliar Japan*, the book he had written in Matsue, was selling in England and in America. He was no longer poor and if anything happened to him, he wanted them to inherit whatever money he had, and there was only one way to ensure this.

"I need to become a Japanese citizen, Setsu."

"Really?"

"Yes, your family will have to adopt me."

"I'm sure we would be happy to do that. But what would that make us? Will you be my brother, or my son? Will I then be your Little Mama?"

He laughed.

"No, you will be my wife. I will be your Japanese husband. Our son will be legitimate and, if anything happens to me, you will be legally entitled to inherit all my worldly goods."

She took a moment to answer.

"Is something wrong? Are you sick?"

"No, I'm not sick but I'd like to do it soon. It is a difficult and lengthy process."

Her eyes welled up and judging from this unusual show of emotion, he realised that she had been aware of her precarious predicament but perhaps did not want to make any such demand of him.

"I can't ask you to give up your own citizenship."

"That would be no great sacrifice for me. All my life I've been wandering. I've never known where I belonged. I wouldn't be giving up anything precious and, if it makes you and Kazuo secure, I want to do it."

They walked along quietly together until she stopped, said a little prayer in front of one of the statues of *Jizo*, and then turning to him asked:

"What name will you take?"

"Your family name: Koizumi."

"Of course. I meant your first name?"

He had thought long and hard about this. While in Matsue he had visited the remote Yaegaki Shrine, a place where the deities of Wedlock and Love resided. Young people in love made the arduous pilgrimage there and confided their secret hopes and wishes to the trees. The temple took its name from a legend that told of a god who fell in love with a princess and saved her from an eight-headed dragon. One of the most ancient Japanese songs told of eight clouds rising, the eight clouds of Izumo that rose up and formed a fence for the lovers to live safely within.

"Yakumo," he said.

With the index finger of his right hand, he wrote on his left palm the four characters that would spell his new name: Koizumi, meaning little spring; and Yakumo, meaning eight clouds. She understood the reference and a small smile flitted across her face.

Chapter Thirteen

Kumamoto, Japan, 1894

By the time Kazuo was a year old, the streets of Kumamoto were thronged with men in white uniforms. Bugle sound and the rumble of artillery filled the air. For the third time in history the Japanese army had subdued Korea, and the Imperial declaration of war against China was published in newspapers printed on crimson paper. All the military power of Japan was in motion. The first line of reserves had been summoned and troops poured into Kumamoto. Barracks, inns and temples could not accommodate them, thousands were billeted on the citizens and still there was not enough room even though special trains were carrying regiments north as fast as possible to the port of Shimonoseki.

Considering the scale of the movement, it surprised Hearn that the city was so quiet. The troops were as silent and gentle as his Japanese boys in class. There was no swaggering, no reckless gaiety, but he suspected that under the calm exterior smouldered all the fierceness of the old feudal days.

"You're very quiet, Danna-sama," said Setsuko one night as they prepared for bed. "Something has upset you."

"I keep expecting a knock on the door. We're going to have to accommodate soldiers. I hate disruption."

"We have enough room. It won't be for long."

"Yesterday I read a report in the newspaper about a man who shot himself on being refused the chance of doing his military service."

"Yes, it happens."

"In the West, a man would be delighted to be able to go home to his family."

"Really?"

"And today there was a piece about a soldier who committed *hara kiri* because he wasn't permitted to go to the front."

"He must have felt deeply sad not to be able to die for the Emperor."

"But why kill yourself when you have a chance to live. If you're not at the front, you might survive the war."

"I suppose he couldn't live with the shame. Do you remember Furumatsu-san in Matsue?"

"Yes, of course. His wife died in the cholera epidemic?"

"That's right. Well, he wanted to join the army but he couldn't find anybody to take care of his daughter. So he killed her."

"What? But she was only…"

"Eight years old."

Hearn was speechless.

"He joined his regiment before the facts were known and went straight to the front to seek death in battle so that he could join her in the afterworld."

To hide his bewilderment, he extinguished the light and lay rigid beside her, trying to fathom what he had just heard. She sensed his tension.

"You mustn't think badly of Furumatsu-san," she said. "He had *samurai* blood in his veins. His grandfather and Oji-san fought together. Such an act was not unheard of in feudal times. Before battle, *samurai* sometimes killed their wives and children, in order to banish thoughts of them."

"I cannot begin to understand—"

"You see," she continued, "there were three things a warrior should not think about on the battlefield: home, loved ones and his own mortality. After such an act of ferocious heroism—"

"Is that what you call murdering your family? Ferocious heroism?"

"In this instance, yes. After such an act, a warrior is ready to do his duty. He is ready for the hour of the 'death fury'. He gives and takes no quarter."

Sleep did not come easily to him that night.

Over the next few weeks he witnessed Buddhist priests addressing squadrons in the courtyards of the temples, and great ceremonies performed in the parade ground of Kumamoto castle. Thousands were placed under the protection of *Amida*, Buddha of Light. Hearn watched soldiers being consecrated by the laying of a naked razor blade on each young head: a symbol of voluntary renunciation of life's vanities. At Shinto shrines, he heard endless prayers being offered up to the gods of armies and to the memory of the heroes who had fought and died for the Emperor in ancient days. Sacred charms were distributed to the troops: they were narrow, and cleverly designed so that they could be slipped into the lining of a uniform.

Keen to pay her respects, Setsuko went with him to Honmyoji, the famous monastery that housed the ashes of the great warrior, Kato Kiyomasa, conqueror of Korea, enemy of the Jesuits and protector of Buddhism. There, the pilgrims' chanting of the sacred invocation, *namu myo ho renge kyo*, resounded like the roar of surf. She bought a souvenir in the shape of a tiny shrine that held a miniature image of Kiyomasa, and she told him about the mysterious disappearance of the deified warrior's armour. It seemed that the helmet and sword, which had been preserved in the main shrine for three hundred years, vanished shortly after war was declared. Some said that they had been sent to Korea to stimulate the heroism of the army. Others talked of hooves echoing in the temple at night and the passing of a mighty shadow as Kiyomasa rose from the sleep of centuries to lead the armies of the Sons of Heaven to conquest once more.

At school, the staff room talk praised the Emperor, how he sent presents and paternal words of affection to his troops. The people followed his august example. According to the newspaper reports, every steamer that left for Korea was laden down with provisions, tobacco, *sake* and gifts of all kinds. Those who could afford nothing costlier sent straw sandals. Even children made little contributions, and they were not refused lest the universal impulse of patriotism be in any way discouraged. Special subscriptions, made voluntarily, were collected in every street for the support of the families of the reserves, the married men who had been obliged to leave their wives and children without the means to live. With all this love and support, Hearn did not doubt that the soldiers would perform more than the simple duty demanded. Amidst all this activity the people remained singularly quiet. He realised that this public calm was characteristically Japanese; the more profoundly their emotions were called into play, the more self-contained they seemed.

One day, Manyemon, the old servant who had come from Matsue with Setsuko's aunt and uncle, came to his study door. It was unlike him to enter this side of the house; he knelt down and spoke from the far side of the *shoji* screen.

"Master, there's a soldier at the entrance who wishes to see you."

"Oh, Manyemon, I hope they are not going to billet soldiers on us. Tell him the house is full."

"I did. He says he knows you and begs to speak with you."

Curious, Hearn put down his pen and followed Manyemon to the entrance where a fine young man in uniform stood waiting. When he saw Hearn he smiled, took off his cap and bowed. The smile was familiar but Hearn could not place him.

"*Sensei*, have you really forgotten me?"

Seeing the puzzled look on Hearn's face, the soldier let out a little laugh and then volunteered his name.

"Kosuga Asakichi."

Hearn's heart leapt when he realised that standing before him was a former student of his from Matsue; it was almost four years since he had seen him. He held out both hands in welcome.

"Come in. Come in. How big and handsome you have grown. No wonder I didn't know you."

The young man blushed as he slipped off his shoes and unbuckled his sword.

"I am so glad to find you at home. I got permission to come and bid you goodbye. You are as famous here as you were in Matsue."

Asakichi stayed for dinner and they talked of happy times in Matsue.

"You will drink a little *sake* with me."

"I would love to share a drink with you, *Sensei*, but I promised mother I wouldn't drink while I was in the army."

"Perhaps some coffee after dinner then?"

"Yes, please, if it's not too much trouble."

Hearn learned that after graduating Asakichi had returned to his people, wealthy farmers. A year later, all the boys in his village who had reached the age of nineteen were summoned for military service. At first he had been stationed in Nagoya, then in Tokyo, but on hearing that his regiment was not to be sent to fight, he applied for a transfer to the Kumamoto division.

"I'm so glad I did. We leave tomorrow," he said, his face radiant with joy.

Hearn had never seen such joy before, except once: in Mattie's eyes on the morning they married.

"I remember you once declared in class that you wished to die for the Emperor," said Hearn.

"And now my chance has come, not only for me but for several of your old students."

He listed off the names of classmates who were already in Korea.

"Oh, and our drill master is there too. Do you remember him?"

"Lieutenant Fuji."

"Yes."

"I thought he had retired from the army."

"He is with the reserves. He had another son born since you left us. Now, he has two boys and two girls."

"Then his family must be very anxious about him."

"No, not at all. To die in battle is very honourable and the government will take care of the families of those who are killed. Our officers have no fear, unless they have no son. It's very sad to die if you have no son."

"Do you mean sad for the wife and the rest of the family?"

"No, I mean for the man."

"But how is it sad for him?" asked Hearn.

"The son inherits. The son maintains the family name. The son makes the offerings to the dead of food and drink without which the spirit would suffer. But not only that, *Sensei*. Every man needs someone to love him after he is dead."

"I can't imagine how the love of the living could make me happy after I die. I can't even imagine myself conscious of love after death."

"Then you must think it very strange that we should love the dead."

"No, I think it's beautiful."

"Those who fall in battle will be honoured. Even the Emperor will honour us. We will be loved and worshipped by all the people."

He said 'we' quite naturally as if it were a foregone conclusion that he would die.

After dinner, Setsuko came with coffee and sweet cake. She did not linger but complimented Asakichi on how well he looked in his soldier's uniform.

"Your family must be very proud of you," she said, bowed deeply and then quietly closed the *shoji* screen.

Sitting facing each other on flat cushions on the *tatami* floor, they talked until darkness fell. There were some seeming contradictions in the young man's beliefs but Hearn felt it was not the time to challenge him. Buddhists believed that the dead must make a long dark journey to the *Meido*, a place where souls are tested and await judgement before they move on to the next life. Shinto followers believed that the souls remained in the world with their families. Hearn wanted to know, if the dead were in the *Meido*, why were offerings made to the ancestors in temples and before the family shrines as if they were really present.

"We think of a soul as one and as many. We think of it as a person but not as a substance. We think of it as something that can be many places at once, like a moving of air."

"Or of electricity," said Hearn.

"Yes."

"I see."

Asakichi told him how before he left Tokyo, he marched on a military excursion to a shrine where the spirits of heroes were worshipped. It was a beautiful, lonesome place among the hills shaded by tall trees. In the dim, cool silence, they stopped before the shrine. Nobody spoke. Then the bugle sounded through the holy grove, like a call to battle, and they all presented arms. Asakichi told Hearn how he was overcome with emotion and when he looked around he saw that all his comrades felt the same way.

"I don't know what causes it, but whenever I'm in a great shrine tears flow from my eyes," said Asakichi.

It was not the first time Hearn had heard of the sentiments evoked by the sacred traditions and the solemnity of the ancient shrines. Asakichi was describing the ancestral feeling of the race: the vague but immeasurable emotion of Shinto.

The plaintive call of bugles echoed through the city and filtered into the little room where they sat. They fell silent. From Kiyomasa's fortress soared a sound as loud as thunder: the singing of ten thousand men. Asakichi listened, swaying his shoulders in time to the rhythm. It was a song of brave hearts and of the everlasting, pure and holy Imperial Realm.

"*Sensei*, I must go. I don't know how to thank you enough or to tell you how happy this day has been for me. But first, please accept this."

From his pocket he took a small envelope and handed it to Hearn.

It contained a photograph of himself: a proud young man in military uniform. Hearn had to fight hard to contain his emotions.

"Long ago you asked me for a photograph. So I brought this for you."

"Thank you. I will treasure it."

At the entrance Asakichi buckled on his sword and asked what he might send from Korea.

"A letter, please, after the next great victory."

"If I can hold a pen, I will write."

Asakichi first bowed, then gave the formal military salute before striding away. Feeling desolate, Hearn watched him until he disappeared into the darkness. He could hear the soldiers singing and faintly, in the distance, the roll of trains bearing away so many young hearts and so much extraordinary loyalty to the bloody war in China.

Some weeks later a solemn Manyemon came to his study with a Japanese newspaper and pointed to a name in the middle of a long list of those fallen in battle. Hearn squinted at the list but could not read the tiny characters.

"Kosuga Asakichi," said Manyemon.

Sorrow descended like a great weight on his soul.

"Please, come with me."

Hearn followed him to the room where he had dined with Asakichi. Manyemon had decorated the alcove as if for a festival, filling vases with flowers, lighting little votive lamps, and placing several sticks of burning incense in a small bronze cup. Approaching the alcove Hearn was moved to see Asakichi's photograph propped up on a small stand and before it was spread a miniature feast of rice, fruits and cakes.

"It would please his spirit if you would honour him with some words."

Manyemon left him alone, and he sat and stared at the photograph. And he did talk to Asakichi and the young man seemed to smile back at him through the rising haze of curling incense.

Chapter Fourteen

Kumamoto, Japan, 1894

As the war in China dragged on, he became increasingly conscious of a change in attitude towards foreigners; while people were not overtly hostile, he felt thoroughly unwelcome. On more than one occasion, he had been hissed at on the street; he could not tell Setsuko, knowing that it would upset her.

The atmosphere in school had become unbearable. Hearn heard the word *gaijin* frequently whispered in corridors when he passed, and not in a kind way. Conversations stopped when he entered rooms; people moved away from him as if he were contagious. He felt so isolated that he found himself craving the company of Westerners again, with all their prejudices, conventions and berserk whiskers. He was convinced that he was being spied on, and this was confirmed one day while taking lunch with one of his students in the nearby cemetery when he discovered a fellow teacher hiding behind a tombstone listening to their conversation. A newly converted Christian, he had been responsible for more than a few resignations. Hearn thought him a nasty piece of work.

His paranoia was further compounded when his contract at the school, which was due for renewal in April, was not renewed. Expecting to receive it at any moment, he said nothing but by June, convinced that they were trying to get rid of him, he wrote a testy letter of resignation to the director. When Setsuko came to his study with lunch, she saw the address on the envelope.

"You'll be there tomorrow, won't you? Why not hand it—"

"I never want to set foot in that damned school again. Post it, please."

She usually just delivered lunch and left him to get on with his work but she sank to her knees with the envelope in her hands.

"And don't put it in a drawer, Setsu. Send it immediately."

"Yes, of course. What does it say?"

"Nothing a polite, well-bred woman like you would want to hear."

"Then perhaps it is the kind of letter you might regret sending in a day or two?"

"I don't care. I've made up my mind. I'm resigning before they throw me out."

"If you feel you must resign, perhaps you should try to do it quietly, in a way that will leave no black mark on your character."

"Enough."

Placing the letter back on his desk, she said,

"Why don't you go and talk to the headmaster? Sakurai-san is a civilised man. It might help to discuss the situation with him."

She bowed and left before he could reply. Of course she was right. The letter would burn bridges. And such a sudden departure might go against him in the future if he needed a job in another government school or university. He fumed for a few moments then crumpled the letter into a ball and flung it at the wall.

It took all his self-control the next day not to burst into the headmaster's office and confront him; blunt aggression seldom received the desired results, especially not in Japan. He made an appointment and went to see him later that afternoon. It would have been easier to have the conversation in English, where he felt free to be more direct, more assertive, but Sakurai-san did not speak English. A precise, gentle man of quiet disposition, Sakurai-san had studied in France. Rather than fumble in the formal Japanese, at Hearn's request, they spoke in French. Initial pleasantries dispensed with,

Hearn got to the point.

"I was just wondering if perhaps you might be able to enlighten me as to why my contract has not been renewed?"

The headmaster seemed genuinely surprised. He leaned forward.

"Hasn't it?"

"No."

"Well, I'm terribly sorry. It's clearly just an oversight, Hearn-san. You've been here so long…"

"Three years."

"Is it three years?"

"If it's not being renewed—"

"No, no, no. It is a terrible mistake. I really am sorry. I'll see to it immediately."

Hearn was not to be appeased by the headmaster's seemingly genuine regret for the oversight.

"Oh, I don't know…" said Hearn, turning to look out the window.

The muffled sound of students marching up and down in rigid formation could be heard through the closed window. It was an uncomfortably hot, humid day; they must have been sweltering in their military uniforms.

"I'm not sure I can continue to teach here much longer."

"The contract will be on your desk tomorr—"

"It's not just because of the delay with the contract."

"Then why? Please tell me what—"

"The fact is… This sounds childish but… Nobody likes me here. Nobody talks to me. People stop talking when I enter the staff room – most noticeably, staff members with Christian connections. I think you know who I mean."

The headmaster let out a small sigh, sat back, and as they were speaking French, he made the quintessential French gesture of bewilderment, floating his hands in the air and scowling.

"And perhaps you have heard the words 'morally deplorable' whispered about me," said Hearn. "The missionaries have our sanctimonious friend brainwashed. Don't tell me he hasn't suggested to you that I am trying to corrupt the students."

"There are intrigues in all academic circles, Hearn-san."

"Perhaps but—"

"The students talk positively about you. You inspire them with your wonderful lectures. They do like you. Perhaps they just don't know how to show it."

"Well, that's good to hear."

"I would hate to lose…"

At the call of a bugle, the students saluted their drill master and then dispersed. The headmaster opened the window and sat back down at his desk.

"As I was saying, I would hate to lose you, Hearn-san. If any of the staff are rude to you, tell me and I will make sure it doesn't happen again. Please, you will stay with us, won't you?"

Feeling somewhat placated but without committing to staying on for another two years, he left the headmaster's office. There were only three weeks left in the term. He would get through them and then try to figure out how best to handle the situation during the summer break.

Mostly he dined alone in his room but that night he joined the family in the kitchen. He sensed unhappiness among them and wondered if it was because of the burglary some weeks earlier, which had unsettled them all. It had happened on the night when the entire household was out hunting singing insects. This was a popular pastime. Equipped with lanterns to attract them, and light bamboo cages in which to trap them, everybody knew which insects to look for. The little creatures would be brought home and placed amongst the garden shrubbery so that the family could enjoy their music. It evoked memories and sensations of rural peace, of woods and hills, of flowing water, starry nights and sweet country air.

That night Oka-san had insisted on carrying Kazuo on her back and, on the way home, to everyone's surprise, she recited a famous romantic poem about a woman listening to insect song while waiting in a garden for her lover to come. It was a heartfelt rendering and when she finished they gave her a round of applause but she did not seem to hear it. Perhaps haunted by sad memories, she was gazing up at the moon and, somewhat distracted, she tripped and fell. Fortunately, she managed to twist around so that Kazuo was not hurt. The night did not end well. Oka-san got a nasty cut on the side of her face, and then they returned home to find that the house had been broken into. They were astonished. In all their time in Matsue, nothing like this had ever happened. The rooms had been turned upside down, presumably in a search for money, which fortunately Setsuko kept very little of in the house. Only a small amount of cash had been taken, but personal items had been rummaged through. There was a sense of having been violated as well as considerable apprehension that the thieves might return.

The following morning he came upon Hanako and Oka-san squatting in the garden. They had found the footprints of the burglars and were placing burning *moxa*, small cones of plant fibre, on each footprint. He was puzzled. *Moxa* was usually used to heal people. Burning *moxa* was placed on a patient's skin and left to smoulder, and the heat supposedly stimulated the flow of energy and blood, and promoted healing.

"The *moxa* will burn the burglars' feet and they won't be able to run very far," explained Hanako.

"It will slow them down. The police will have a better chance of catching them," said Oka-san.

The word 'nonsense' was on the tip of his tongue but he said nothing. What right had he to mock their simple beliefs.

"I see," he said.

He left them to it. The burglars were never caught.

What with the robbery, frequent earthquakes, tremendous thunder storms and the general ugliness of the city, the entire household was sick of Kumamoto – so much so that the uncle and aunt who had come to live with them were already making plans to return to Matsue. Setsuko and her mother said they would also be happy to leave Kumamoto. It eased his conscience to know that, if he decided that they should go, he would not be disrupting their worlds merely because of his own dissatisfaction.

As was the custom after dinner, Setsuko read the newspaper aloud for the family but mostly for the benefit of Hanako and Manyemon who were illiterate. One report of a tragic *joshi*, lovers' suicide, moved them deeply. Intrigued by the story, Hearn temporarily forgot his own woes.

According to this report, a farmer saw a couple crossing the rice fields near his house. They were heading for the railroad tracks just north of the village railway station. The early express train from Tokyo was due and he could see the plume of smoke rising from the advancing train. The two people began to run along the tracks. The farmer was not overly alarmed because they stepped off the tracks as the train approached and stood hand in hand off to the side.

As the train drew near, the couple stepped onto the tracks. The train driver could see them clearly as they were only a hundred yards ahead, and he described how they wound their arms around each other and lay down, cheek to cheek, straight across one of the rails. Despite frantic attempts to halt the speeding train, the wheels, like an enormous blade, sliced through both bodies.

The girl, Oyoshi, was eighteen. He, Taro, was seventeen. They had been childhood friends, had recently fallen in love and had hoped to marry. Ignoring their wishes, her parents made arrangements for her to marry an elderly widower, a farmer who was known to have speculated in rice during a time of famine: a crime that peasants never forgive. He was wealthy but many unpleasant stories were known about him. It was said that on the night of his first marriage, he had been forced to honour *Jizo*.

Hearn knew that it was still customary in some provinces on the occasion of the marriage of a very unpopular farmer, for a band of sturdy young men to force their way into the marriage feast carrying a statue of *Jizo* borrowed from a roadside or from a nearby cemetery. A large crowd follows them. They deposit the stone *Jizo* in the middle of the celebration and demand that offerings of food and *sake* be made to it at once. This means a big feast for themselves, and it is apparently more than dangerous to refuse. All the uninvited guests have to be served until they can neither eat nor drink any more. The obligation to give such a feast was not only a public rebuke, it was also a lasting public disgrace.

Though it had happened some thirty years earlier, Oyoshi had heard the story. She knew it was hopeless to protest and a few days before the wedding she and Taro disappeared. Letters from both were found hours after their deaths. The newspaper article ended with an account of how the village people put bamboo cups full of flowers on the single tombstone of the united pair in the local Buddhist cemetery. People burned incense sticks and unhappy lovers prayed there.

Setsuko put down the newspaper and there was silence. Hanako slowly shook her head in dismay. Oka-san was weeping quietly. Hearn wondered if she was remembering the sad time when, on her wedding night, her husband and his secret lover committed *joshi*.

"No good ever comes of a lusty old man forcing a young woman into marriage," said Setsuko's aunt.

Oka-san flashed her a reprimanding glance.

"I'm sorry, I didn't mean… Besides, Hearn-san is not so old and—"

"And nobody was forced," said Setsuko.

Manyemon intervened to lighten the moment by telling a story about a miserly old man who wanted a beautiful young wife. He found one, and to his delight it seemed that she only ate two grains of rice a day.

"One night he returned home earlier than usual and heard strange noises coming from inside the house. It sounded like a wild beast savaging a carcass, slobbering, grunting and chewing with gusto."

Manyemon paused for dramatic effect. He sipped some tea. They urged him to continue.

"Alarmed, he crept to a spot where one of the *shoji* screens was damaged. He peeped in and was shocked to see his wife devouring vast quantities of rice and fish, shoving all the food into a hole in the top of her head under her hair."

"I know," said Hanako. "He had married a mountain demon."

They all laughed except Hearn who was still puzzled by the newspaper report.

"Did you say that Oyoshi and Taro's tombstone was in a Buddhist cemetery?" he asked.

"Yes," said Setsuko.

"But I thought Buddhism forbids *joshi*."

"Yes, it does," said Manyemon. "But in this case... Well, I think the couple deserve profound respect."

They all nodded in agreement.

"They suffered so much," said Oka-san.

Hearn went back to his room and wrote down the sad story of Oyoshi and Taro. Then, feeling certain that his days in Kumamoto, and perhaps in Japan, were numbered, he realised it was time to start looking for a new position. But he hated asking for anything, begging favours, and so he postponed the task and instead wrote to Watkins, answering his letter of some months earlier.

Kumamoto, June, 1894

Dear Old Dad,

I was happy to hear from you and to know that you think of me. I often find myself thinking about you. The other night I dreamed of that dear little shop of yours and heard the ticking of the old clock like far away footsteps on a pavement. Does the clock still tick? I am ashamed that I write so seldom. It's not that I have forgotten you or that I care less for you. I'm so busy here there is little time to dwell on the past, on faces and places that seem now to be gone forever.

Here in Kumamoto the problem of existence forever stares one in the face with eyes of iron. Independence is so hard to obtain. The missionaries, the institutions, the cliques, the humbugs all work against the man who tries to preserve independence of thought and action. I am forty-four now and I feel old, immemorially old, older than the moon. I ought never to have been born in this century. I live forever in dreams of other centuries and other faiths and other ethics. I live in my books and smoke my pipe and I am happy to tell you that being in the company of one woman has not killed me with ennui as I always thought it would. On the contrary, Setsuko is the dearest wife and mother – and of course my son continues to delight.

I have not been getting rich, but I am at least trying to prepare the foundations for the security of my family and for ultimate independence. My efforts in this regard are endlessly foiled by my difficulty in having to work at anything other than writing. I am in a perpetual quandary. Though there is so much I love in Japan, sadly I feel my time here may be coming to an end. Don't be surprised if you hear a knock on the door some day and find me once more outside your printing shop begging for employment.

Goodbye for a little while, with my best love to you,
Lafcadio Hearn

When he had finished the letter, he composed one to Chamberlain and several more to acquaintances he had made when he first arrived in Yokohama. Finally, he wrote to some old friends in America to see if suitable employment could be found for him there – anywhere but New York, he stressed. Just writing the name caused it all to come back to him: the city walled up to the sky and roaring like a monster. He had walked too many miles along those hard streets, never treading on earth, knowing that below those huge concrete slabs lay cavernous tunnels heaving with water, steam and fire. On either side of the streets, high grey buildings shut out the sun, and slivers of sky were barely visible through tangles of ugly electric cables.

He recalled the sense of panic he felt when living there, panic caused by the city's enormous energy, its architectural utterance announcing a new industrial age. And there was to be no halt to the thunder of wheels, the roar of machines and the storming of human feet. Back and forth, up and down they went, heights too dizzying, distances too great for the use of limbs. It was life without sympathy, power without pity.

He looked out at his simple but lovely garden and thought how pleasant it was to live close to the soft green earth. He slid open the screens. The *semi*, Japanese crickets, were in great voice. They were particularly wonderful singers and they seemed to have a different song for each month during the warm season. They began their song with a wheezy sound that swelled into a crescendo and then slowly died away; it never failed to soothe him.

He had learned that insect melody was highly regarded, not just in domestic life, but in literature as well, and it suggested to him that the Japanese aesthetic sensibility had developed in directions that remained almost unexplored in the West – except perhaps by the rarest of poets. So much could be learned from people in whose minds the simple chant of a cricket could awaken whole swarms of tender fancies. The West could boast of being more technologically advanced but when it came to nature, the Japanese were millennia ahead.

And yet it saddened him to think that even in a country like Japan, with its sophisticated culture, there was no shortage of greedy industrialists. The old courtesy, the old faith, the old kindness was vanishing like snow in the sun. The Meiji government was lapping up everything the West had to offer. As soon as the doors had opened, Westerners barged in, and it seemed to him that this blind aggressive industrialism would ruin Japan. Once the damage had been done, only then would they – and he increasingly thought of Westerners as 'they' – begin to understand the charm of what they had destroyed.

He filled his pipe and stood in the open doorway wondering how it would work if he did get an offer of employment in America. Would they all go together or would he go first, set up home and then send for them. It turned out that Setsuko had a surprisingly adventurous nature, but he knew that she would be loath to part from her mother. He could not see Oka-san leaving Japan. And what about Hanako and Manyemon? What would become of these two loyal old servants? If they did not want to come, he could send money to support them.

Or, it occurred to him, he might just resume his travels alone. They had saved some money. The family could go back to Matsue. They would be fine for at least a year or maybe more given Setsuko's frugality. It would only be for a while and perhaps he could take Kazuo with him. He broached this possibility with Setsuko as they prepared for bed that night and was met with a stern, startled look that put an instant end to that plan. She would never let him take the child away.

Sleep would not come. Images of Saint Pierre flitted in and out of his mind, tempting, glorious ones. How good it would be, he thought, to live again without rules and stifling etiquette, to be able to speak his mind and give offence knowing that whoever was on the receiving end would give just as good back. There was often hurt in such exchanges but there was also clarity. He had not quite got to terms with the rules of engagement in Japan; the constant need for restraint was draining, especially when he was feeling low. Much as he loved and admired Japan, there were times when he felt the fire in his soul being smothered.

All his life he had been a creature of circumstance, drifting along in the direction of least resistance, resolving to love nothing yet always loving too much. And when things had fallen apart, he had moved on and the past had taken on the unreal quality of a dream. He asked himself, if the life he was living now might someday come to an end and fade into a hazy memory. Even as he posed the question, he knew this would not happen. He sensed in some dim way that he was here to stay.

Chapter Fifteen

Kobe, Japan, 1895

Word went out that Hearn was looking for a new position and it was not long before offers came in. The most interesting one came from *The Kobe Chronicle*, who promised him the freedom to write whatever he wanted in the editorials. He had accepted the position and moved his family to Kobe that October. Work at the newspaper was enjoyable and it was a relief to be in the company of uncomplicated, like-minded American colleagues. The only problem was that working all day at the newspaper and then going home to write at night put a huge strain on his eye. It had been especially bad during the winter months. Curiously, he discovered that a hot bath helped restore clear vision and as the weather warmed, his sight improved.

Setsuko was pleased with Kobe and with the house she had found for them. It was not the kind of house he would have chosen but she liked it. Clean, bright and newly built on a hill overlooking the city, the ground floor was Japanese style and upstairs was Western. It was strange to be sleeping in a bed again. Having become accustomed to rolling out of the *futon* onto a welcoming *tatami* floor, he had fallen out of the bed twice in the first week there.

One fine May morning, he stepped onto the balcony outside his bedroom and gazed over the tiled roofs of houses that sloped down to the port. Everywhere he looked he saw extraordinary shapes quivering and fluttering in the air: tied to tall bamboo poles were giant *koi*, Japanese carp, made of vibrant coloured paper and cloth. The cables holding them up were fastened within the heads of the fish and wind entering through their open mouths inflated their bodies and kept them undulating, rising and falling, twisting and turning like real fish.

He realised it was 5th May, the Festival of Boys, and *koi* flying above a house signified the presence of boys within. They also symbolised the hope of the parents that their sons would win their way through the world against all obstacles, just as real *koi* ascend swift rivers against the stream. In honour of Kazuo, Manyemon had put up one in their own garden. It was about fifteen feet long and had an orange belly and a bluish-grey back. The rustling of its motions as it flapped against the sky reminded Hearn of the sound of wind in a cane field. He was aware that this year *koi* symbolised something more than mere parental hope: they symbolised the trust of a nation regenerated through war. China had been defeated. The war was over.

Beyond this colourful spectacle of flying fish, he could see in the distance the great warship, Katsushima Kan, which had returned from China and was anchored in the bay. A grey steel fortress on a clear blue sea, she was by no means a colossus but she had fought valiantly. The previous day he and Setsuko had boarded the ship along with hundreds of other sightseers. It showed none of the scars of battle – all damage had been repaired – but here and there dark stains were still visible on the deck and people looked at them with tender reverence knowing that only a few months earlier these decks had been covered with brave men's blood.

While he stood there lost in thought, Setsuko came with his breakfast and placed it on the little table just inside the Western-style French doors.

"How's your headache," she asked.

"Better."

"Good. Are you free tonight?"

"Why?"

"Manyemon is going to see the regiments arriving home. You might find it interesting."

"Perhaps," he said as he came in.

Breakfast consisted of beef steak and a little ale. He had been thrilled to discover Bass ale in plentiful supply in Kobe; not that he drank much but a small amount in the morning set him up for the day. He only ate Japanese food at lunchtime, and it still amazed him how anyone could survive on such frugal fare. While he ate, she laid out his clothes.

"You seldom go to the foreign clubs anymore."

"Why would I? To hear people who have neither fine feelings, nor anything interesting to say, talking nonsense? Or to kill time playing tedious games of cards? Or to see pretty girls whom I can't marry?"

Playfully, she flashed him a censorious look.

"In truth, dear wife, the shrill voices of foreign women jar upon the comfort of existence."

It pleased her to hear this.

"You said the German club had a fine library."

"I've exhausted it."

"You receive so many invitations, surely—"

" I assure you, my presence is only required because I am thought to be famous. They want me to amuse them, to entertain them, to sing for my supper. You think these invitations are proof of kindly interest. Not a bit of it. It's precisely the same kind of curiosity that impels men to look at strange animals, a six-legged calf for instance."

"Oh, nonsense."

"It's true."

"But you used to enjoy the clubs."

"I suppose they were a novelty at first. But now…"

Despondent, he put down his knife and fork and sighed.

"So much of my life has been wasted, Setsu, sinfully wasted, and I shall have to work like a demon until I die to make up for it."

"There's no need—"

"I only write one article a day."

"No, I mean, no need to work at night. You made more than enough this year. And the publisher said your books will bring in twice as much next year."

"I have to write. And it's not just for the money. Perhaps I shall never do anything remarkable but every now and then I come upon a few truths and that that makes it worthwhile."

He wondered if she noticed that he was having regular fits of despondency and disgust with his work. The two books he had written about Japan, *Glimpses of Unfamiliar Japan* and *Kokoro*, seemed deeply flawed to him now and a third was well under way. One day he would think he had done well, the next that he was a failure. Any criticism, no matter how slight, cut deeply. He also felt sure that the moment he felt satisfied, progress would stop.

For Hearn writing was not something voluntary. It was not pleasurable. He was forced by a curious necessity. When idle, his mind tortured him with recollections of unpleasant things said or done in the past. To escape these thoughts, he would immerse himself in his work, write page after page and then throw them aside. The next day, he would rework and rewrite them until they began to arrange themselves into a coherent whole. The result would be an essay or a new chapter and he would have no idea how it had been written. Pain was of exceeding value to him; checks, failures and mockeries goaded him on. He wondered if anybody else wrote like this. It struck him as being a peculiarly morbid way of working.

Hearn now fell silent and Setsuko followed his gaze to a print on the wall of a girl with a sweet shyness in her downcast gaze. Cherry blossoms falling from the branch above seemed to pass through her and the folds of her *kimono* melted into the mist. She was a tree fairy: the spirit of the cherry tree. He had bought it some months earlier because there was something magical about it.

"I'd love to see her," he said.

"She only appears fleetingly at twilight, or sometimes in the early morning, gliding about her tree. Better not to look for her."

"Why not?"

"Whoever sees the tree fairy falls in love with her."

He laughed.

"Anyway, you're not likely to see her. She's very shy. When approached she vanishes back into the tree trunk."

He got up and moved closer to the print to study it.

"Has it faded?" he asked.

She joined him and peered at the print.

"I don't think so."

"It seems somehow... The colours seem less vivid."

"It looks the same to me."

On hearing Kazuo crying in a nearby room, she hurried to the door.

"What shall I tell Manyemon about tonight? Will you—?"

"Yes, I'll go with him."

"I'll come back to help you dress."

There was no point in arguing with her. She took endless pleasure in serving him and he had to admit that he enjoyed her attentions. The closeness of her, the relaxed quietness, the easy silence between them never failed to soothe him. Why would he ever emerge from this cosy cocoon, unless work necessitated it? He hated socialising. The effort of being agreeable, the fear of doing something gauche, and having to give, or receive, vacuous compliments strained his nerves.

A few moments after her departure he heard her gentle motherly words and the boy stopped crying. He leaned into the picture to examine it and became perplexed. The colours were definitely less vibrant. It occurred to him as he dressed for work that either Setsuko was mistaken or there was something wrong with his eye, his sole window to the world.

After work that evening he accompanied Manyemon to see the regiments return. Arches of greenery had been erected over the streets the troops were to pass through from Kobe Station to the great Minatogawa Shrine, which had been built by the Meiji government just twenty years earlier. Manyemon told him that the shrine housed the spirit of the respected *samurai* lord, Kusunoki Masashige.

"And who is this fellow?" he asked. "I've never heard of him."

"Oh, he is famous. All boys learn about him. He was a great military strategist who lived hundreds of years ago and he was known for his unselfish devotion and loyalty to the emperor," said Manyemon. "So it is a good place in which to honour our soldiers."

"I see."

Hearn and Manyemon waited outside the shrine where a huge triumphal arch had been constructed. On each façade, welcome greetings had been painted in gold, and on the top was a huge globe surmounted by a hawk with outspread wings. During feudal times, Hearn knew that falconry had been a great sport. He asked Manyemon what was the significance of the hawk on this occasion.

"Last year a hawk, a sign of victory, landed on the mast of one of our cruisers and allowed itself to be petted and fed. So this bird of good omen was presented to the emperor."

The battalions came along the street in regular columns. The crowd thickened about them but, strangely, there was no cheering, nobody spoke, the hush was broken only by the marching feet of the passing troops. Hearn could scarcely believe that these were the same men he had seen going to war just a year earlier. Though the faces were haggard and grim, the dark blue winter uniforms torn and frayed and the boots worn out, the strong swinging stride was the stride of hardened soldiers. Neither joy nor pride lit up their faces; they hardly glanced at the welcoming flags and decorations.

Ordinary people had subscribed thousands of *yen* for the honour of serving the soldiers their first meal upon their return. Hearn knew this. And he saw now that the tents in which the soldiers would eat had been festooned. Welcome, comfort and gifts of sweetmeats, cigarettes and little towels printed with poems in praise of valour awaited them. As he watched them enter the shrine under the triumphal arch, a great weight descended on him. Turning to Manyemon, he said,

"Last year I saw many regiments in their white summer uniforms on their way to war. They looked like students I used to teach: fresh-faced boys from school. I couldn't help feeling that it was cruel sending them into battle."

"There was no need to fear for them. They gave an excellent account of themselves," said Manyemon.

"But they were only boys. I was thinking of the fever and frost, the Manchurian winter. These were probably more to fear than the Chinese."

"The troops did their duty and are proud and happy to be home."

They did not look happy to Hearn. He knew they had probably seen and done unspeakable things.

"It must be sad for them. Tonight when they hear the bugle call, they'll think of their comrades who will never return."

"All our dead return, Master. They know the way from China and from Korea and from out of the bitter sea. They come back. All of them."

"I would like to believe that, Manyemon."

"It's true. And they will hear the bugles again on the day when the armies of the Sons of Heaven are summoned to war against Russia."

Manyemon was right. War would come again. No sooner had the terms of the peace treaty with China been announced when Russia interfered, backed up by France and Germany. The army wanted to fight, but the navy was weak and the government knew that any battle with these three powers would be costly. Japan capitulated, and returned the seized lands to China in exchange for a compensatory increase in the previously extracted war indemnity.

Japan seemed to have yielded, but Hearn suspected it was a ruse. It was *jujutsu* carried out at a national level. He had seen this ancient art of self-defence practiced in the training hall of the school in Kumamoto. Force was never opposed with force, rather the power of the attack was redirected back at the attacker and even skilled small men overcame strong muscular opponents with ease. It had baffled him. Ingenious technique enabled the weaker man to win. It was a way of thinking in curves and circles as opposed to the direct, confrontational way of Westerners.

And there was plenty of evidence to support his theory. He had read about the arrival of Commodore Perry's Black Ships thirty years earlier. They had come to force an end to Japan's two-hundred-year-old policy of isolation. Instead of resisting and fighting a battle they could not win, Japan invited the unwelcome foreigners in. This was not benign hospitality; the plan was to learn from them. And they did. In two short decades, Japan was transformed from a feudal society into an industrial one. Now, with Western technology and modern weaponry, they were strong. Hearn believed it a wise decision by the government not to respond to Russia's current provocation. War was averted, but the national pride had been wounded. He had no doubt that they would build up the navy and take on Russia when they were good and ready.

Thinking about *jujutsu*, it amused him to think about how he himself was out-manoeuvred at every turn by his wife. They rarely fought and it was not because she always agreed with him; it was because she never directly disagreed. She would listen and seem to agree, and then quietly manipulate matters until he came around to her way of thinking. This concept of conquering by yielding permeated every aspect of Japanese life, but there was one enemy who knew nothing of peace, or of treaties, that Japan had not banked on: cholera. It followed the returning armies home and invaded the victorious empire, killing about thirty thousand people that summer. The smoke and the smell from the funeral pyres blew down from the hills into his garden. The entire household prayed to be spared and Kazuo was not allowed out.

It was a horrible time – much worse than the outbreak he had experienced in Matsue. He saw cholera patients being taken from their houses, removed by force in spite of the tears and cries of the families. The Sanitary Law forbade the treatment of cholera in private houses. Disregarding the fines and penalties, people tried to hide their sickness because the designated cholera hospitals were overcrowded and badly managed. When the police discovered unreported cases, they came with litters and coolies. He watched from his balcony as his neighbour's wife followed the litters bearing her husband and son away until the police forced her to return to her desolate little shop. It closed and would probably never open again.

A few days after that episode, Oka-san came and sat with him while he was playing with Kazuo.

"His hair is getting lighter. And his eyes… What colour would you say they are?" she asked.

"Blue. Just like my father's."

"Not like yours."

"No, I have my mother's dark eyes."

"The first time I noticed that his eyes had changed colour, I was shocked. I had never seen such strange eyes. It was like looking at a ghost."

"I suppose the pale colour must seem strange."

"We're used to them now. They're pretty."

From the folds of her *kimono*, she produced a number of small wooden figures. Kazuo watched her line up little carved Chinese soldiers, bent over kowtowing to an illustrious Japanese general.

"I wonder what colour your next child's eyes will be?" she said.

"There'll be no more children, Oka-san."

"Really?"

The very thought of another child alarmed him. Much as he loved his family, whatever hope he had of leaving, even for a few months, would be further complicated if there was another mouth to feed. More children would also mean that he would be obliged to work in jobs he had no great interest in purely for the salary; a writer's income could not be depended on. There would be no more children. He had often cursed himself for having had even one and then immediately admonished himself as the boy was the greatest joy of his life.

"It would be nice for Kazuo to have a little brother to play with," she said.

"I don't think—"

"But if anything happens to Kazuo—"

"He'll be fine, Oka-san. We'll continue to keep him in until the epidemic ends."

"Yes, but if anything should happen... Setsu would be childless. She'd be very unhappy."

"We'll continue to be vigilant. Nothing will happen," he said in a voice harsher than intended.

Oka-san knew better than to pursue the matter.

"I pray every day for all of us and for an end to this sickness," she said, turning her attention to Kazuo.

As quickly as it had begun, the cholera epidemic ended. The ordinary life of the street went on by day and by night as if nothing had happened. Itinerant vendors, with their bamboo poles, baskets, buckets and boxes wandered the streets calling out their usual cries. Religious processions went by chanting fragments of sutras. The blind shampooer blew his melancholy whistle. The private watchman banged his heavy staff on the flagged pavements. The boy selling sweets still tapped his drum. Children played as usual; their friends may have vanished but they chased one another with screams and laughter. They caught dragonflies and tied them to long threads and sang jolly little songs about cutting off Chinese heads.

Chapter Sixteen

Kobe, Japan, 1895

One day in late October, Fujimoto-san, a government official, came to the house to discuss Hearn's application for citizenship, which they had lodged soon after Kazuo's birth. An officious little man with no sense of humour, his questions to Hearn were neither important nor interesting. It was obvious he only wanted to speak to Setsuko.

"How long have you known this man?" asked Fujimoto-san.

"Since 1891. It will be five years next Spring."

"And has he been kind to you?"

"Yes, he has."

"Do you think he will always be good to you, Koizumi-san?"

She looked at Hearn and smiled.

"Yes, I know he will."

"And do you think you will always be content to have such a husband?"

"What do you mean, Fujimoto-san?"

"Well, let's just say, he's... eh... He's not Japanese."

"I think my wife might have noticed that," said Hearn.

She glanced at him and there was a slight upturning at the sides of her lips; it was not a smile but a gentle reprimand. Hearn remained silent after that.

"Of course I'm sure I will be content with my husband."

"He's not your legal husband."

"I'm hoping, with your kind help, he soon will be."

"Is that your earnest opinion, Koizumi-san?"

"Yes."

Fujimoto-san sipped the tea Hanako had brought and, having formulated his next question, he patted his lips with the napkin and replaced the little cup soundlessly on the lacquered tray.

"Koizumi-san, did you make the application on your own free will, or under pressure from your relations?"

"There was no pressure made."

"Whose idea was it to apply for citizenship for Hearn-san?"

"It was his idea and I was very happy to make the application for him. All the family think it a good thing."

"Did Hearn-san force you to make it?"

Hearn raised his eyebrows in indignation but said nothing. He would like to have shown this wretch the door right there and then, but restraint was called for – he smouldered silently.

"No, he certainly did not," she replied. "He never forces me to do anything."

Fujimoto-san stared long and hard at Hearn, taking in the grey hair, the crow's feet, the sunken blind eye and the protruding myopic eye. Watkins had told him that the habit he had of turning away from people, always showing only his functioning eye, made him look furtive. He assumed the official was wondering what this nice young woman was doing with such an ugly old foreigner. Clearly unhappy with the situation, Fujimoto-san made notes, gathered up his papers and, after much obsequious bowing which government officials seemed to excel at, he went on his way. Hearn could not help thinking that, under the veneer of civility, Fujimoto-san was a brute who would have liked nothing more than to see Hearn off on the next departing ship.

A week after the interview Setsuko was summoned to Fujimoto-san's office and told to come alone. Hearn accompanied her to the building and waited outside in a rickshaw, smoking his pipe and contemplating the worst. What would they do if the application were refused? It pained him to think of Setsuko and Kazuo condemned to a life in legal limbo and possible poverty.

When she emerged an hour later, she explained that Fujimoto-san had been concerned that she really had been forced into making the application by her tyrannical foreign husband. He had asked her the same questions again, and she had given the same answers and assured him that it was her deepest wish that Hearn become a Japanese citizen.

They heard nothing for a month and were beginning to fear that the application would be refused. Night after night he lay awake worrying about what they would do if it was refused. On one such sleepless night, she reached over and stroked his hair.

"You need to sleep, Danna-sama."

"Perhaps I've not been over-prudent."

"In what way?"

"When I was offered that position in Tokyo…"

"At the university?"

"Yes. I didn't reply respectfully to the offer."

They had discussed this while still in Kumamoto and they went over it again in bed that night. She had been keen for him to take the prestigious position as it would have been good for his reputation. Though she did not say it directly, he knew that she wanted to live there. She thought of Tokyo just as a French woman thinks of Paris. She imagined the beautiful Tokyo of the old picture-books and bank bills. She knew the names of all the famous bridges, streets and temples, and these were associated in her mind with plays, famous stories and legends. He was not as informed as she was about the capital city. All he could think of was the atrocious weather there. Tokyo earthquakes were particularly fearsome, and he imagined the large foreign presence and Japanese officialdom there would be oppressive.

The curt note he had written in Kumamoto declining the offer of the university job had been a mistake. Government departments more than likely shared files on foreigners, and he suspected that he might be thought of as somebody who did not respect the great institutions of Japan. Luckily, he had left the school without a stain on his character thanks to Setsuko. At her suggestion, instead of storming out, he had cited ill health as the reason for his resignation and he had given them ample notice. Whatever the cause of the delay with the application, it was creating problems for them. Anticipating a speedy resolution, he had foolishly arranged for money orders for royalties from overseas publishers to be made out in his new name and they could not be cashed because Koizumi Yakumo did not yet legally exist.

Until the matter of his citizenship was settled, he could not relax and he blamed the onset of headaches on nervous anxiety. He continued to spend his days at the newspaper and then work at home at night. The headaches got worse and became extremely painful when he moved his eye. Setsuko was concerned. His right eye, his 'Cyclops Eye' as he called it, became badly inflamed and she begged him to see a doctor. The limited vision he had was deteriorating, and one day at work the pain on the right side of his head got so bad he fainted. The doctor diagnosed severe optic neuritis and told him that if he did not rest, he might go blind.

Kobe, January, 1896

Dear Old Dad,

How nice to hear from you. I find it difficult to write letters. I have very few correspondents. True men are few, and the autograph hunters, the scheming class of small publishers and people who want gratis information about commercial matters in Japan are not considered by me as correspondents. They never get answers. I have two or three dear friends in this world, you being the oldest and the dearest. To you, I do my best to reply.

I've had some trouble. The last few months were spent in a darkened room with compresses over my precious eye. Given the choice between blindness or rest I naturally chose the latter. I have never put down my pen for such an extended period; it was torture to be alone with my demons in the dark and thoughts of the rascal I was came back to me. How did you ever put up with me? When I think of all the mean, absurd things I did to annoy you and to scandalise you, I can't for the life of me understand how you did not want to kill me. I know your wife did. I have lost more than a few friends because their wives hated me. But what an idiot I was, a detestable young man. I like to think I have changed, but sometimes ghostly reminders of my despicable old self surface, and I am filled with self-loathing and torturous doubt about my abilities. I wish I were near you. You always encouraged me. I wish I could make up for all the vexation I caused you.

I'm over the worst of the neuritis. I can see again, the headaches have stopped and I am able to write and read for a short time every day. There remains a black spot at the center of my vision. My doctor said it will go away but warned me that I cannot go back to working both day and night. The strain on my eye would be too great so I have had to quit the newspaper. The upside to this awful situation is that I can now devote all my time to writing.

You know how hopeless I am with money, but Setsuko has managed to save enough so I need not worry about earning for at least a year. You always said I would amount to something while others, less kind, insisted that I would end my days in jail or at the end of a rope. Hopefully your prediction will come true. My books are selling; I am finally getting noticed in England and America – for the right reasons.

The only joy during that dismal confinement was the approval of my application for citizenship. It came in December and I was adopted into the Koizumi family. I am now officially a Japanese citizen. This settles all legal questions as to property as well as marriage under Japanese law. It is a great relief to know that if anything happens to me, Setsuko and Kazuo will be secure.

I want to build my sweet wife a house, either here or in nearby Kyoto. But I hesitate. I know I must create a base here in Japan but where to do it? My heart is back in Matsue but the winters there prohibit me from returning. Life here in Kobe is tainted by Western influence. Carpets, pianos, windows, curtains, brass bands and churches, how I hate them. And white shirts and all Western clothes. Would I had been born a savage. The curse of civilised cities is upon me and I can't get away from them. You like all these things, I know. I'm not expecting any sympathy but I thought you might like to know about the effect on me of a half-return to Western life. I never knew how much I could hate all that we call civilisation. I never could have conceived just how ugly it is without having had a long sojourn in Old Japan – by that I mean Matsue, where the best of Old Japan can still be seen.

I still dream of Saint Pierre. You never did come to visit me in my delightfully ramshackled little house. Perhaps someday we might yet manage to meet there, or somewhere where we could take things easy, rest by running streams, feel mountain winds blow, hear birds and the whisper of leaves, and bask under the stars, away from horrible cities, abominable noises, sickness and humdrum machines. If we both could strike our tents, move a little nearer to nature, I could tell you strange stories and theories gathered during my unexpectedly long sojourn here in the Orient.

Ever with affectionate regard to you,
Koizumi Yakumo.

P.S. Did I mention that in Japan the surname comes first? Here I am now called Koizumi-san by the general rabble but you, dear friend, can call me Yakumo, or whatever name you choose.

During the miserable days of confinement there had been nothing to do but reflect on his long life. It seemed like a hundred years since he left Ireland. He had been eighteen when he last saw Aunt Sarah. Twenty-eight years had passed since then. He tried to picture her wrinkled old face, but all he could remember clearly was the voluminous black dress, the crucifix dangling, the spotless white collar around her neck and the little white bonnet she wore over her steel grey hair. She was austere but she had been kind, and he regretted that he had never shown her any appreciation. It was unlikely that he would ever return to Ireland; he would never be able to pay his respects at her grave in that lovely little seaside town of Tramore. One night, he wrote her name on a card and lay it beside the drawing of his mother that James had sent him just before he left for Japan. He placed flowers before this makeshift altar, burned incense and whispered to their spirits; he liked to think that they were out there somewhere listening.

Thinking about the past sometimes distressed him so much he felt unwell; it was a deep, probing, cruel nausea that brought back the sense of isolation and fear that had prevailed during his early childhood. He could still see himself, face pressed to the windowpane, watching his mother's carriage disappearing into the morning mist; the clip-clop of horse hooves on hard ground always brought this image to mind.

Another memory that haunted him was of having his face pushed against a metal bird cage. He must have been about three at the time, and his tormentor, a strong little girl who was a year or two older than him, held him there while the parrot squawked and shrieked and yanked at his long dark hair. Where it happened, he could not remember – probably it was in a neighbouring house in Dublin – but the more he screamed and the louder it squawked, the more she laughed. On hearing the commotion, the girl's mother arrived and she also laughed at the sight of the hysterical little boy.

There were fleeting images of happy times too, mostly by the sea, but they were overshadowed by dominant memories of being alone and afraid in cold, cavernous old houses and of being mocked and treated with suspicion. There had been a brief time in his early teens, away at boarding school in England, that he had been happy but it did not last long. When he lost his eye, he lost all confidence and, from that time on, he somehow felt persecuted.

Aunt Sarah's bankruptcy added to his misery; as her only heir, it catapulted him from man of means to pauper. Whipped out of his expensive school, he was sent to live with the former maid, Catherine, now married to an English navvy and living in a clean but tiny house in the shabby East End of London. Wallowing in self-pity, he would disappear for days on end; drinking, whoring, begging, stealing, sleeping on the streets and in workhouses. Ever the loyal servant, Catherine tried to help. He had been sent to her because Aunt Sarah was ill – just how ill she was Hearn had no idea – and was unable to deal with a sullen, spoilt teenager. Catherine could not deal with him either. He abused her hospitality, seduced one of her nieces and then left in haste before her husband could boot him out the door.

Molyneux made sure the unruly nineteen-year-old Hearn did not trouble Aunt Sarah by paying for his ticket to America. The first few months in New York were spent in an alcoholic haze, and he quickly squandered the small amount of money Molyneux had given him. His clothes became worn and filthy. His hair grew long and unkempt. He probably stank. In an attempt to hide his deformity, he took to wearing a ridiculous wide-brimmed hat. Within months of arriving, the educated young man had turned into a drunken beggar, and by the time he arrived in Cincinnati to seek the promised help from Molyneux's sister, she wanted nothing to do with him.

And then he met Henry Watkins, who saw him for the lost boy he was and became the father he had never had. In return for his kindness, Hearn tormented the old man. Once, he even tried to poison his dog for some perceived slight. It still shamed him to remember it.

Sitting in the darkened room, with nothing to do but think, he remembered over and over again how he had treated people shoddily, used them for his own gain and then discarded them. Always on the defensive, he had insulted and hurt friends who disagreed with him, and blatantly flaunted his disregard for their opinions, sensibilities and morality. Looking back, he liked to think that he was no longer that person. With age, he hoped he had gained a modicum of wisdom, perhaps some humility and compassion. Was this not a natural development that came with maturity? Or had Japan civilised him?

Having resigned from the newspaper, being at home day and night made him aware of how hard Setsuko worked – this was something he had never thought about before. The entire household fussed over Kazuo. There was no reprimanding him, no scolding the little emperor. The boy's needs and wants ruled the house and Setsuko got no rest, and no sleep except when Kazuo allowed it, and yet it was a joy for her. She had already taught the two-year-old how to be polite, how to ask for things while making the correct hand gestures, how to smile at the appropriate time and how to prostrate himself before his father first thing in the morning and last thing at night. It was all done with love and patience.

At home he could be himself. Everywhere else he was constantly on guard against the world and though he had an easy relationship with members of the household, Setsuko was the only person to whom he bared his soul and he did so only with the certainty that she would not give him away.

Apart from Setsuko, there was no one he could confide in except Watkins and he was thousands of miles away. Nishida-san, of course, was a good friend but unfortunately he was in Matsue. He was fond of Chamberlain but their exchanges were mostly academic, and most of his other relationships were based on self-interest and were dependent merely on power or position for their degree of intensity. Any pleasure that might result from them was false. Depressingly, he saw society as a tedious masked ball.

Setsuko had been brought up, chiefly at home, in the old-fashioned way and Hearn tried to picture her domestic education: an education that cultivated simplicity of heart, grace, manners, obedience and love of duty. Though poor, she was refined and all refined girls were taught never to show jealousy, grief, or anger even under compelling circumstances. Having been trained to depend on the mercy of her husband, the expectation, the hope, would have been that she would marry a husband with a similar background, delicate in discernment, able to divine her feelings and never to wound them. But she married Hearn and he did not fall into this category. He asked himself the question, how did she tolerate him? Did she have unspoken desires, needs, or dissatisfactions that she felt unable to articulate and that he failed to observe?

The unusually forthright exchange he had had with Oka-san regarding the matter of more children came to mind. He reasoned that if Setsuko wanted more children and felt she could not make such a demand to him, it was more than likely she would have confided in her mother. Oka-san probably felt justified in interfering as Hearn, being a foreigner, was probably oblivious to Setsuko's subtle hints.

Through the translucent paper in the *shoji* screen he could see her soft shadow in the next room, kneeling in front of the alcove, silently arranging flowers. He was living with a creature of grace and loveliness, and he had never before felt so at peace with the world. How could he show his gratitude? She managed the household with wonderful economy but seldom asked for anything for herself. Despite her protests, he began to buy her fine silk *kimono*, not just one, sometimes five at a time. It pleased him to see her daintily dressed, like a beautiful butterfly robed in the folds of its colourful wings.

It troubled him that Setsuko seldom went out. Her only relatives lived far away in Matsue, so she had few visits to make. She seemed to like being at home, minding Kazuo, arranging flowers for the alcoves or for the gods, decorating the rooms and feeding the tame goldfish in the garden pond; they would lift up their heads when they saw her coming. In an attempt to show his love and gratitude, he began to take her to the theatre, to side shows and other places of amusement. One night they went to see a travelling show which boasted exotic exhibits: the Skeleton of the Devil, the Claws of a Goblin and a Giant Rat as large as a sheep. The skeleton turned out to belong to an orangutan with horns ingeniously attached to the skull. The Goblin's Claws were shark's teeth. And the rat was in fact a tame kangaroo, but having never seen or heard of one before, the spectators were astonished. What he could not understand and what astonished him most was the sight of a young woman who stretched her neck to a length of about two feet, making ghastly faces during this impossible performance.

"She has *nuke kubi*," said Setsuko. "She has a head that detaches from her body and prowls about by itself at night."

"I have to see this," he said.

They waited but the head did not detach. On the way home, she told him the story of a young man who woke one night and saw his wife's head rise from the pillow. Her neck grew longer and longer like a great white serpent, while the rest of her body remained motionless. The man watched as the head, supported by an ever-lengthening neck, entered the next room and drank all the oil in the lamps. Hearn was not surprised to hear that the young man had fled in fear. He could not wait to get home to write about it.

Another time, when the weather was warmer, they visited Sakai, a town near the mouth of the Yamato River. An important seaport since medieval times, it was now famous for forging the finest *samurai* swords. Hearn was there to buy a sword, but also for the swimming. His doctor had recommended that he take more exercise. The sea air and swimming would strengthen his lungs. He swam every morning and evening, and in the afternoons they visited keyhole-shaped burial mounds, which dated back to the fifth century. Setsuko told him that the largest mound was believed to be the grave of Emperor Nintoku.

"It's the largest grave in the world," she said.

"What's in it?" he asked.

"Who knows? The emperor's sword and armour, I suppose. Some

treasure maybe. Nobody has entered since it was built fifteen hundred years ago. We will never know."

Encircled by three moats, it took them an hour to walk around the perimeter.

That night as they prepared for bed, she laid her hand on his naked chest.

"Swimming has brought out all your muscles."

"In so short a time? Is it noticeable?

"Yes. You must go to the sea whenever you feel poorly. It's good for you. You could bring Kazuo here."

"It's too dangerous for him. The currents change three times every day. Some of them are very strong. You have to be careful."

"I hope you are."

"I am. I throw straws in the water to see the way of the current near shore. I don't go out too far anymore. There are cross-currents going the other way. It's tricky."

Setsuko extinguished the light and lay down. The sword he had bought earlier in the week lay in its scabbard by the alcove, and he could not resist another look at it before bed. He pulled it from its sheath; the blade glinted in the dimly lit room. It was a magnificent old weapon and he wondered how many poor souls it had dispatched. It would not be the worst way to die, he thought. Sakai blades were said to be the sharpest in the world and, yielded by a skilled hand, there would be no fumbling or hacking, it would be all over in a split second.

One of the graves they had visited that afternoon contained the remains of eleven *samurai* who were ordered to commit *hara kiri*, for killing some foreigners. Smiling to himself, he wished they could come back again to kill a few more, perhaps clear the country of the plague of Westerners who were destroying it. From his travels around the country, it was evident to him that contact with Westerners, particularly in the port cities, was causing the poorer classes of the Japanese to lose their natural politeness, their native morals and even their capacity for simple happiness.

Aware that Setsuko was watching him, he replaced the sword in its sheath. As he lay down, he caught a glimpse of her face before she turned away from him. Unusually quiet all night, she seemed strangely sad and, by the sound of her breathing, he could tell that she was not about to drift away into a peaceful sleep.

"What's wrong, Setsu."

"Just… The graveyard made me think of…"

She paused and took a deep calming breath.

"Of…?"

"Of Oji-san," she said.

"He was a fine man. I often think of him, especially when the plum tree blossoms."

Oji-san had given them the little plum tree when they married. It was a simple present yet worthy of a prince. He had tended it lovingly for years and when he presented it, every branch and spray was a snowy dazzle of blossoms.

"Oji-san once had to do something…" said Setsuko. "I've never spoken of it."

"I'm listening if you'd like to—"

"Promise me you will never write about it."

"I promise."

She turned to face him and, though the room was dark he could see her features in the soft half-light of the moon. She told him how Oji-san's grandfather had been buried with his sword. It had been a gift from his feudal lord and the mountings on the weapon were made of gold. At a time of great poverty, when the family were on the brink of starvation, Oji-san had the grave opened. He replaced the gold hilt of the sword with a common one, and he removed the precious ornaments from the lacquered sheath.

"Why didn't he just take the sword?" he asked.

"He couldn't take it. His grandfather might need it."

"But—"

"Oji-san said he saw his grandfather's face as he sat erect in the great red clay urn. He was a *samurai* of high rank, you see, so he had been buried according to the ancient rites sitting upright in an urn."

"Not cremated?"

"No. Oji-san said his features were still recognisable after all those years, and that he seemed to nod a grim assent to what had been done when Oji-san gave him back his sword."

She was now weeping quietly. He wiped her tears away.

"He did what was necessary to save the family. Don't feel ashamed, Setsu."

"Oh, I don't feel ashamed. I feel only love and gratitude to my great-great-grandfather. And I'm sure it made the other ancestors happy that he was able to help us."

He was baffled. She truly believed that her deceased great-great-grandfather still needed his sword and that the dead had feelings. Drawing her close, he felt her tremble as she struggled to control the emotion the memory had evoked. It was clear that the family circumstances had been desperate through no fault of their own. The centuries-old *samurai* way of life had been wiped out by the stroke of an official pen. He had endured hard times himself but his downfall had been, for the most part, of his own making. She had been the hapless victim of a changing world. Wrapping his arms around her, he determined, in as much as he could, to make up for ancient miseries, to give her whatever her heart desired.

Their love making that night was extraordinarily gentle and intense. Long after she had fallen asleep, he lay awake thinking about how her love for her ancestors was a real and powerful phenomenon. The idea of it was utterly alien to his way of thinking. He did not believe that it was possible for the living to have an active relationship with the dead. In the West, if you were profoundly religious, you thought of the dead as removed from the living; they were either in limbo, in heaven or in hell. If you happened to be irreligious, then you did not believe in ghosts or spirits; the dead were simply gone.

He lay there wondering if there were to arise within him the absolute certainty that his ancestors were with him – seeing his every act, knowing his every thought, hearing every word he uttered, able to feel sympathy for him or anger with him, able to help him and love him, and that they also needed his love – if he could believe this, he was quite certain that his concept of life and duty would be vastly changed.

Setsuko snored sweetly. He got up, lit his pipe and stood smoking, looking out over the water. The town was silent, the moon cast a pale band of golden light across the rippling sea, a pathway to the heavens, and it occurred to him that this feeling of grateful, reverential love for the ancestors was probably the most profound and powerful emotion in Japan. It directed national life and shaped the national character. Filial piety depended on it. Family love was rooted in it. Loyalty was based upon it. And as he drew on his pipe, he realised that a sense of duty extended not only to parents and blood relatives but to grandparents and great-grandparents and all the dead gone before them. And in time of national peril, this love extended to the whole nation as if they were one great family. It was a feeling much deeper than patriotism as he understood it, and it made Japan's armies formidable.

This combined sense of love, loyalty and gratitude extended infinitely into the past and was not less real, though perhaps slightly more vague, than the feelings extended to living relatives. He watched the sea and, lulled by its perpetual motion, it came to him that the ancestors never became a mere memory. Here, the dead were present and existed side by side with the living.

~

Back in Kobe, Setsuko was always reluctant to part from Kazuo, but they had another maid now, and Oka-san encouraged her to accompany her husband on his excursions; the boy would be safe at home. It was the first time since their marriage that he had not been either sick or working too hard, and during this time he came to understand Setsuko more and more.

On summer nights they went out together to see the shimmering fireflies, and in autumn they spent a week wandering around Kyoto marveling at the astonishing crimson foliage of the maple trees. Situated in a valley surrounded by wooded mountains, the city had been the capital until thirty years earlier and there were endless gardens, temples, shrines and palaces to visit. In Nijo Castle, they delighted in the nightingale floor which chirped as they walked on it. Three rivers ran through the city and everywhere the play of water leaping cold and clear from streams and waterways could be heard.

It was a magical week. Ablaze in autumnal colour, Kyoto was like a dream of five hundred years ago. And always floating on the air was the plaintive sound of unseen flutes blowing softly, an ancient tone of peace and sadness blending just as cold light turns to blue over a dying sun.

Nine months after the trip to Sakai their second son, Iwao, was born.

Chapter Seventeen

Tokyo, Japan, 1897

*D*ear Old Dad,
    Awful weather. In Kobe, just before we left, the river – usually a dry sand bed – burst its banks after rain, swept away whole streets, wrecked hundreds of houses and drowned many people. Then there was a tidal wave in the north; it was two hundred miles long and destroyed almost thirty thousand lives. A considerable part of East Central Japan is still under water at this moment, river water. Lake Biwa rose and drowned the city of Otsu. The deforestation of the country is probably the cause of these terrible visitations. I blame this hideous industrial age, the reckless consumption of profiteers and the wastefulness of the rich who casually devour what nature has taken centuries to create. The insatiable cannibals of civilisation are more cruel than those of savagery, and they require much more flesh.

    You can see by my address that we have moved. I am currently employed as Professor of English Literature at Tokyo Imperial University. You were right; it seems I have finally amounted to something. I partly owe this prestigious position to Professor Chamberlain's kind recommendation and partly to my books. The Japanese seldom notice literary work by foreigners, unless they are giants, but for some curious reason, they pay considerable attention to mine! Perhaps it involves a little narcissism on their part as my recent work is all about them and is generally flattering.

I only arrived here a few weeks ago, so at present I can give you no valid impressions. Everything is a blur, but so far the position does not seem disagreeable, rather the reverse. In fact I am afraid to express my satisfaction. Former pupils from Matsue and Kumamoto gather round, welcoming me. The other professors move in separate and never-colliding orbits. I can teach for years, if I please, without ever seeing any of my colleagues.

Setsuko found a wonderful old house, an hour by rickshaw from the university so the chances of anyone casually dropping in are unlikely. It's a yashiki, an old-fashioned house, full of surprises of colour, beauty, quaintness and peace. Here, I can happily hide away from the world. I wasn't sure about the location until I heard the boom of a big bell coming from a nearby temple. I went to see the bell. It's about nine feet high and five feet in diameter. The shape is not like our bells which broaden towards the opening; the diameter is the same all along its magnificent ornate length. It hangs from the roof in a lofty open shed and is rung by means of a heavy swinging beam, like a battering ram. Strike it and an enormous, extraordinary and beautiful sound rolls out over the city, and the tone continues to billow and echo for at least ten minutes. I love these old bells. They awaken strange ancient memories in me. When I die I want to be buried within hearing of a great bell.

The other night I went to a little-known part of Tokyo, to a street ablaze with lanterns about thirty feet high. I bought a number of cages full of night-singing insects and fireflies and I am now trying to make a study of them. The music made by these creatures is extraordinary. These little orchestras give to city dwellers the delight of being in the country. This is a refinement of sensation, is it not? Only poetic people could create the illusion of nature where there is only dust and mud.

Speaking of mud… No, I must not say too much about the mud, the bad roads, the horrible confusion caused by the laying-down of new water pipes. The weather is vile and Tokyo is hideous. But Setsuko is as happy as a bird making its nest. She is fixing up her new home and is too busy with our two sons to notice what an ugly place it is. On the other hand, here we find everything very cheap, except rent. But even that is much lower than in Kobe, very much lower. I pay only $25 a month for a very big house. There's lots of room for you to come and visit me. Please come. I will look after you very well and take you to see things that would delight and amaze you.

Affectionate regards,
Yakumo

For months following his arrival in Tokyo, he walked the city from one end to the other, hoping to find evidence of elegant old Japan. What he found was, for the most part, detestable. The quarter of the foreign embassies looked like a well-painted American suburb. Walking on, he found square miles of indescribable squalor, followed by sprawling military parade grounds trampled into a wasteland of dust and bounded by unsightly barracks. His heart lifted somewhat when he came to a great park, full of strange beauty; the shadows all black as ink. He paced square miles of streets of flimsy shops which, he was told, burnt down once a year. Then more squalor, then rice fields and bamboo groves and then more streets.

Tokyo was a city of undulations. Immense silences, green and romantic, alternated with chaotic areas crammed with factories and railroad stations. Miles and miles of water pipes interrupted traffic on the principal streets. Efforts to lay the pipes underground had been slowed by endless official interference. Gigantic reservoirs were ready but there was no water in them. Streets melted under rain, water pipes sank, the freshly dug holes filled with water, drowned drunken men and swallowed-up playful children. To think of writing in the dead waste and muddle of this mess was difficult for him. He felt like a caged insect himself but he was unable to sing. Anything he wrote soon found its way into the wastepaper basket.

Work at the university was enjoyable however, and the household was content. His income was secure. The publication and popularity of his two books on Japan had rekindled interest in his earlier work; *A Year in the West Indies, Youma, Chita, Some Chinese Ghosts*, even the cookbook he had written in New Orleans, were all selling. Soon, they would buy a house, or build a new one in the old style, and when the family was financially secure, he would indulge himself with a little foreign travel, just a few months. Every now and then he felt a longing, like a bird impatient for the migrating season. He remembered how, as a young man, he thought he would drift forever until he got old, stooped and grey, and died. That was all he had wanted: just to go wherever he pleased, to keep to himself and to never bother anybody. In idle moments, he daydreamed about seeking a passage on some tropical vessel and sailing hither and thither like a ghost on the wandering wind.

The first summer in Tokyo was made bearable by taking lots of trips to nearby places of interest. He was always glad to escape the city, even on short trips by rickshaw out into the infinite network of rice fields where, above all the little ditches and canals, there was a silent flickering of tiny lights, a zigzagging, soundless flashing of emerald, rose and azure steel: the flight of dragonflies. These magnificent insects thrived in abundant wetlands and laid their eggs on the surface of the water. The larvae that emerged from the eggs were dull and grey but when they shed their outer layers, the adults emerged, transformed into vibrant, swift creatures of indescribable colour and beauty.

"Aren't they wonderful," said Setsuko as they walked along a canal bank one sunny summer day. "We love our dragonflies."

"I've noticed. There seem to be almost as many poems about them as there are dragonflies."

"Japan used to be known as the Island of Dragonflies. Did you know that?"

"No, I didn't."

"They mean many things to us. They're a symbol of change and of mental and emotional maturity. They're also a symbol of death."

"Why is that?"

"We think of a person's soul as being like a dragonfly because it breaks away from its earthbound form, spreads its wings and is free. Some people say that a dragonfly is the soul of a departed ancestor who comes back to visit a loved one."

An image flashed before him of Oji-san greeting the black dragonfly that hovered around him a few days before he died. He felt a sudden rush of tenderness towards the old man, who had remained cheerful and serene until the end.

"That's lovely, Setsu. I'll write that down as soon as I get home."

"I will expect a share in the royalties."

"You can have it all."

His instinct at that moment was to reach out and hold her hand, but he knew that it would make her uncomfortable though there was no one in sight. He remained very still, gazing out over the rice fields. She moved past him and as she did, she laid a gentle hand on his arm; it was the lightest of touches but it thrilled him.

Kazuo, who was now four years old, had no respect for dragonflies, but they fascinated him; he ran about chasing them and when he caught one he pulled off its wings.

"Oh, the poor thing," said Setsuko. "Now he can't fly."

The child was puzzled.

"In your next life, you might come back as a dragonfly and you'll need your wings."

The boy tried to stick the wings back on the dead insect and when it failed to revive, he grew sad.

"I'm sorry," he said.

The boy was upset and Hearn kneeled down to console him.

"When I was a boy, we believed that little people flew about the countryside using dragonflies as horses," he said.

"They must have been very small people," said Setsuko.

"Yes, they were tiny. We called them fairies. They rode on the backs of dragonflies, and they got up to all kinds of mischief."

He told Kazuo the story about the fairy who came down the chimney and fell into the pot of boiling water. Kazuo forgot his sadness and listened with wide-eyed delight. The story had terrified Hearn as a child. He was glad that Kazuo was made of sterner stuff, the result, he assumed, of having a warm and loving environment in which to grow.

Late in September on one of their explorative journeys out of Tokyo, they came upon the fishing village of Yaizu. Curving along a little bay, Yaizu was sheltered from heavy seas by an extraordinary rampart built in the form of terraced steps. On each level, the loose stones of which it was constructed were kept in position by a sort of basket work, woven between stakes. Yaizu supplied *katsuo*, bonito, to the entire country. It was a huge part of the Japanese diet, and they were so plentiful in the local waters it was said that even the poor discarded the fish heads.

The day was overcast. Setsuko sat on a wall and watched while he climbed the high ramparts. Looking over the town, a broad space of grey tiled roofs and weather-worn grey timbers under a low sodden sky, he found himself suddenly hurled back in time to the soft grey landscape of his Irish childhood. More evocative even than the scene were the salty wafts of bracken and kelp, sea air and fish that filled his nostrils.

Between the ramparts and the sea there was no sand, only a grey slope of stones and boulders that rolled with the surf. He imagined it would be difficult to get past the breakers on a rough day. Once when he was very young, in Greystones – a small seaside resort named for its long pebbled beach – while paddling he was struck by an unexpected wave. A spray of stones hit him like buckshot, took the legs from under him and left him stunned, struggling to right himself on the shifting seabed. He had not forgotten it. Stronger now and an accomplished swimmer, he could not wait to swim here.

Joining Setsuko, they strolled for a while and then sat on the harbour wall looking out over the water. There was a grand view of jagged mountain peaks, and beyond them, the haunting spectre of Mount Fuji, its tip obscured in the clouds, towered over everything. The bay was filled with strange-looking fishing boats, all heading for shore and Hearn guessed that they could carry a crew of forty or fifty men. He could tell by the sturdy look of them that they could ride a rough sea.

"They seem to be in a hurry," said Setsuko.

"They are. There's a storm on the way."

There was great activity in the harbour that afternoon. It seemed as if the entire town had gathered to help get the boats out of the water. Hearn was right, a typhoon was coming. Men, women and children of all ages helped create a kind of slipway by laying a long line of wooden frames on the ground. Thick ropes were attached to the flat-bottomed boats and Hearn joined in to help as they hauled the boats onto dry land. In time to a rhythmic chant, they pulled the heavy boats away from the harbour into the shelter of adjacent streets.

Setsuko was not as enamoured of Yaizu as he was. She was keen to get home to Kazuo and Iwao, but he insisted they stay the night. He wanted to watch the storm. The only inn was full, but they were directed to accommodation in rooms above a fishmonger's shop at the harbour. The fishmonger, Yamaguchi-san, a thin weathered man with an honest, friendly face, showed them three adjoining rooms overlooking the sea. Hearn took an immediate liking to him and paid twice the price he asked for the accommodation. Setsuko looked around the bare rooms with dismay. There was nothing pretty about them, the *tatami* mats were dirty, there was no hanging scroll in the alcove, and only a common little table shoved into a corner. As soon as Yamaguchi-san left, she inspected the bedding.

"I can't stay here," she said.

"It's too late to go home. And look," he said, directing her attention to the view.

She did not turn to admire it.

"There are fleas in the *futon*," she said, stepping back.

"But the swimming will be glorious when the storm abates. Who cares about a few fleas."

"I do, I—"

"Setsu, a little patience—"

"I don't want to stay here. And that smell... What on earth are they cooking downstairs?"

He sniffed the air. It was not pleasant; a tired odour of fish, radish and something he could not name permeated the room. He had smelled worse. All he had to do was open the window and gaze out to sea, and the smell and the fleas were forgotten. But just then, a plump flea landed on her hand. She brushed it off with a cry of disgust.

"Oh, damn it. Why should a strong woman like you tremble before a little flea? We're not due back for another two days. I'd like to stay."

"Well, you can stay here alone."

"Alright, I will."

They walked in silence to the train station, but she missed the last train back and refused to speak to him for the rest of the night.

Yamaguchi-san's wife served them a passable meal of rice, fish and pickles which they ate in silence. Drinking *sake* and smoking his pipe, he sat at the open window and stared at the waves crashing against the ramparts. The little house trembled. He never watched the ocean roll or heard its thunder without feeling solemn; it made him forget everything else. Beyond the pounding of the nearer waves, he could hear the deep base sound of surf further out to sea, a ceaseless muttering that brought to mind the trampling of cavalry, soldiers marching, armies on the move. At some point he joined Setsuko and fell into a deep sleep. She lay awake beside him scratching until dawn, and then she crept away to catch the first train home.

When he woke, the sea was calm. Setsuko had left him a short note saying that he should come home when he tired of his blood-sucking friends. For the next two days he did nothing but swim and wander around the town in the simple blue and white *yukata* and straw sandals given to him by Yamaguchi-san. At the harbour, he was delighted to discover that both morning and evening, fishermen bowed towards Mount Fuji, clapped their hands and prayed to the great mountain for protection. They were happy to show the curious foreigner their catches: crabs with legs of astonishing length, balloon fish that blew themselves up in the most absurd manner and various other creatures with such extraordinary shapes that he could scarcely believe them real without touching them.

The big boats with holy texts on their prows were not the strangest objects on the beach. Even more remarkable were the bait baskets made of split bamboo. They were six feet high and eighteen feet round with one small hole in the dome-shaped top. He saw them from a distance arranged along the sea wall to dry and he mistook them for huts, not unlike the stone beehive huts he had seen in County Kerry. There were also great wooden anchors shaped like ploughshares and shod with metal; iron anchors with four flukes; giant wooden mallets used for driving stakes; and various other implements still more unfamiliar of which he could not even imagine the purpose. The strangeness of everything gave him a weird remote sensation. It was as if he was far away in time.

As in Matsue, the life of Yaizu had not changed for centuries. Here too, the people were frank and kind, honest to a fault, innocent of the world, and loyal to the ancient traditions and to the ancient gods. Only a few hours by train from Tokyo, he knew that he had found a haven, a place where he could swim and grow strong and relax and forget about work and officialdom and the oppression of city life.

When he arrived home Setsuko greeted him at the front door with a large box of flea powder and led him straight to the bath.

"May I have your clothes please?" she said.

"Certainly, madam."

He stripped off, and when she saw that he was covered from head to toe in flea bites, she laughed.

"A small price to pay," he said in the most indignant voice he could muster. "I've rented the rooms for the next few weekends, and for a month next summer."

"Well, unless you can find somewhere better to stay, you will be going alone."

She held his clothes at arm's length and took them away for cleaning, leaving him to soak his chewed up flesh in the hot tub.

CHAPTER EIGHTEEN

Tokyo, Japan, 1902

Life had settled. Hearn was content, more than content, he was happy and he was writing again. Since he discovered Yaizu, a calmness had washed over him and whenever he had a few free days he went there. Sometimes he went just for a single night, to sit and dream and gaze out over the ocean. The rooms above the fishmonger's shop had become a home from home, and the Yamaguchis a second family. Their children played with his children. Setsuko seldom came but when she did, she came in a whirlwind of flea powder. If she was not there, Yamaguchi-san's wife cleaned and cooked for him. To encourage her to join him, he bought a new set of *futon* to replace the old ones and that somewhat alleviated the flea problem; but the smell of fish and other mysterious concoctions, which she found objectionable, still floated up from the shop.

Three years earlier, another son, Kiyoshi, had been born. One warm April evening shortly after his birth, Hearn was sitting on the moon-viewing platform, enjoying the delicate sight of the crescent moon beyond the blossoming cherry tree, when Oka-san appeared in the garden with Kiyoshi in her arms. She was humming a lullaby to the baby and Hearn moved over to make room for her but she did not sit down.

"No, no, we just came out to smell the blossoms," she said.

She reached up, plucked a cherry blossom from a low hanging branch and held it close to the baby's nose. As she strolled around the garden, she whispered in Kiyoshi's ear.

"*Mitsugo no tamashi hyaku made.*"

It was not quite a whisper, Hearn could hear her repeating the proverb which translated as: the soul, or character, of a three-year-old child lasts a hundred years. In other words, a child's character was formed in the first three years of life. By now, he was used to Oka-san's subtle interference. Clearly, she had overheard conversations between himself and Setsuko about the possibility of his taking a few months abroad. She need not have said anything. He had already decided to wait before taking the much longed-for trip back to Saint Pierre.

~

Those years had passed quickly. Kiyoshi was now three, and it was time for him to go. At last, they had found a suitable site and overseeing the building of the new house would keep Setsuko occupied while he travelled. He would sail from Japan to San Francisco, and then take a train to Cincinnati to see Watkins. Perhaps, if the old man were well enough, he would come with him to Saint Pierre. If not, he would travel on alone, by train to Memphis and then sail down the Mississippi to New Orleans, as he had done all those years ago when he was a destitute young man fleeing scandal. He was no longer angry with the world. Now, sober and reflective, he was looking forward to seeing his old world with new eyes.

From New Orleans he would take one of those light, narrow steamers, built especially for bayou travel, and sail from island to island to Martinique. He could hardly have picked a more difficult place to get to from Japan, but he had lots of time. After a few idle months in Saint Pierre, he planned to sail across the Atlantic Ocean and on to Greece where he would try to find his mother's grave. Having fulfilled his duty, he would then travel through the Suez Canal and back to Japan.

After six years of service, professors at the Imperial University were entitled to nine months' paid vacation so he could well afford this indulgence. But most importantly, Setsuko understood how important it was for him to make this trip; she knew that he would not be at peace until he had done it.

Giving the university plenty of notice, he informed them of his plans well in advance. He was due to sail in early July and to return the following March. Now, there were only three months to go until his departure and, as of old, the anticipation of the journey filled him with joy. He could see himself, in a crumpled linen suit, a small travelling bag in hand, wide-brimmed hat on his head, stepping onto the steamboat at Yokohama. The image was clear in his mind; at last, he would be on his way.

In May, he took Kazuo to Yaizu for the weekend. The boy was nine years old now and loved the sea as much as his father did. Though some years earlier, remembering how he himself had learned to swim, Hearn had carried Kazuo on his shoulders into the water and, despite his protests, he had thrown him in. Kazuo struggled, panicked and choked and Hearn only pulled him out at the last minute. Yamaguchi-san had come running to the water's edge.

"That's wrong, Hearn-san. It will only make him afraid of the water," he called out.

Kazuo had cried hysterically and escaped into Yamaguchi-san's strong arms. The fishmonger took charge of the boy, and by leaving him free to follow his natural impulses, and by gently coaxing him, Kazuo eventually overcame his fear. Now, he swam with his father every day. Hearn felt especially responsible for his timid eldest son who reminded him so much of his younger self. Protective towards him, he was determined to give him every possible support, though in the case of swimming, his efforts had been misguided.

The two younger boys, who had inherited predominantly Japanese features, were sturdy and unlikely to cause anxiety, but Kazuo was delicate. He had brown hair and blue eyes and an endearing tendency to pronounce the words of poems in English – which he had learned by heart – with a queer little Irish accent. Hearing Kazuo recite, it surprised Hearn to realise that, unbeknownst to himself, he must have still had a hint of an Irish accent that the boy had picked up.

In Kazuo's face, he saw a living composite of generations and generations of faces and Hearn liked to think of these varying expressions as evidence of the souls within him. Sometimes he caught a glimpse of himself or Setsuko or a grandparent, at other times he took on the appearance of more remote family members. Occasionally, there would appear peculiarities of expression that neither he, nor Setsuko, could account for. Turn by turn, one soul or another would float up from the depths within the child, surface on his face and transform it. Hearn never tired of watching these ever-changing faces, these reminders of the ancestors.

On their second day in Yaizu, as they swam to shore, they saw Setsuko standing on the beach waiting for them. He could tell by her solemn air that something was wrong. His immediate thought was that Oka-san, who had been ill, had died; but in such an event, she would not have left her mother's side, she would have sent Manyemon. When they emerged from the water he discovered that, as he suspected, she had brought bad news.

She sent Kazuo back to Yamaguchi's house, sat with Hearn on the beach and showed him a copy of the morning newspaper. On the front page was a photograph of Mount Pelée on Martinique. Three days earlier, on the morning of 8th May, an eruption sent an avalanche of boiling ash down the side of the mountain. Saint Pierre was buried within minutes and virtually everyone, some twenty-eight thousand people, perished. Unable to believe what Setsuko was telling him, Hearn stared at the newspaper. He had friends there. Friends who had arranged for him to rent a house on the waterfront. He had pictured himself smoking his pipe on his veranda overlooking the quayside. The beautiful city with its steep winding streets and warm flagstones, glorious palms and white cathedral spires could not be gone.

"It seemed the people died instantly," she said.

"Were there no survivors?"

Setsuko consulted the newspaper again.

"There were a few. A prisoner, who was locked in an underground cell, and some sailors whose boat managed to stay afloat, but they were badly burnt. All the other boats in the harbour capsized and the crews were lost."

She folded the newspaper and passed it to him. He stared at it with utter incomprehension.

"What if…" she said.

He looked up from the newspaper and saw that she was as pale as a ghost.

"What if you had been there?" she said.

At his request, she took Kazuo back home to Tokyo and left him alone with his grief. Desolation and despair overwhelmed him. He could see the happy faces of his friends. He could hear their voices. He remembered clearly summer mornings bathed in rose coloured light and golden evening sunsets. Alone, he drank too much *sake*, sang the island folk songs and wept. And then he wondered what he was weeping for. For the people of Saint Pierre, for the lost paradise, or for himself? Saint Pierre was to have been the high point of his trip. Now, it was gone; his dream had faded into blackness and silence. He was filled with self-pity and then with shame for dwelling on his own selfish sorrow. All those people, all those beating hearts, stilled forever.

Yamaguchi's wife brought him dinner but he could not eat. The question he kept asking himself was, why had he so desperately wanted to go there? What was this need to return to the past? His life was now idyllic, and yet he was tormented by the need to go back, to tread old familiar paths, to relive his youth. He remembered how the folk heroes, Oisín and Urashima, had both found happiness in magical lands, and yet they had hankered for their old lives. It was a hankering that led to their undoing. They had left paradise and gone home, only to realise when it was too late, that home, as they remembered it, did not exist anymore.

He knew in his heart that he could never go back now. Not just because there was nowhere to go back to, but because the past did not exist. The devastation of Saint Pierre made him realise that he had everything he needed in Japan. The idea that he could leave and, for whatever reason, not return to his three sons, to Setsuko, was too distressing to contemplate. He decided to postpone his travels indefinitely.

Standing at the window, he looked out across the sea to Mount Fuji, another mighty volcanic mountain, and before closing the window he prayed that it would remain benign. Quietly, he gathered up his things and, so as not to seem ungrateful for Yamaguchi-san's kindness, he wrapped up the uneaten dinner and tucked it into his bag. He headed for home, determined to cherish what was most important to him: his family.

Chapter Nineteen

Tokyo, Japan, 1902

In June, shortly before he had been due to set out on his planned
but now cancelled travels, he was informed by an official at the
university that, as a Japanese citizen, he was no longer entitled to
a foreigner's salary. Foreign professors earned twice, sometimes
even three times, as much as their Japanese colleagues. He had not
informed them that instead of travelling, he had decided to devote
that time totally to writing but the promised vacation money was
also rescinded. That July, over an open-air lunch at Chamberlain's
favourite *sushi* cart, he asked his old friend for advice.

"Yes, I was aware, and so must you have been, that there was
disgruntlement amongst the Japanese academics that you were
having your cake and eating it, so to speak," said Chamberlain on
hearing of his predicament.

"But, why now? They've known for years about my status."

"I expect they've been asked to tighten their belts. There's another
war coming, you know."

"They offered to renew my contract but at terms so derisory that it's
impossible for me to accept. So the long and the short of the matter
is that, having worked for twelve years in the Japanese educational
system, I am to be driven out of the service and practically banished
from the country."

"Come now, Hearn, you're exaggerating. There are other ways to make a living. There are other universities."

Seeing their empty plates, the *sushi* master placed two more artistic morsels in front of them. It was sweltering. Chamberlain signaled for more green tea.

"Oh, I'm just tired," said Hearn. "I'm fifty-three. I've no energy. I'll never be rich."

"If that's what you want, you should write a novel."

"That's what my publishers tell me. But you know as well as I do that literary success of any enduring kind is only achieved by refusing to do what the damned publishers want, by refusing to write what the public wants, and by absolutely refusing to write anything to order."

"An admirable sentiment," said Chamberlain. "But it's not the way to make money, if, as you say, that's what you want."

"No, but it is the only way to achieve literary sincerity. Of course I would like to have millions and give it all to my wife, but the truth is you get what you wish for only when you have stopped wishing for it."

"Well, whatever about a novel, you might try to make your writing more accessible," said Chamberlain. "Perhaps if you did, your books would sell more."

"What do you mean?"

"Well, you do use rather a lot of Japanese words."

"So?"

"Your readers don't speak Japanese, Hearn. How do you expect them to understand?"

Hearn bristled. Yes, there were some Japanese words in his texts but when he used them, he did so for a reason. Strange words were compelling and exotic. They whispered and rustled; they wept and raged and rioted. How could Chamberlain fail to understand that words did not need to be fully intelligible to move the heart of the reader?

Over the years he had come to like *sushi* but lunch ended on a somewhat sour note. The criticism smarted, and he went home feeling annoyed with Chamberlain and furious that, even if he wanted to, he would struggle to write a novel. He could write an essay on some topic of which he was quite ignorant by simply studying the subject, but a novel could not be written by studying. It had to come from within, from some sensation deep inside. The two short novels he had written had met with popular success, but that was before he came to Japan, and he had known even then that it was a direction he did not want to pursue. Dredging up deeply buried emotion was traumatic for him.

Perhaps if he tried, he might manage to coax out one more novel, or a volume of little fictional stories. That might suffice to secure a steady income flow. It saddened him to acknowledge that fiction was all the feeble-minded masses seemed to care about, not essays, however clever, nor whimsical titbits, nor travels; made-up stories were all readers seemed to want. Though comfortable enough, he knew fiction could make him rich – something he now realised he would never be.

One thing he knew though, beyond all doubt, was that it was absolutely useless for him to try to force work. If inspiration did not come, he was better off doing nothing. In this dark state of mind, he decided never to write another line about Japan. After all his efforts to promote Japan, to explain her beauty to the rest of the world, he was being treated appallingly by the Ministry of Education and was effectively being forced out of the university in spite of protests from the press and from his students, who had stood by him.

To make matters worse, he burst a blood vessel, and was not allowed to talk. Lecturing was out of the question and he was not altogether sorry. Though someone had once suggested he publish his lectures, he felt they were not worth printing. They were formless lectures, dictated on the spot, not from notes. He believed he was no scholar, nor even a competent critic. There were scores of men who could do his job better than he could.

Feeling useless and a failure, he escaped to Yaizu, where day after day, out he swam, and as the water deepened beneath him, he could feel cold currents rising and the fleeting touch of fish. To right and left they leapt and dived swiftly and the further out he swam, the more numerous they became. Gulls flew low about him, circling with their screeching cries. Once, for just an instant, his feet touched something both heavy and lithe that rushed passed. Fear overcame him and he turned to shore.

Alone, one warm night at his open window looking out over the vast Pacific Ocean, he thought how curious it was that what was veiled by the light of day became visible at night. The star-filled sky made him forget his disillusionment. Moved to tears, it occurred to him that it was not the loveliness of the scene that was making him weep, it was the longing of past generations quickening in his heart. Perhaps the beauty he saw before him had no real existence. Perhaps it was the presence of the dead, all those innumerable souls within him, that made it seem lovely. He imagined the ghosts of his ancestors crowding to the windows of the house of life, like prisoners towards some vision of bright skies, free hills and glimmering streams. Beyond the iron bars of their ghostly cells, they glimpsed the magnificence of the great night sky with its hundred million suns burning eternally. But this glorious sight came to them filtered through the generations, through him, only as dreams of home to a hopeless exile; of childhood bliss to desolate age; of remembered vision to the blind.

He sat there listening to the murmur of the ocean and wondered if the souls within him longed in vain to live again, to touch again, to feel the joy of limbs entwined in love. For a while, the vast shining world seemed not quite so hateful.

Setsuko and the children visited frequently but Hearn spent almost the entire summer in Yaizu, returning home only for *Bon*, the Festival of the Dead, to make the offerings to the ancestors and to celebrate with the family. He stayed for the first two days of the festival and then returned to Yaizu for the third and final day. There were no little Ships of Souls like the ones he had seen in other places launched at Yaizu. Instead, simple lanterns carried the spirits of the ancestors away and he wanted to see them.

He was tired when he reached his rooms above Yamaguchi-san's shop and after dinner he fell asleep. It was late when he woke and he hurried to the beach, but when he got there the festival was over and everyone had gone home. Out at sea he saw a procession of lanterns floating away on the tide, too far away to be distinguished except as points of light. They were moving slowly and it occurred to him that he could easily swim out to them. He left his *yukata* and a towel on the beach and plunged naked into the water. The sea was calm and beautifully phosphorescent, and every stroke kindled a stream of yellow fire.

He swam fast and overtook the lantern fleet sooner than expected. Knowing that it would be improper to interfere with them, to divert them from their silent course, he contented himself with keeping close to one of them. The bottom was a thick plank, perfectly square and measuring about ten inches across. On each corner was a slender upright post about sixteen inches high and these were supported by a cross beam. The four sides had plain translucent paper insets, and inside each lantern a candle flickered.

Every whisper of wind and ripple of wave scattered the frail glowing shapes ever more widely apart. Each little lantern with its fading glow seemed afraid, trembling on the current that was bearing it into the outer blackness. And he wondered if he himself were not also lost upon a deep and dim sea, separating further and further from others as he drifted to his inevitable end.

As he swam, he began to doubt whether he was really alone. Was there something more than a mere flickering light in the lantern that rocked beside him; some presence that haunted the dying flame and was watching him. A faint cold thrill passed through him. Old superstitions came back to him: vague warnings of danger during the Festival of the Dead. It occurred to him that if any evil were to befall him out here in the dark, meddling or seeming to meddle with the lights of the dead, he himself might become the subject of some ominous future legend. He whispered the Buddhist formula of farewell to the lanterns and quickly made for the shore.

On reaching the beach, he was startled to see a white shadow before him, and he had a strange feeling that he was about to meet his death until a light flared beside the figure. It was Yamaguchi-san, who had come to look for him.

"Is the water not cold out there?"

"Not really," said Hearn as he dried himself.

"Even *kappa* drown sometimes," he said.

"Yes, I know it was foolish of me but I wanted to see the lanterns."

"You should have asked. I could make one for you. This is no time to go swimming. We were worried about you."

Hearn felt bad that Yamaguchi-san had been worried. He knew that eating cucumber was believed to protect against *kappa*, the amphibious green demons who were known to assault humans in water, so he said,

"There was no need to worry, I ate a cucumber before I swam."

"You weren't afraid?"

"No. Well, perhaps a little."

"The sea has a soul and hears everything, Hearn-san. It's better not to speak of your fear when you're out there. If you say that you are afraid, the waves will suddenly rise higher."

"Yes, I've often felt that the sea is alive," said Hearn as he put on his *yukata*. "In order to be able to think of it as a mere body of water, I have to be on dry land."

"Come, let's have some *sake* together and wish the ancestors a safe journey."

Usually at that time of year the sea grew rough, and the following morning he saw that the surf was running high. All day it grew, and by the middle of the afternoon the waves were wild and wonderful, and he sat on the sea wall and watched them until sundown. Each wave was long, slow rolling, massive and just before breaking, a towering swell would crack along its length, then fall and flatten, shaking the wall beneath him.

Yet the power, the mystery and beauty of the sea did not lessen the gloom that had enveloped him since the news of Saint Pierre. Nature was cruel. He had not been smothered in a cloud of boiling ash, but earthquakes were a frequent occurrence in this part of Japan, and weather watchers were predicting a big one. Was it his fate to be devoured by the cracked earth, or buried under the rubble of falling buildings? If not, he might burn to death in the fires that follow, or drown in a *tsunami* that earthquakes often trigger. A life that could be snuffed out in an instant seemed to him pointless.

Since moving to Tokyo he had felt, as never before, how utterly dead Old Japan was and how ugly New Japan was becoming. The charm of Old Japan, which had been the focus of all his work, was fading fast and would soon be gone forever. It seemed useless to write about things that had more or less ceased to exist. He could not, in all honesty, put himself forward as an authority on Japanese history, or on any specialised Japanese subject. The value of his work depended on impression and suggestion, rather than upon any crystallisation of fact. What he was doing, he consoled himself, was keeping some sort of record of a vanishing world.

In this morbid frame of mind he wandered home, and as he neared the fishmonger's shop he noticed people gathering on the quayside and went to investigate. All he could see were the backs of two women seated on the ground in the middle of the crowd. One of them unwrapped her *shamisen* and played while the other sang. He stood transfixed. All the sorrow and beauty, all the pain and sweetness of life thrilled and quivered in their remarkable performance, and he realized that, notwithstanding all the changes that had taken place, the heart of Old Japan was still beating. A great sense of tenderness filled him and he looked around and saw that, touched by the pathos and the beauty of the music, many were moved to tears.

When the performance ended and the crowd dispersed, he talked to the women and learned that they lived in tragic poverty; blighted by smallpox, blindness, a paralyzed husband and children to care for, they scrounged together a living by begging on the streets. He felt ashamed. He had so much. He gave them all the money he had on him and determined that if they could keep going under such dreadful circumstances, then so could he.

CHAPTER TWENTY

Tokyo, Japan, 1904

The idea of climbing Mount Fuji had occurred to Hearn on many occasions. From the ramparts in Yaizu, he could see the great mountain in the distance, and through a telescope he could make out snow-covered cusps at the top, like the petals of a lotus flower, a symbol of purity.

Rising to twelve and a half thousand feet, Mount Fuji was visible from thirteen provinces. It was the most sacred mountain in Japan and to climb it, at least once in a lifetime, was the duty of all who revered the ancient gods. This act of faith could not be performed by all forty million citizens, and so representatives from remote towns and villages were sent to pray and salute the morning sun from the summit. For thousands of years it was scaled every summer by vast numbers of pilgrims, and Hearn knew the legend that said that the sand dislodged during the day by pilgrims' feet returned to its former position by night.

Now back in Tokyo, Setsuko slept beside him but he lay awake in the half-light thinking about Mount Fuji and watching the moon's soft shadows as they crept slowly across the room, blurring all hard edges. This would be a good time to do it, he thought. He was no longer employed at the Imperial University, his new book had been sent to the publisher, and he had time on his hands. Setsuko shifted beside him.

"Are you awake?" he asked.

"Almost."

"I'm thinking of climbing Mount Fuji?"

She rolled over in her *futon* and turned a sleepy face to him.

"You've been unwell. Would it be wise?"

"I don't mean right now but if I harden up in the sea over the next while... Nishida-san might come with me."

"Ah, so you have already made plans."

"No, but I could write to him and suggest it."

"It'd be good for you to spend some time with him."

"It would. And he'd look after me."

"Oji-san climbed Fuji-san once when he was young. It took him a full day to get to the top, and his legs were aching but he said it was worth it. There's a shrine on the summit to the beautiful goddess of the mountain. People have seen her hovering like a luminous cloud over the edge of the crater."

"And her name is...?"

"Princess who Causes the Flowers to Blossom Brightly."

"That's quite a mouthful. Imagine having breakfast with her. Good morning Princess who Causes the Flowers to Blossom Brightly. Could you please pass the pickles, Princess who Causes the Flowers to Blossom Brightly."

She laughed.

"If you go, you must be careful not to joke when you're on the mountain. The princess's ghostly servants wait and watch at the edge of the precipice and hurl down anyone who approaches her shrine with an impure heart."

"Quite right too," he said. "Should I bring Kazuo?"

"No, it can be dangerous. He's only eleven."

"It's dormant, isn't it?" he said with a sudden pang of apprehension. "Have there been recent tremors or—?"

"No, no. It's been over two hundred years since the last eruption. I meant the climb can be dangerous. If you insist on going, promise me you'll take the easiest route, won't you?"

"Of course."

"And maybe in a year or two you can bring Kazuo."

She closed her eyes and was about to nod off again when the faint sound of a child beginning to stir roused her. She was up and gone in seconds. He felt more cheerful than he had for many weeks and lay there mentally composing a letter to Nishida-san.

The trip was soon arranged and they met in Gotemba, a little village three hours by train from Tokyo, made up mainly of pilgrim inns. It was a warm May morning and as he alighted from the train, he looked up at the mountain and wondered what the fuss was about. It did not look dangerous; the slope was so gradual, he imagined he would have no difficulty at all climbing it. Nishida-san had booked them a room at an inn and, by the time Hearn arrived, he had hired a couple of experienced guides to accompany them.

"Do we really need guides? It looks straightforward enough."

"It's very deceptive," said Nishida-san. "Trust me, we need them."

Nishida-san handed him a pilgrim's staff, three pairs of straw sandals, a pair of heavy blue cleft-socks to be worn with the sandals and a straw hat shaped like the mountain.

"Why so many sandals?"

"They wear out on the mountain track. All pilgrims carry several pairs."

It had been a while since they had seen each other, not since Kobe, and they had lots to catch up on over dinner in their room. They sat cross-legged at a low table, dressed in *yukata*, sharing *nabe*, a hot-pot of meat, fish, vegetables and noodles served by a formidable maid who must have been close to eighty.

"So how is Tokyo?" asked Nishida-san.

"I dislike the officials, the imitation of foreign ways, the airs, the conceits. Now, to my poor mind, all that was good, noble and true was in Old Japan. I wish I could go back in time, even back a hundred years, to the real Japan. Somehow, Tokyo doesn't seem like Japan at all. I hate it."

"It can't be all bad."

"Yes, there is one good thing about it. It's near Yaizu and I go there as much as I can. I like little villages."

"And your new book?"

"What can I say? It's finished. Let's hope the publishers like it."

"I'm sure they will."

"You never know. Consider me tenth rate until the literary world has decided my worth."

Nishida-san topped up Hearn's *sake* cup and Hearn topped up Nishida-san's.

"You're too modest."

"No, I'm not modest at all. In fact I'm devilishly conceited. If I tell you that much of my work is very bad, I tell you this, not because I'm modest, but because, as a professional writer, I recognise bad work when I see it."

"Like an honest carpenter, who knows his trade, and tells his customer that something isn't going to cost much because the work is bad, and then points out how the piece is backed with cheap wood underneath."

"Exactly. Things look all right only because you don't know how they are patched together."

"So you're still your most severe critic, even after all your success."

"Let's not talk of work. Tell me about Matsue."

"It's changing too. Better not to go back. You'd expect it to be the same as it was and you'd be disappointed."

"Shall we order more *sake*?"

"We start at four in the morning," said Nishida-san.

"Right. No more *sake* tonight."

"Better not."

They went to soak in the communal bath. Up to their necks in hot water in the enormous steam-filled room, they breathed in the warm, wet scented air of the cedar-cladding, and contemplated the climb.

"It shouldn't be too hard. We travel the first five thousand feet in rickshaws," said Nishida-san.

"Great. That leaves just seven thous—"

"No it leaves five. We're already at two thousand feet."

"Really? On the way here I didn't notice that we were going uphill."

"That's because you were sitting on your bum on the train. If you'd been walking…"

Hearn laughed.

"I was so glad to get your letter," said Nishida-san. "I've been meaning to do this for years. After we've climbed Fuji-san, we can die happy."

Hearn was puzzled by this remark. Nishida-san had three daughters but no son, and he remembered Asakichi telling him that it was considered the greatest calamity to die without leaving a male heir to perform the rites and make the offerings at the household shrine.

"Oh, I forgot to tell you, I have a son," said Nishida-san, as if reading his mind.

"You didn't say in your last let—"

"We adopted him into the family just a few months ago and he has married my eldest daughter. There's a grandchild coming."

"That's excellent news. Congratulations."

Relaxed from the bath they returned to their room. Servants had cleared away the dinner dishes and laid out their bedding. It was nine o'clock and they were hoping for a good night's sleep but groups, returning late from the mountain, partied and sang in the adjoining rooms; raucous singing and drunken laughter kept them awake for hours. At three-thirty, just as he was about to nod off, maids arrived with a light breakfast of fish, rice and soup. Then one of the guides arrived to inspect their clothes, and he instructed Hearn to undress and put on heavier undergarments.

When he had first imagined the trip, he thought it would be just him and his dear old friend Nishida-san; two men on the mountain at ease with each other. It had turned into an elaborate expedition. They had a rickshaw each, and each rickshaw had three runners – two to pull and one to push. There were three guides laden with provisions and bundles of heavy clothes. Hearn could not imagine what they were for as they were due back that evening.

They set out into the black morning. It was slightly chilly and there was a fine rain. As they rolled along the country road, soon the lights of Gotemba vanished behind them. The only thing clearly visible was the hazy glow of the swinging paper lantern of the lead runner. Wan grey light slowly diffused the moist air as the day struggled to dawn through the drizzle. Their way lay through thin woods. Occasionally they passed houses with high thatched roofs that looked like farmhouses, but there was no cultivated land to be seen. There was no sign of the mountain either.

At some point he noticed that the road was black, black with sand and cinders, volcanic cinders. The wheels of the rickshaw and the feet of the runners sank into it with a crunching sound. The black road curved across a vast grassy area. Here and there he could see black patches. Little true soil meant that there were no farms and there was no water. He learned later that the eruption two hundred years earlier had covered the entire district with six feet of ash. Volcanic destruction was not eternal destruction though; eruptions could fertilize and he knew that the Princess who Causes the Flowers to Blossom would make the wasteland bloom again in a few hundred years.

The rain stopped, the sky cleared and the sun came out and Mount Fuji appeared right in front of him, stupendous, startling, as if newly risen from the earth – a vast blue cone, warm blue, almost violet through the mists not yet lifted.

When the rickshaws could go no further, they advanced on foot. They followed a track, a yellowish track made from thousands of cast-off straw sandals which had been flung aside by the pilgrims who had climbed before them. At first the ascent was through ashes and sand but then large stones mingled with the sand and the way became steeper. There was nothing firm, nothing resisting to stand on; loose stones and cinders rolled from under their feet. Now he was glad of the staff. Almost every stone that he tread on turned under him and he kept slipping. He wondered how the guides never slipped, never made a false step. Their broad brown feet always poised on the shingle at exactly the right angle. They were much heavier men than him but they moved light as birds. With great difficulty he followed the zig-zagging path, and barely made it to the fourth of the ten stations. It was 10.30 a.m. and they still had another four thousand five hundred feet to go.

After a short rest they were off again, up ever higher and into a white fog. They passed through clouds. The slope became very rough. It was no longer soft ashes and sand mixed with stones but only stones, pumice and fragments of lava – all sharp and angled as if purposely designed to skid out from underfoot when trodden upon. He slipped many times, but the guides stayed close and never allowed him to fall. Dislodged rocks seemed to roll down soundlessly behind him. He looked back but could see nothing. Their noiseless vanishing gave him a strange feeling, like the sensation of falling in a dream.

Without the guides they would not have made it, and he realised that he was not fit enough for this mountain. When the staff began to hurt his hand, one of the guides unwound a long cotton belt from around his waist and gave him one end to hold; he draped the other end over his shoulder so that he could pull Hearn up the mountain. Another guide positioned himself behind Hearn and, between the two of them, they pushed and pulled and constantly propped him up. He felt deeply ashamed to cause them so much trouble with the summit still miles away.

"Try not to stoop," said the guide behind him. "You must walk upright and when you step put your heel down first."

He obeyed and found it a little easier, but he was still panting and sweating profusely. Strong gusts of wild wind blew in their faces and with it came black dust; he tied his hat on tightly. The guide suggested that he close his mouth and only breathe through his nose. He did as he was told and soldiered on, stopping for a small rest at every turn of the path. When his first pair of sandals disintegrated, he tossed them aside and put on a fresh pair.

The mountain had ceased to be blue, blue of any shade. It was black, charcoal black: a frightful heap of ashes, cinders and slaggy lava. The grim black reality became more and more sharply defined. It was a nightmare. Mount Fuji, the fairest of earthly visions, the vision he had seen from the SS *Abyssinia* fourteen years earlier, had dissolved into a spectacle of horror and death.

At one point, as they skirted a snow-filled gully, Nishida-san brought him a large ball of curious-looking snow. It was not soft and flaky but a mass of transparent globules, like glass beads. He ate it and revived a little, then continued up a slope strewn with ever increasing numbers of cast-off sandals.

Unable to speak for weariness, he somehow made it to the eighth station where he collapsed in a heap, his heart beating loud and hard as in a high fever. He could not walk another step. Progress had been slow, and the head guide decided that because of Hearn's fatigue they would stay the night and proceed to the summit in the morning.

The station was a wooden hut half buried in the mountain. It was clean and comfortable, but there were no windows or any opening other than the door. It was freezing cold and he learned the value of the heavy robes the guides had carried. He crawled in, wrapped himself up and lay on the floor. Nishida-san joined him; he was tired but not nearly as exhausted as Hearn.

"Great fun, eh?" said Nishida-san.

"Hilarious," said Hearn.

The two men laughed.

"You hungry?"

"I'll be starving as soon as I recover. Any chance of a big fat steak and a glass of ale?"

"Afraid not."

They dined on *zosui*, a dish of rice and eggs with a hint of meat. Plain as it was, it went down a treat after the day they had put in.

"By the way, I was told to tell you not to go out after dark," said Nishida-san. "If you must go out, bring one of the guides with you."

"Over the years I've noticed that whenever I'm told not to go out at night, it's usually because of some silly superstition."

"Oh no. Nothing silly about this. When a strong wind runs around the mountain, it blows the big rocks away like pebbles. Didn't you notice the extraordinary protective walls around the hut and the way the roof is purposely weighed down."

Hearn had been too tired to notice anything on the way in, but he looked up into the black rafters and saw bundles of wood, packages of sandals, and other indistinguishable things stowed away or suspended in the air; they made eerie shadows in the lamplight.

"A lava-block falling from the upper regions would come down like a shot from a cannon. You don't want to be in its path, Hearn-san."

"Indeed I do not."

After dinner the door was closed and barred. He lay down between the guides, and he could tell by their heavy breathing that they were asleep within minutes. It was really cold, even under his three quilts. Outside, the wind roared and hissed. The hut did not move but sand trickled down between the rafters and small stones on the roof shifted after each gust like the clatter of shingle on a beach.

After a fitful sleep he rose just before dawn and hurried out, hoping to be one of the fortunate mortals to be able to boast that from Mount Fuji he had seen the first glimmer of the sun as it appeared over the horizon. He was disappointed. Heavy cloud blocked the view and he could tell by the burning edges of the cloud, glowing like charcoal, that the sun has already risen. He had missed it.

At 6.40 a.m. they started out for the top. This was the roughest stage of the journey and every bone in his body ached; every step was torture. They proceeded through a wilderness of lava blocks, the path wound its way between ugly outcrops like rotten teeth. Wilder and steeper it became, and he found himself sometimes climbing on all fours. There were barriers that they could only surmount with the help of ladders. They passed a chilling place, a black landscape littered with heaps of rocks, like the little piles of stones that the ghosts of children build in Buddhist pictures of the underworld. Nishida-san told him it was called *Sai no Kawara*, The Dry Bed of the River of Souls.

Two agonizing hours later they reached the dismal top. There were stone huts, a Shinto shrine, an icy well and beyond them the huge dead crater. It was about half a mile wide, a horrible cavity with yellow crumbling walls streaked and stained from centuries of scorching. Hideous overhanging cusps of lava projected out several hundred feet above the opening. He had seen these monstrosities through his telescope from Yaizu. Through the soft illusion of the blue spring light, they had looked like the snowy petals of a lotus flower. Standing there on the cindered tips, there was nothing magical about them. He felt nothing but disappointment.

But then he became aware of other pilgrims, earlier climbers, poised on the highest crags, with their faces turned to the east. They clapped their hands in Shinto prayer and saluted the mighty day. He turned to face what they were facing and found himself gazing out over hundreds of miles at the faint dreamy world far below. It was a golden world draped in the fairy vapours of morning and marvelous wreaths of hazy cloud. The immense poetry of the moment entered into him like a thrill. Even as he looked he knew that the colossal vision before him had already become an unforgettable memory, a memory of which no luminous detail would ever fade.

On the way down they took a different route. The path was all sand and would have been murderous to climb but was effortless to descend. He even found that it was easier to run. A few hours later they were soaking in the thermal waters of an outdoor pool, warm and relaxed, easing their aching joints. A servant came with a little wooden tray bearing a flask of hot *sake*. She filled two little *sake* cups and floated the tray across the steaming water to them. Nishida-san picked up one and put it in Hearn's hand.

"To Fuji-san," he said, raising his cup in the direction of the mountain which was rapidly vanishing into the thickening mist. "We'll go again next year."

"After you," said a dubious Hearn.

Nishida-san let out a great belly laugh. They downed their drinks and Nishida-san poured more, and as he did, he began to hum a little song Hearn had not heard since he left Matsue. It was the funny one about the raccoon dog whose enormous testicles swing back and forth even when there is no wind. He laughed and joined in.

Back in their room, they were both exhausted but giddy with achievement. The maids brought dinner and an endless supply of *sake*, and they got very drunk, sang and laughed and most likely kept their neighbours awake until they both collapsed into a deep sleep in the early hours of the morning.

Chapter Twenty-One

Tokyo, Japan, 1904

*D*ear Old Dad,
   Almost eight years ago, when we arrived in Tokyo, I instinctively felt that I was heading into a world of intrigue, but what kind of intrigue I had no conception of. Here, foreigners seem to live in a state of perpetual panic. Everybody is uneasy and afraid of everybody else, afraid to speak not only their minds, but to speak about anything except irrelevant matters. They huddle together and talk loudly, all at the same time, about nothing, like people in expectation of a possible catastrophe, or like frightened peasants making noise to drive away ghosts.

I am now employed at Waseda University and, as before, I avoid my colleagues as much as possible. But every now and then I am obliged to be part of the world. The Emperor paid us a visit earlier this year and I had to don a frock coat and top hat. Staff and students, stood for hours in sleet and snow, horribly cold as no overcoats were allowed, and for this torture we were twice permitted to bow before His Majesty! Needless to say, the event did not do much for my poor lungs. I will never wear that confounded hat again, though it did add a foot to my diminutive stature.

And now we are at war again. Sometimes when I'm out walking, people spit on the ground in front of me; the Japanese are very skillful at this. Or they hiss, or whisper to each other about the damned foreigner, just loud enough for me to hear. I suppose it's only to be expected. At a time like this, they see all foreigners as the enemy. It's strange though, because I don't consider myself a foreigner. It's only when I catch a glimpse of myself in a mirror that I'm reminded of it.

Yaizu is my great escape. Some of the local men have been summoned to war, including several pleasant acquaintances, so the town is a little lonesome now. When they were going away, one of them gave Kazuo a clay model of a Russian soldier's head and he said, "When I come back, I will bring you a real one." An inappropriate thing to give or to say to a child, you may think, but he was sincere and meant well.

The summer was dry, hot and bright, but a few weeks ago it rained in a peculiar way and the lightning, spectacular though it was, killed several people. And the other day, the cherry tree in our garden blossomed out of season. This upset the family, Setsuko especially, as it was seen as a bad omen. I wonder has the war something to do with the disturbed state of the atmosphere. After one particularly heavy rainfall we got news of a great victory, so now, whenever it rains hard, Setsuko says, "Ah, the Russians are in trouble again." There will be many casualties of this war on both sides, but the people are cheerful and brave. Nobody seems to have any doubt as to the results of the campaign: Russia must lose Manchuria.

I am writing again after a long indolent period and a brief foray into ghost stories and fairytales, which amused the children and gave me much to think about. Curiously, the ghost stories which I've been collecting since I came to Japan, I put together in a book in no time at all, and it's selling better than books I slaved over for years. Of course I should write more of them but that would be far too sensible. Instead, I have been immersed in a new book; in fact I've finished it. Of course it won't sell but who knows. It's called 'Japan: An Attempt at Interpretation' because that's what it is, an attempt to unravel this intriguing country.

The other day, my dear wife suggested that I take Kazuo to Ireland for a short while so that he might see where I grew up. She is opening up to the idea of travel. Whatever about the other children, who are predominantly Japanese, I believe that Kazuo should be educated in Paris, and she hinted that, at some point, we might all live in France for a year or two. That would please me greatly.

Setsuko is happy. The boys are thriving. Suzuko is nine months old now. Her eyes have again changed colour, from blue to brown, like my own, but her hair remains chestnut. She is strong like her mother and is crawling about, opening drawers and, like me, causing much trouble. I'm fine, a little tired but I always feel like this when I finish a book. I enclose a photograph taken at the university recently. You will spot me easily as I'm the only person in profile. Everybody else is looking directly at the camera; I alone looked down and to the side so that the camera couldn't capture forever my hideous sunken eye. In my foolish attempt not to be seen, I merely managed to stick out even more.

Japan is changing rapidly and the changes are not beautiful. I try to keep within fragments of the old atmosphere that lingers here and there in temples and shrines, in obscure little streets and gardens. My home will always have its atmosphere of a thousand years ago; but in the raw light outside, the changes are ugly and sad. As for me... I'm like a flea in a wash bowl. My best chance is to lie quiet and await the coming of unpredictable events.

May all good fortune be with you, my dear old friend.

With love,
Yakumo

He reread the letter and sat wondering about his new book: a collection of essays that summed up all his thoughts about Japan. The effort of writing it had nearly killed him and of late he had been wondering if he had been bewitched like the heroes of the old folk tales who had travelled to enchanted lands. Was everything as charming as he had believed? The old kindliness and grace of manners had, after all, been cultivated for a thousand years under the edge of the sword. The common politeness and rarity of quarrels came about when, for generations, social disruption had been met with extraordinarily vigorous punishment. And what of the winning smile? Was it still charming when you knew that in the past underlings had to smile in the face of pain, for not to, might cost you your life. Countless restrictions had once ruled this land and yet, he could not help but admire the results: the amiability of manners, the daintiness of habits, the delicate tact displayed in pleasure giving, and the strange power of presenting outwardly, under any circumstances, only the best and brightest aspects of character. Even the most cynical would find poetry in Shinto: in the lamps kindled nightly before the names of the dead in the household shrines, in the tiny offerings of food and drink for the ancestors, in the welcome fires lit to guide the spirits of the dead home during the Festival of the Dead, and in the little Ships of Souls prepared to bear them back to their resting place. Shinto was, and had always been, the very life of the people, the motivation and directing power of their every action.

Rising above his conflicted feelings was a sense that, notwithstanding how this world had come into being, he had glimpsed paradise, and it gave him hope for the future, for a higher future where people would behave with instinctive unselfishness and have the common desire to find joy in making others happy. It would be a world of perfect sympathy where people had a universal sense of moral beauty. To have seen Old Japan was to know that such a possibility existed.

He flicked through the proofs of his new book and hoped that it would go some way towards explaining this highly evolved but often misunderstood civilisation to Westerners. But would they understand? He hoped so. From the moment he arrived in Japan he had delighted in and appreciated what he saw all around him, but it had taken him years to understand the hearts and emotions of the people.

One particularly baffling incident stood out in his mind. In May 1891, an assassination attempt was made on the Russian Prince Nicholas who was visiting Japan on a diplomatic mission. The assassin, one of the Japanese policemen tasked with guarding him, attacked the prince with a sword and managed to scar but not kill him. He was living in Matsue at the time and he had been astonished by the intensity of the shame even the poorest peasant felt, that a guest in their country could have been treated this way.

The Emperor announced his sorrow in the national newspapers, and the entire country went into public mourning of the type that usually follows some great calamity or national peril. He remembered being surprised when theatres, pleasure resorts and banqueting halls closed. There were no flower displays, and not even the tinkle of a *shamisen* could be heard in the silent quarters of the *geisha*. The faces on the streets ceased to wear the habitual smile.

Following this immense sympathy came the spontaneous desire to right the wrong, to make compensation for the injury done. Hundreds of thousands of letters and telegrams of condolence and curious gifts were sent from all over the country to the wounded prince. Innumerable messages were forwarded to his father, the Czar, by ordinary people. Hearn recalled being stopped on the street by an old merchant who asked him to compose a telegram in French to the Czar, expressing the profound grief of all the citizens of Japan for the attack on his son. He was a poor man and the telegram cost him a large sum of money but he was determined to send it.

Forty million people were sorrowing but one young girl was sorrowing more than others. Her name was Yuko Hatakeyama. She was ruled by emotions and by impulses of which, at the time, he could only guess the nature in the vaguest possible way. He knew now that her feelings were dominated by one supreme emotion: loyalty. The English word 'loyalty' did not convey the emotion adequately.

What she was feeling was more akin to mystical exaltation, a sense of uttermost reverence to the distressed Emperor.

Hearn read about the girl in the newspaper. She was a young seamstress and she rose one dawn, fulfilled her duties, put on her prettiest clothes and travelled to Kyoto. There she booked into a lodging house, sat up through the night until the heavy darkness just before dawn and then set out into the silence. The streets were dimly lit, the only sound the click-clack of her wooden sandals echoing through the empty streets. Only the stars looked down on her.

When she arrived at the deep gates of the Kyoto Prefectural Office, she slipped into the shadows, knelt down and whispered a prayer. Then, according to the ancient tradition, she bound her *kimono* tightly about her, tying the knot just above her knees for, no matter what might happen in the instant of blind agony, she must not be found in death with limbs indecently composed. She secured the knot and then she slit her throat.

She was found at sunrise in a pool of blood. Her belongings consisted of a small purse with just enough money for her funeral and two farewell letters: one to her brother, and one to high officials requesting that they petition the Emperor to cease from sorrowing because a young life, albeit an unworthy one, had been given in voluntary expiation of the wrong done to the Russian prince. Her story was printed in all the newspapers and she was praised as a valiant and patriotic woman. The Emperor heard of her sacrifice, knew that his people loved him and ceased to mourn.

Hearn understood now that the beauty of self-sacrifice alone was the motive and that ecstatic loyalty was part of the national life. It was Shinto. It was in the blood, inherent as the impulse of an ant to perish for its little republic; unconscious as the loyalty of bees to their queen.

An uncomfortable, familiar feeling in his chest caused him to sit back in his chair. This had happened a few times lately and he had got used to it. Taking a few deep breaths, he lay on the floor and waited for the sensation to pass. The first time it happened, Setsuko sent for the doctor but by the time he arrived he was perfectly well again and the doctor could find nothing wrong with him. Better not to mention it rather than alarm her again.

Setsuko had not heard the scratch of his pen for some time, and neither could she hear him pacing up and down. As an excuse to check on him, she brought him tea and a piece of the plum pudding she had made some months earlier but had just opened. He loved plum pudding; she had learned how to make it even though the ingredients were difficult to source. When she arrived in his study and found him lying on the floor, she let out a little gasp of distress. He smiled up at her and sniffed the air.

"What's that I smell? Is it whiskey?" he asked.

"Yes, I'm afraid I might have put too much in the pudding."

"There can never be too much whiskey."

He got up and relieved her of the slice of plum pudding and sat back at his desk.

"My dear little wife, you go to so much trouble for me. I can never thank you enough."

"It's no trouble."

"Did you taste it?" he asked.

"No. I felt drunk just smelling it."

She glanced over his desk which was piled high with proofs and letters and on the floor under the desk was another huge pile of other papers.

"You're very pale. Are you alright?" she asked.

"I'm fine."

"You don't usually lie on the floor?"

"I was just resting."

Though he was not at all hungry, he took a small bite of pudding and made suitably appreciative noises.

"When you've finished your tea, would you like to go for a walk? It's a lovely evening."

"I can't. I have to finish checking these proofs. Then I've a few letters to write and more than a hundred compositions to look through. Then I have at least another day's work packing and sending out prizes."

He did not eat any more of the pudding and she noticed how unusually distracted he seemed.

"Perhaps you should leave all this until after the weekend. You look tired."

"I am tired."

"Why don't you go to Yaizu tomorrow? Rest and swim. It will do you good and you always come back refreshed."

He took her advice and the following morning caught the first train. He swam, a short, effortful swim and then strolled along the ramparts. The warm September day was drowsy and tender blue, and there were just a few wisps of cloud floating over the sea. Beyond the town, the hills were hazy shapes melting into the sky. A sudden memory came to him of a place and time in which the sun was larger and brighter. Whether it was of this life, or a phantom memory, or a dream, he could not tell; but he knew that the sky was very much bluer and nearer the world then. The sea was alive and used to talk to him, and the wind made him cry out for joy when it touched him.

As he walked slowly along, he remembered too that the days were much longer in that magical world, and every day brought new wonders and pleasures. Time and place were gently ruled by his pretty mother who thought only of ways to make him happy. Sometimes he would refuse to be made happy and that always caused her pain. And then he would try very hard to be sorry. At bedtime, she would lie down beside him and tell him stories that made him tingle with pleasure. And when the pleasure became too great she would sing a strange little song to which he always fell asleep.

He stopped and looked around. On the right, fields of rice and barley stretched to the far off hills. On the left, fishing boats rode the shining sea. Everything was steeped in dazzling white sun. He was curiously breathless, and the familiar sensation in his chest came again. This time it was extremely unpleasant and he had to sit down.

What had previously been just an uncomfortable feeling, not unlike indigestion, turned into pain. Hands on his knees, he took deep breaths and focused on Mount Fuji off in the distance. He had been there. He had seen the bleak reality of the sacred mountain: silent and black, a spectre of death that hovered over everything. But from where he was sitting now, it was magnificent. It was all illusion, a glorious illusion: just like life. And it occurred to him that, just as the sand disturbed by climbing pilgrims resumed its former position each night leaving no trace of the pilgrims' struggles, soon he would be gone from this world and the elements would rearrange themselves to fill the space he had occupied, as if he had never been. There would be no trace left of his brief life, except perhaps his books, but even they would succumb to damp and mould, and eventually rot and disintegrate and disappear.

Even the effort of sitting straight was exhausting. He collapsed back and lay on the rampart staring up at the sky. There was one little white cloud overhead. Perhaps it was not a cloud at all; perhaps it was the mist that escaped a thousand years ago from Urashima's lacquered box. The legends of Oisín and Urashima had touched something deep in his heart. He shared with them the mutual longing to return to the familiar. The temptation had been great but he had stayed put. And he knew he had done the right thing.

A faint persistent knocking sound reached his ears. The noise grew louder. He managed to turn his head to the side and he saw Kazuo running towards him in his little wooden sandals. The sea breeze blew aside his *yukata* as he ran, baring his slender legs to the knee; the long sleeves fluttered and flapped. The boy called to him but his words floated away on the warm air. In his cupped hands he had something to show his father; a black dragonfly escaped his grasp and flew to Hearn. It zig-zagged around him and then came to rest on his chest and, in that moment, an icy chill ran through him.

He could still see the gracious little figure of his son leaping in the light between the summer silences of field and sea. A delicate boy with the blended charm of two races. How softly vivid everything seemed: the shadows of grasses and little stones, the boy's smiling face, the patter of his quick light feet. But quickly as he ran, the boy came no nearer. Those little sandalled feet would never, ever reach him.

AFTERWORD

LAFCADIO HEARN is considered one of the first great Western observers of the Japanese way of life. His books and essays shed enormous light on this highly evolved but often misunderstood civilisation. As he detested anyone editing his work, I see myself as an uninvited ghost writer, who has shamelessly plundered the best of his writing, edited and rearranged it in a way of which he would have thoroughly disapproved.

Black Dragonfly is based on Hearn's life and work but is a work of fiction. I have taken random sections from his letters, essays and books and woven them together to create a story that hopefully gives insight into his character and inner thoughts. I did not want to just reproduce his work. I wanted readers to be with him as he experienced life in Japan with all its delights and difficulties. I have turned his prose into imagined conversations he might have had with his family and friends. They are fictional conversations but the words are mostly his. Liberties have been taken with characterisation. In order to enrich the plot, some events that he recorded have been ascribed to characters who did not experience them. The letters to Watkins are also a mixture of actual letters and my own imaginings. Throughout the book, I rearrange and fill gaps to smooth out the narrative. To put everything of his into italics or quote marks would have made for a cluttered read but be sure that the best of the writing in *Black Dragonfly* is Hearn's. Any mistakes are my own.

I believe that Hearn blossomed in Japan. He did his best work there. After a lifetime of wandering, he found what he had lacked in his youth: a stable base and a family to love and support him. In 1904, after fourteen productive years there, he died of heart failure at the age of fifty-four, leaving a legacy of work chronicling every aspect of life in a unique and ancient culture that was rapidly vanishing as the modern world encroached. His final book, *Japan: An Attempt at Interpretation*, was published posthumously and hailed as a masterpiece. He is buried in Tokyo.

I am particularly indebted to the following:

Lafcadio Hearn. *Letters from the Raven; Chita; Glimpses of Unfamiliar Japan; Out of the East; Kokoro; Writings from Japan;* and *Japan: An Attempt at Interpretation*

Koizumi Setsuko. *Reminiscences of Lafcadio Hearn*

Jonathan Colt. *Wandering Ghost: The Odyssey of Lafcadio Hearn*

Paul Murray. *A Fantastic Journey: The Life and Literature of Lafcadio Hearn*

Vera McWilliams. *Lafcadio Hearn*

Elizabeth Bisland. *The Life and Letters of Lafcadio Hearn, Volumes I and II.*

Acknowledgements

Thank You:

My sister, Linda Curran, who is my first sounding board, proofreader
and constructive critic; Jenny Wright, editor and friend, who took
long walks with me on many a grim day and gave me the confidence to
send *Black Dragonfly* out into the world; Niall MacMonagle, who was
endlessly generous with his knowledge and expertise; Jean Callanan,
book midwife, friend and a source of support and encouragement
for many years; Roh-Suan Tung, Markéta Glanzová, Julia Sam and
all at Balestier Press for publishing this labour of love; Linda Scales,
friend and legal advisor; Sarah Yagi, my oldest friend in Japan for her
insight and wisdom; Shoko and Bon Koizumi and staff at the Lafcadio
Hearn Memorial Museum, who were most hospitable during my
time in Matsue; Robert Nicholson at the Writer's Museum, Dublin,
for sharing his desk with me as I trawled through ancient editions of
Hearn's work; Kelli Marjolet and Annien Rossouw who save me when
technology overwhelms; Hajime Morita, kind friend and guide in
Tokyo; and all the others who have helped along the way with advice,
recommendations, suggestions, support, introductions, cups of tea
and other comforting libations, including Professor Mary Gallagher,
Junko and Duncan Hamilton, John Harris, Cormac Kinsella, Carol
Lannigan, Arthur Lappin, Colm MacGinty, Dr. Elaine Mahon, Paul
Murphy, Maki Mutai, Jasmine Daines Pilgrem, Gordon Snell; and
lastly, a huge thank you to Terence, who is always there for me.

JEAN PASLEY writes mostly for film but also for stage and radio. Her screenplays have won numerous awards and include *How About You*, based on a Maeve Binchy short story. Her most recent screenplay as co-writer, *The Bright Side*, won The Audience Award at Cork International Film Festival 2020. She lived in Japan for many years but now lives in Dublin, next door to one of Lafcadio Hearn's childhood homes. This is her first novel.

The year is 1890. Western influences are flooding into Japan. A nomadic Irishman arrives to record this unique culture before it vanishes.

In this richly imagined novel, late nineteenth century Japan is brought vividly to life. Based on the remarkable experiences of the Irish writer, Lafcadio Hearn, and drawing on his letters, essays and books, Jean Pasley explores not only Hearn's stark, lonely childhood in Ireland and his scandalous time in America but also how Japan changed him and how he went on to become one of Japan's most celebrated and cherished writers.

'A lavish, beautiful testimony to the life and achievements of Lafcadio Hearn, the writer who opened our eyes to Japan's intricate, extraordinary art and literature, and to its rituals, sometimes exquisite, sometimes scarifying, always uniquely the country's own. Pasley is a true writer, and *Black Dragonfly* a book to read and remember.'
Frank McGuinness

'This is the story of the writer, Lafcadio Hearn, a complex and troubled man, as he tries to come to terms with his life and at the same time, negotiate the ancient, mysterious and fast-changing civilisation of nineteenth century Japan. Handled with great delicacy and empathy, from start to finish, *Black Dragonfly* is a pure pleasure to read.'
Christine Dwyer Hickey

'One of the most engaging and insightful books I've read in a long time. Written with vivacity and elegance, *Black Dragonfly* is a profound love letter to the fading elegance of an ancient civilisation skilfully captured in this alluring and absorbing tale.'
Manchán Magan

Balestier Press
www.balestier.com

ISBN 978-1-913891-05-3
90000
9 781913 891053